SPIRITS

PRAISE FOR *UNCLEAN SPIRITS*

'Fascinating without being overbearing . . . it is unique enough that it stands out from the rest of the urban fantasy genre . . . Every character in *Unclean Spirits* has a strong voice, and that makes this great story even better . . . A must-read for any urban fantasy lover'
Fallen Angel Reviews

'Hanover gives us a smart heroine coming into her own, which is how I like my urban fantasy. Jayné Heller is going places'
Carrie Vaughn, *New York Time* bestselling author

'Smooth prose and zippy action sequences'
Publishers Weekly

'Jayné is a fresh, likable heroine who grows from being a direc-tionless college student into a vigorous, confident leader as she discovers and accepts her mission in life . . . With a solid concept and eclectic cast of characters establishes, I have high expecta-tions for Book 2 of the Black Sun's Daughter'
The Sci Fi Guy

'Between the novel's energetic pacing, Jayné's undeniable charm, and the intriguing concept behind the riders, *Unclean Spirits* is a solid entry in the urban fantasy genre'
Fantasy Book Critic

BY M. L. N. HANOVER

The Black Sun's Daughter
Unclean Spirits
Darker Angels
Vicious Grace
Killing Rites

UNCLEAN SPIRITS

THE BLACK SUN'S DAUGHTER

1

M.L.N.HANOVER

www.orbitbooks.net

ORBIT

First published in Great Britain in 2012 by Orbit
First published in the United States in 2009 by Pocket Books
a division of Simon & Schuster, Inc.

Copyright © 2008 by M. L. N. Hanover

The moral right of the author has been asserted.

Excerpt from *Darker Angels* by M. L. N. Hanover
Copyright © 2009 by M. L. N. Hanover

A CIP catalogue record for this book is available from the British Library.

ISBN 978-0-356-50122-2

Typeset in Garamond 3 by Hewer Text UK Ltd Edinburgh
Printed and bound by CPI Group (UK) Ltd, Croydon, CR0 4YY

Papers used by Orbit are from well-managed forests
and other responsible sources.

MIX
Paper from
responsible sources
FSC
www.fsc.org FSC® C104740

Orbit
An imprint of
Little, Brown Book Group
100 Victoria Embankment
London EC4Y 0DY

An Hachette UK Company
www.hachette.co.uk

www.orbitbooks.net

To John Constantine

Introduction

It was raining in Denver the night Eric Heller died. The clouds had rolled in late in the afternoon, white pillars ascending toward the sun with a darkness at the base that was pure threat. Seven minutes after five o'clock—just in time for the rush-hour traffic—the sky opened, rain pounding down onto the streets and windows. It was still going three and a half hours later. Falling water and flashing lightning hid the sunset, but Eric could feel it. It was a side effect; he could always feel the dark coming on.

'Something's happening,' the voice from his cell phone said. 'Something big.'

'I know, Aubrey. I'm on it.'

'I mean really big.'

'I'm *on* it.'

Across from Eric in the dim orange light of the bar, a man laughed and the waitress smiled a tight little smile that didn't reach her eyes. Eric tapped his glass, the tick-tick-tick of his fingernails sounding like the rain against the window.

'Okay,' Aubrey said. 'But if there's something I can do, you'll tell me. Right?'

'No question,' Eric said. 'Take care of yourself, okay? And maybe fly low for a while. This might get a little messy.'

Aubrey was a decent guy, which meant he did a lot of decent-guy things. Eric's present job didn't call for that skill set. He needed a hard-ass. And so he was sitting in this bar in one of the worst parts of Five Points, waiting for someone he'd never met while a monsoon beat the shit out of the city. And while Coin and the Invisible College did something in the dangerous almost-reality of the Pleroma. Something big.

'You want another one, Pops?' the waitress said.

'Yes,' Eric said. 'Yes, I do.'

He'd finished the other one and moved on to a third when the door swung open. The curl of rain-chilled air moved through the bar like a breath. Then five men walked in. Four of them could have been simple violence-soaked gangbangers. The fifth one, the big sonofabitch in sunglasses, had a rider. Eric couldn't tell by looking whether it was a *loupine* or *nosferatu* or any of the other thousand species of unclean spirit that could crawl into a human body, but he could feel power coming off the man. Eric's hand twitched toward the gun in his pocket, wanting the reassuringly solid grip under his fingers. But that would be poor form.

The big sonofabitch approached and loomed over Eric, just close enough to be a provocation. The other four split up, two standing by the door, two lounging close to Eric with a fake casual air. Apart from the radio blaring out a hip-hop tune, the bar had gone silent.

'You're Tusk,' Eric said. 'Nice belt buckle you've got there. Shiny.'

'Who the fuck are you, old man?' the big sonofabitch asked. His breath smelled like creosote. *Loupine*, then. A werewolf.

'My name's Eric Heller. I'm looking for someone to do a job for me.'

'We look unemployed?' the big sonofabitch asked. The two who weren't by the door smiled mirthlessly. 'You think some Anglo motherfucker just come in here and whistle, we gonna jump?'

Eric reached up and plucked the sunglasses off the big sonofabitch. The black eyes met his. Eric pulled his will up from his crotch, up through his belly and his throat, pressing cold qi out through his gaze. The big sonofabitch tilted his head like a dog hearing an unfamiliar sound. The others stirred, hands reaching under jackets and shirts.

'I'm looking for someone to do a job, friend,' Eric said, pressing the glasses into the man's blacksmith-thick hand. 'If it's not you, it's not you. No offense meant.'

The big sonofabitch shook his head once, but it wasn't really a refusal. Eric waited.

'Who are you?' the *loupine* asked. The humanity had left the voice. Eric was talking straight to the rider now.

'Eric. Alexander. Heller. Ask around,' he said. 'I can offer you the Mark of Brute-Loka. Might be useful to someone in your position.'

The black eyes went wider.

'What do you want for it? You want someone killed?'

'I want someone killed,' Eric agreed softly. Everyone was quiet. Quiet as the grave. 'You want to talk about it here with all these nice people around? Or should we go some-place private?'

'Chango,' the big sonofabitch said. One of the men by the door stepped forward, lifting his chin. 'Get the car.'

Eric swilled down the last of his drink, and the big sonof-abitch stepped back enough to let him stand. Eric dropped two twenties on the table. A very generous tip. It always paid to be kind to the help.

Outside, the rain had slackened to merely driving. A black car pulled up to the curb, Chango at the wheel. The *loupine* and his three homies clustered around Eric, ignoring the downpour. Two of the three minions got in the back with Eric stuck between them. The *loupine* had a short conversation with the last guy, then took the front. The last gangbanger spat on the street and went back into the bar as the car pulled away. They drove east toward Park Hill. Eric didn't speak.

For the first time that night, Eric felt that the plan was coming together. The muscle was the last piece he needed. The trick now was to fix the timing. The whole thing had to come together like clockwork, every element in place just when it needed to be there. Him, and the *loupine*, and the old-timer.

The driver sneezed. The thug to Eric's left murmured, 'Gesundheit,' and Eric's spine crawled with fear. Since when did Five Points gangbangers say *gesundheit*?

What the fuck was he sitting next to?

As casually as he could, he brought a hand to his mouth. He crushed the fresh sage and peppermint leaves in the cuff and breathed in the scent. His mind clicked into trance, the aroma acting as trigger. His eyes felt like they'd been washed clean. Everything around him was intensely real, the edges sharp, the textures vibrant. He could hear the individual raindrops striking the car. He felt each fiber of his shirt pressing against his skin. And the glamour fell away from the others. The ink of their markings seemed to well up from inside them like blood from a cut. The driver was entirely bald, labyrinthine tattoos rising from his collar and crawling up over his ears. The two beside Eric were just as marked, their faces covered with symbols and sigils.

It had been a setup from the start. The contact, the face-down at the bar, the creosote breath. There were no gangbangers. No *loupine*.

One of them glanced at Eric.

'He knows,' the guard said.

The big sonofabitch in the front was still a big sonofa-bitch. He turned, looking over his shoulder. His lips were black, his eyes set in a tangle of something half Arabic script, half spiderweb.

'Mr. Heller,' he said, as if they were meeting for the first time. His voice was low as tires against asphalt. With his senses scraped raw by the cantrip, Eric could feel the man's breath on his skin.

'This isn't what you boys think it is,' Eric said.

'We know what you've been doing, Mr. Heller,' the other man said. 'It stops tonight. It stops *now*.'

With a despairing cry, Eric went for his gun.

1

I flew into Denver on the second of August, three days before my twenty-third birthday. I had an overnight bag packed with three changes of clothes, the leather backpack I used for a purse, the jacket my last boyfriend hadn't had the guts to come pick up from my apartment (it still smelled like him), my three-year-old laptop wrapped in a blanket, and a phone number for Uncle Eric's lawyer. The area around the baggage carousel was thick with families and friends hugging one another and saying how long it had been and how much everyone had grown or shrunk or whatever. The wide metal blades weren't about to offer up anything of mine, so I was just looking through the crowd for my alleged ride and trying not to make eye contact.

It took me a while to find him at the back of the crowd, his head shifting from side to side, looking for me. He had a legal pad in his hand with my name in handwritten letters—'JAYNE HELLER.' He was younger than I'd expected, maybe midthirties, and cuter. I shouldered my way through the happy mass of people, mentally applauding Uncle Eric's taste.

'You'd be Aubrey?' I said.

'Jayné,' he said, pronouncing it *Jane*. It's actually

zha-*nay*, but that was a fight I'd given up. 'Good. Great. I'm glad to meet you. Can I help you with your bags?'

'Pretty much covered on that one,' I said. 'Thanks, though.'

He looked surprised, then shrugged it off.

'Right. I'm parked over on the first level. Let me at least get that one for you.'

I surrendered my three changes of clothes and followed.

'You're going to be staying at Eric's place?' Aubrey asked over his shoulder. 'I have the keys. The lawyer said it would be okay to give them to you.'

'Keys to the kingdom,' I said, then, 'Yes. I thought I'd save the money on a hotel. Doesn't make sense not to, right?'

'Right,' Aubrey said with a smile that wanted badly to be comfortable but wasn't.

I couldn't blame the guy for being nervous. Christ only knew what Eric had told him about the family. Even the broad stroke of 'My brother and sister-in-law don't talk to me' would have been enough to make the guy tentative. Much less the full-on gay-hating, patriarch-in-the-house, know-your-place episode of *Jerry Springer* that had been my childhood. Calling Uncle Eric the black sheep of the family was like saying the surface of the sun was warmish. Or that I'd been a little tiny disappointment to them.

Aubrey drove a minivan, which was kind of cute. After he slung my lonely little bag into the back, we climbed in and drove out. The happy crowd of families and friends fell away behind us. I leaned against the window and looked up into the clear night sky. The moon was about halfway down from full. There weren't many stars.

'So,' Aubrey said. 'I'm sorry. About Eric. Were you two close?'

'Yeah,' I said. 'Or . . . maybe. I don't know. Not close like he called me up to tell me about his day. He'd check in on me, make sure things weren't too weird at home. He'd just show up sometimes, take me out to lunch or for ice cream or something cheesy like that. We always had to keep under my dad's radar, so I figure he'd have come by more often if he could.'

Aubrey gunned the minivan, pulling us onto the highway.

'He protected me,' I said, soft enough that I didn't think Aubrey would hear me, but he did.

'From what?'

'Myself,' I said.

Here's the story. In the middle of high school, I spent about six months hanging out with the bad kids. On my sixteenth birthday, I got very, *very* drunk and woke up two days later in a hotel room with half a tattoo on my back and wearing someone else's clothes. Eric had been there for me. He told my dad that I'd gotten the flu and helped me figure out how to keep anyone from ever seeing the ink.

I realized I'd gone silent. Aubrey was looking over at me.

'Eric was always swooping in just when everything was about to get out of control,' I said. 'Putting in the cooling rods.'

'Yeah,' Aubrey said. 'That sounds like him.'

9

Aubrey smiled at the highway. It seemed he wasn't thinking about it, so the smile looked real. I could see why Eric would have gone for him. Short, curly hair the color of honey. Broad shoulders. What my mother would have called a kind mouth. I hoped that he'd made Eric happy.

'I just want you to know,' I said, 'it's okay with me that he was gay.'

Aubrey started.

'He was gay?'

'Um,' I said. 'He wasn't?'

'He never told me.'

'Oh,' I said, mentally recalculating. 'Maybe he wasn't. I assumed . . . I mean, I just thought since my dad wouldn't talk about him . . . my dad's kind of old-school. Where *school* means *testament*. He never really got into that love-thy-neighbor-as-thyself part.'

'I know the type,' he said. The smile was actually pointed at me now, and it seemed genuine.

'There was this big falling-out about three years ago,' I said. 'Uncle Eric had called the house, which he almost never did. Dad went out around dinnertime and came back looking deeply pissed off. After that . . . things were weird. I just assumed . . .'

I didn't tell Aubrey that Dad had gathered us all in the living room—me, Mom, my older brother Jay, and Curtis the young one—and said that we weren't to have anything to do with Uncle Eric anymore. Not any of us. Not ever. He was a pervert and an abomination before God.

Mom had gone sheet-white. The boys just nodded and

looked grave. I'd wanted to stand up for him, to say that Uncle Eric was family, and that Dad was being totally unfair and hypocritical. I didn't, though. It wasn't a fight I could win.

But Aubrey knew him well enough to have a set of spare keys, and he didn't think Eric was gay. Maybe Dad had meant something else. I tried to think what exactly had made me think it was that, but I couldn't come up with anything solid.

Aubrey pulled his minivan off the highway, then through a maze of twisty little streets. One-story bungalows with neatly kept yards snuggled up against each other. About half the picture windows had open curtains; it was like driving past museum dioramas of the American Family. Here was one with an old couple sitting under a cut glass chandelier. One with the backs of two sofa-bound heads and a wall-size Bruce Willis looking troubled and heroic. One with two early-teenage boys, twins to look at them, chasing each other. And then we made a quick dogleg and pulled into a carport beside a brick house. Same lawn, same architecture. No lights, no one in the windows.

'Thanks,' I said, reaching around in the seat to grab my bag.

'Do you want . . . I mean, I can show you around a little. If you want.'

'I think I'm just going to grab a shower and order in a pizza or something,' I said. 'Decompress. You know.'

'Okay,' he said, fishing in his pocket. He came out with a leather fob with two keys and passed it over to me. I took

11

it. The leather was soft and warm. 'If you need anything, you have my number?'

'Yeah,' I said. 'Thanks for the lift.'

'If there's anything I can do . . .'

I popped open the door. The dome light came on.

'I'll let you know,' I said. 'Promise.'

'Your uncle,' Aubrey said. Then, 'Your uncle was a very special man.'

'I know,' I said.

He seemed like he wanted to say something else, but instead he just made me promise again that I'd call him if I needed help.

There wasn't much mail in the box—ads and a water bill. I tucked it under my arm while I struggled with the lock. When I finally got the door open, I stumbled in, my bag bumping behind me.

A dim atrium. A darker living room before me. The kitchen door to my left, ajar. A hall to my right, heading back to bedrooms and bathrooms and closets.

'Hey,' I said to nothing and no one. 'I'm home.'

I never would have said it to anyone, but my uncle had been killed at the perfect time. I hated myself for even thinking that, but it was true. If I hadn't gotten the call from his lawyer, if I hadn't been able to come here, I would have been reduced to couch surfing with people I knew peripherally from college. I wasn't welcome at home right now. I hadn't registered for the next semester at ASU, which technically made me a college dropout.

I didn't have a job or a boyfriend. I had a storage unit in Phoenix and a bag, and I didn't have the money to keep the storage unit for more than another month. With any luck at all, I'd be able to stay here in the house until Uncle Eric's estate was all squared away. There might even be enough money in his will that I could manage first and last on a place of my own. He was swooping in one last time to pull me out of the fire. The idea made me sad, and grateful, and a little bit ashamed.

They'd found him in an alley somewhere on the north side of the city. There was, the lawyer had told me, an open investigation. Apparently he'd been seen at a bar somewhere talking to someone. Or it might have just been a mugging that got out of hand. One way or another, his friend Aubrey had identified the body. Eric had left instructions in his will for funeral arrangements, already taken care of. It was all very neat. Very tidy.

The house was just as tidy. He hadn't owned very much, and it gave the place a simplicity. The bed was neatly made. Shirts, jackets, slacks all hung in the bedroom closet, some still in the plastic from the dry cleaner's. There were towels in the bathroom, a safety razor beside the sink with a little bit of soap scum and stubble still on the blade.

I found a closet with general household items, including a spare toothbrush. The food in the fridge was mostly spoiled, but I scrounged up a can of beef soup that I nuked in a plain black bowl, sopping up the last with bread that wasn't too stale. The television was in the living room, and I spooled through channels and channels of bright, shining crap. I didn't feel right putting my feet on the couch.

When I turned on the laptop, I found there was a wireless network. I guessed the encryption key on my third try. It was the landline phone number. I checked mail and had nothing waiting for me. I pulled up my messenger program. A few names appeared, including my most recent ex-boyfriend. The worst thing I could have done just then was talk with him. The last thing I needed was another reminder of how alone I was. I started typing.

Jayneheller: Hey. You there?

A few seconds later, the icon showed he was on the other end, typing.

Caryonandon: I'm not really here. About to go out.
Jayneheller: OK. Is there a time we can talk?
Caryonandon: Maybe. Not now.

His name vanished from the list. I played a freeware word search game while I conducted imaginary conversations with him in which I always came out on top, then went to bed feeling sick to my stomach.

I called the lawyer in the morning, and by noon, she was at the door. Midfifties, gray suit, floral perfume with something earthy under it, and a smile bright as a brand-new hatchet. I pulled my hair back when she came in and wished I'd put on something more formal than blue jeans and a Pink Martini T-shirt.

'Jayné,' she said, as if we were old acquaintances. She

pronounced it *Jane* too. I didn't correct her. 'This must be so hard for you. I'm so sorry for your loss.'

'Thanks,' I said. 'You want to come into the kitchen? I think there's some tea I could make.'

'That would be lovely,' she said.

I fired up the kettle and dug through the shelves. There wasn't any tea, but I found some fresh peppermint and one of those little metal balls, so I brewed that. The lawyer sat at the kitchen table, her briefcase open, small piles of paper falling into ranks like soldiers on parade. I brought over two plain black mugs, careful not to spill on anything.

'Thank you, dear,' she said, taking the hot mug from my hands. 'And your trip was all right? You have everything you need?'

'Everything's fine,' I said, sitting.

'Good, then we can get to business. I have a copy of the will itself here. You'll want to keep that for your files. There is, I'm afraid, going to be a lot of paperwork to get through. Some of the foreign properties are complex, but don't worry, we'll make it.'

'Okay,' I said, wondering what she was talking about.

'This is an inventory of the most difficult transfers. The good news is that Eric arranged most of the liquid assets as pay-on-death, so the tax situation is fairly straightforward, and we get to avoid probate. The rest of the estate is more complicated. I've also brought keys to the other Denver properties. I have a copy of the death certificate, so you only need to fill out a signature card at the bank before you can do anything with the funds. Do you have enough to see you through for a day or two?'

She handed me a typewritten sheet of paper. I ran my finger down the list. Addresses in London, Paris, Bombay, Athens . . .

'I'm sorry,' I said. 'I don't want to be a pain in the ass, but I don't understand. What is all this?'

'The inventory of the difficult transfers,' she said, slowing down the words a little bit, like maybe I hadn't understood them before. 'Some of the foreign properties are going to require more paperwork.'

'These are all Uncle Eric's?' I said. 'He has a house in London?'

'He has property all over the world, dear. Didn't you know?'

'No,' I said. 'I didn't. What am I . . . I mean, what am I supposed to do with this stuff?'

The lawyer put down her pen. A crease had appeared between her brows. I sipped the peppermint tea and it scalded my tongue.

'You and your uncle didn't discuss any of this?' she said.

I shook my head. I could feel my eyes growing abnormally wide. 'I thought he was gay,' I said. It occurred to me just how stunningly underqualified I was to execute anybody's will, much less something complex with a lot of paperwork.

The lawyer sat back in her seat, considering me like I had just appeared and she was maybe not so impressed with what she saw.

'Your uncle was a very rich man,' she said. 'He left all his assets specifically and exclusively to you. And you had no idea that was his intention?'

'We didn't talk much,' I said. 'He left it to me? Are you sure? I mean, thanks, but are you sure?'

'The majority of his titles are already jointly in your names. And you're certain he never mentioned this?'

'Never.'

The lawyer sighed.

'Ms. Heller,' she said. 'You are a very rich young woman.'

I blinked.

'Um,' I said. 'Okay. What scale are we talking about here?'

She told me: total worth, liquid assets, property.

'Well,' I said, putting the mug down. 'Holy shit.'

I think lottery winners must feel the same way. I followed everything the lawyer said, but about half of it washed right back out of my mind. The world and everything in it had taken on a kind of unreality. I wanted to laugh or cry or curl up in a ball and hug myself. I didn't—did *not*—want to wake up and find out it had all been a dream.

We talked for about two hours. We made a list of things I needed to do, and she loaned me six hundred dollars—'to keep me in shoes'—until I could get to the bank and jump through the hoops that would give me access to enough money to do pretty much anything I wanted. She left a listing of Eric's assets about a half inch thick, and keys to the other Denver properties: two storage facilities and an apartment in what she told me was a hip and happening neighborhood.

I closed the door behind her when she left and sank down to the floor. The atrium tiles were cold against my palms. Eric Alexander Heller, my guardian uncle, left me more than I'd dreamed of. Money, security, any number of places that I could live in if I wanted to.

Everything, in fact, but an explanation.

I took myself back to the kitchen table and read the will. Legal jargon wasn't my strong suit, but from what I could tell, it was just what the lawyer had said. Everything he had owned was mine. No one else's. No discussion. Now that I was alone and starting to get my bearings, about a thousand questions presented themselves. Why leave everything to me? Why hadn't he told me about any of it? How had he made all this money?

And, top of the list, what was someone worth as much as a small nation doing in a bar in the shitty part of Denver, and did all the money that had just dropped into my lap have anything to do with why he'd been killed?

I took out the keys she'd left me. A single house key shared a ring with a green plastic tag with an address on Inca Street. Two storage keys for two different companies.

If I'd had anyone to talk to, I'd have called them. My parents, a friend, a boyfriend, anyone. A year ago, I would have had a list half as long as my arm. The world changes a lot in a year. Sometimes it changes a lot in a day.

I walked back to the bedroom and looked at my clothes, the ghost of my discomfort with the lawyer still haunting me. If I was going to go face Christ only knew what, I wasn't going in a T-shirt. I took one of the white shirts out of the closet, held it close to my face, and breathed in. It didn't smell like anything at all. I stripped off my shirt, found a simple white tee in Eric's dresser, and put myself together in a good white men's button-down. It classed up the jeans, and if it was a little too big, I could roll up the sleeves and still look more confident than I did in my own clothes. More confident than I felt.

I felt a little weird, wearing a dead man's shirt. But it was mine now. He'd given it to me. I had the ultimate hand-me-down life. The thought brought a lump to my throat.

'Come on, little tomato,' I told the key ring. 'You and me against the world.'

I called a taxi service, went out to the curb to wait, and inside forty-five minutes I was on Inca Street, standing in front of the mysterious apartment.

2

In the middle of the afternoon there wasn't much foot traffic. The address was a warehouse complex converted into living space for the Brie and wine set. Five stories of redbrick with balconies at each level. Tasteful plants filled the three feet between the knee-high wrought iron fence and the walls. According to the paperwork, the apartment Eric owned—the one I owned—was valued at half a million.

I tried to look like I belonged there as I walked in and found my way to the elevators. It was like sneaking into a bar; I didn't belong there, but I did. I kept expecting someone to stop me, to ask for my ID, to check my name against a list and throw me out.

Why, I asked myself, does someone have a house and an apartment both in the same city? It wasn't like he could sleep in two beds at once. Maybe this was his getaway. Maybe it was where his lover stayed, assuming he had one.

The elevator chimed, a low, reassuring bell, like someone clearing their throat. I stepped out, checked the number on the key ring, and followed the corridor down to my left. I started to knock, then stopped.

I stood there, silent, my breath fast. The door shone like lacquer. I could see my reflection in it, blurred and imprecise. I put the key in the lock and turned. I felt the bolt open, but I didn't hear it.

The inside of the apartment was gorgeous and surreal. Wooden floors that seemed to glow, bronze fixtures, windows that made the city outside seem like it had been arranged to be seen from this vantage point. The ceilings were raw beams and exposed ductwork so stylish they looked obvious. Books were stacked on the floor, on the deep, plush couch. History books, it looked like. Some of them were in languages I recognized, some weren't. A whiteboard hung on one wall, covered with timetables and scribbled notes. A huge glass ashtray held the remains of at least a pack of dark brown cigarettes, the scent of old smoke tainting the air. And the art . . .

At each of the huge windows, a glass ball seemed to float in the air. It was only when I got close enough to breathe on them that I saw the tiny cradles, three hair-thin wire strands for each, hanging from the high ceiling. When I turned around, I saw there was one above the doorway too. Candles in thick brass candlesticks covered the dining table in three ascending rows, and a picture framed in burnished metal hung at the mouth of a hallway. It was a picture of a young woman in nineteenth-century clothes, and I wasn't sure from looking whether it was a photograph or a drawing. It seemed as real as a photo, but the eyes and the way she held her hands looked subtly off.

Silently, I went down the hallway. A fair-size kitchen with white tiles and a brushed steel sink and refrigerator and stove. A breakfast bar with ironwork stools to match the fence outside. A bathroom with the lights out. A bedroom, and on the bed, laid out as if in state, a corpse.

I could feel the blood leaving my face. I didn't scream, but I put my hand on the door frame to keep steady. My stomach tightened and flipped. I stepped forward. Whoever he'd been, he'd been dead for a long time. The skin was desiccated, tight, and waxy; the nose was sunken; the hands folded on his chest were fleshless as chicken wings. Blackened teeth lurked behind ruined lips. Wisps of color-less hair still clung to the scalp. He was wearing a white shirt with suspenders and pants that came up to his rib cage, like someone from a forties movie.

I crouched at the side of the bed, disgusted, fascinated, and frightened. My mind was jumping and screeching like a monkey behind my eyes, but there was something wrong. I had touched my nose before I figured it out, like my body already knew and had to give me the hint. He didn't smell like a corpse. He didn't smell like anything. He smelled *cold*.

I had started to wonder if maybe it wasn't a body at all but some kind of desperately Goth wax sculpture when the eyes opened with a wet click.

This time, I screamed.

'You aren't Eric,' it said in a voice like a rusted cattle gate opening.

'I'm his niece,' I said. I didn't remember running across the room, but my back was pressed against the wall now. I tried to squeak less when I spoke again. 'I'm Jayné.'

He repeated my name like he was tasting it. Zha-*nay*.

'French?' he asked.

'My mother's side,' I said. 'People usually say it like Jane or Janey.'

'Monolingual fuckwits,' he said, and sat up. I thought I could hear his joints creaking like leather, but I might have only imagined it. 'You're here, that means something happened to Eric?'

'He's dead.'

The man sighed.

'I was afraid of that,' he said. 'Explains a lot. The little rat fuckers must have sussed him out.'

The skeletal, awkward hand rubbed his chin like it was checking for stubble. When he looked at me, his eyes were the yellow of old ivory. In motion, he didn't look like a corpse, only a badly damaged man.

'Hey,' he said, 'where are my manners, eh? You want a drink?'

'Um,' I said. And then, 'Yes.'

He led the way back to the kitchen. I perched on one of the stools while he poured two generous fingers of brandy into a water glass. I'd seen pictures of people who survived horrific burns, and while he didn't bear those scars, the effect was much the same. I could see it when his joints—shoulder, hip, elbow—didn't quite bend the way they were meant to. He walked carefully. I wanted to ask what had happened to him, but I couldn't think of a way to phrase it that didn't seem excruciatingly rude. I tried not to stare, the way you try not to look at people with harelips or missing hands, but my eyes just kept going back.

Guilt started pulling at me. Even if it was officially my place, coming in the way I had was rude. Clearly Uncle Eric had been letting the guy crash here. He poured a glass for himself, then took a wood cutting board from the cabinet beside the refrigerator and a knife from its holder.

'So,' he said. 'He didn't tell you a goddamn thing about all this, did he?'

'Not really,' I said, and sipped the brandy. I never drank much, but I could tell that the liquor was better than I'd ever had.

'Yeah. Like him,' the man said, and put a cast-iron skillet on the burner. 'Well. Shit, I don't know where to start. My name's Midian. Midian Clark. Your uncle and I were working together.'

If I pretended I was listening to Tom Waits, his voice wasn't so bad.

'What on?'

A scoop of butter thick enough to make a dietitian weep dropped onto the skillet and started to quietly melt.

'That's a long story,' Midian said.

'Was it why he got killed?'

'Yeah, it was.'

'So you know who killed him.'

Midian shifted his head to the side, his ragged lips pressed thin. He sighed.

'Yes. If he got killed, I know who killed him.'

'Okay,' I said. 'Spill it.'

He frowned quietly as he took a yellow onion, half a red bell pepper, and an egg carton out of the refrigerator. I drank more brandy, the warm feeling in my throat spreading to my cheeks. I cleared my throat.

'I'm not blowing you off. I just think better when I'm cooking,' he said. 'Okay. So. There's a guy calls himself Randolph Coin. He came to Denver about a year ago. He heads up a bunch of fellas call themselves the Invisible College, okay? They think that all the ghoulies and ghosties and long-legged beasties you've ever heard of really exist. Vampires, werewolves, zombies. People doing magic. You name it. You like onions?'

'Not really.'

'Not even grilled? Tell you what, just try this. If you don't like it, I'll make another one. So the Invisible College, they also think they know *why* all these things exist. It's about possession. Something coming out of this abstract spiritual world that's right next to ours and worming its way inside people and animals. Hell, sometimes even things. Knives.' He held up the cutting blade. 'Whatever.'

'Demons taking people over,' I said. He looked up, smiling at the skepticism in my voice, as he sliced the onion in neat halves, peeled away the skin, and started dicing the pale flesh.

'Well, yeah, a lot of it is about demons. Or spirits or loa or whatever you want to call them. Seelie Court, Unseelie Court, Radha, Petro, Ghede. Ifrit. Hungry ghosts. All kinds of them. The generic term's riders. They get inside a person, and they change them. Make them do things, make them *want* to do things. Give them freaky powers. Normal people who've got a feel for it and the right training—call 'em wizards or witches or cunning men or whatever—they can do some pretty weird shit, but *nothing* compared to what riders are capable of.'

'So not just demons, but magic too,' I said. He dropped the onion into the spreading pool of butter, where it sizzled angrily. The pepper was next for the block.

'Thing is, kid, the folks that believe that shit? They're absolutely right. That's exactly how the world is. Let me give you a fer instance. I know you're wondering what the fuck happened to me, right? Well, how old do you think I am?'

'I . . . I don't . . .'

'I was born the year they stormed the Bastille. The year of our Lord seventeen hundred and eighty motherfucking nine.' His voice had taken on an angry buzz. The blade in his hand flickered over the cutting board. 'I crossed the Invisible College, and they cursed me. I've been wandering around ever since. Coin is direct apostolic line from the pig fucker who did this to me. He's the only one who can take it back.'

He put the peppers in with the browning onions. Wisps of smoke and steam rose from the black metal.

'I came to Eric because he's the kind of guy who knows things. Helps people. I needed help.'

'You're telling me that a bunch of evil wizards killed my uncle?' I could hear the raw disbelief in my own voice.

His yellowed eyes locked on me. He took an egg from the carton and cracked it deliberately on the countertop.

'I'm telling you the world's more complicated than you thought,' he said. 'And I'm not wrong about that.'

While he whipped eggs in a tiny steel mixing bowl, I sat hunched over the breakfast bar, brandy in my hands. I felt like I'd been on an amusement park ride one too many times. Confused and dizzy and a little sick. We both knew he was giving me time to think. Time, specifically, to decide he was a nut or a liar. My first guess was both. But he was the only thread I had that might lead to Uncle Eric and whoever had killed him.

'Okay,' I said as he poured the yellow-white froth over the peppers and onions, 'let's say I buy it. What were you two going to do? Track this Coin guy down and give him a good talking to?'

'The Invisible College is here for a reason. Every few years, they have to come together to induct new people into the club. They have to call up a rider, open the poor sucker who's signing up for the horror show, and infect them with it. Things start moving just outside the world like sharks coming up for chum. When you get too many riders bumping around, the barrier between the physical world and the abstract gets . . . well, not thin exactly, but *weird*. That started in April. While that's happening, the Invisible College has its hands full. Eric and I were planning to disrupt things before they could eat the new crop of people. And while we were at it, kill Coin.'

'You were going to murder someone?'

He put his hand on the handle of the skillet, flinched back from the heat, and reached for a dishcloth to protect himself.

'Coin's dead, kid,' he said. 'Coin's been dead since the

day they made him Invisible. We were looking to kill the thing that's living in his body.'

He lifted the skillet, and a flick of his wrist spun the omelet in the air, folded it, and caught it. The ragged lips twisted into a satisfied smile. He waited a few seconds, then flipped it to the other side.

'That's how it works with them,' he said. 'You take the unclean spirit inside, and it devours you. It's not always like that. Other kinds of rider, you maybe don't need a ceremony. You get bitten, you pick up the wrong guy at the bar. You get assaulted. Maybe it kicks you out of your body, puts you someplace else. Or it just hangs out in the back of your mind, making suggestions or taking over in little ways so you won't even notice.'

'That's . . .' I didn't know whether I was going to say horrible or gross or implausible. Midian shrugged.

'Yeah, well,' he said. 'Thing is, the Invisible College bastards? They're strong, and they're smart, and they're organized. Every one of them that penetrates into the world makes Coin stronger, and the stronger he gets, the more he can protect his own. Think Amway, but for demonic possession.'

'And killing the thing inside Coin would fix you?'

'Killing that fucker would undo everything it's done in the physical world. Me and a whole lot of other things besides. He's the center of the whole damn infection. Here, lemme get you a fork. Blow on it a little, it's still hot.'

The taste was more than a few eggs, onions, and peppers seemed to justify. It was lush and hot and rich. He smiled at my reaction and slid the rest onto a plate for me.

'That's really good,' I said through my mouthful.

'There's a secret to it. Always drink some brandy first. There. Enjoy. So, yeah, we were looking to break the Invisible College's back. Get rid of Coin, disrupt the induction. It'd be just like penicillin taking out a case of the clap. We both knew it was dangerous. I don't know how they got to Eric, but I'm dead sure they did. Your average mugger would have been out of his depth with him. Guys like Eric don't die at random. He got hit.'

I took another bite of the omelet, chewing slowly to give myself time to think. On the one hand, everything Midian said was clearly insane. A two-hundred-year-old man cursed by demons. A cabal of evil wizards planning to engineer the demonic possession of a new batch of cultists. And my uncle in the middle of it all, dead because someone caught wind of his plan.

On the other hand, if anyone had asked me a week before what my uncle did, I would have guessed wrong. And even if every word coming out of Midian's mouth was crap, it seemed to be crap he believed. And so maybe this Coin guy believed it too. I'd had enough experience with the kind of atrocities that blind faith can lead to that I couldn't discount anything just because it was crazy. If Coin and the Invisible College believed that they were demon-possessed wizards and that Eric was out to stop them, that could have been reason enough to kill him. Things don't have to exist to have consequences.

I was lost in bitter memories for a moment. The flare of a match brought me back. The deathly face was considering me as he lit a cigarette.

'I'd think it was bullshit too if I was you,' he said. 'You doubt. I respect that. Doubt's important stuff.'

He took a long drag, the coal of his cigarette going bright and then dark. Long, blue smoke slid out of his mouth and nostrils as he spoke. It didn't smell like tobacco. It was sweeter and more acrid.

'Thing is, kid, you gotta doubt the stuff that *isn't* true. You go around doubting whether pickup trucks exist, you'll wind up on the curb with a lot of broken bits.'

I put my fork against the side of the plate and looked up at him.

'I'm taking this to the police, you know,' I said.

'Won't do you any good. They're just going to think you're nuts. They have an explanation that suits them just fine.'

'All the same—'

A hard tap came from the front room. Both of us turned to look. The little glass ball that hung over the door had fallen. It rolled uneasily along the unseen slope of the floor-boards. While we watched, the ones over the windows fell too, one-two-three. Midian grunted.

'When you came in,' he said, 'you didn't drop something behind you? Ashes or salt, something like that?'

'No,' I said. 'Nothing.'

Midian nodded and took another drag of his cigarette.

'That's too bad,' he said.

With a bang like a car wreck, the front door burst in.

3

Four figures poured into the front room. They wore pale shirts and loose pants, almost like a karate gi. Their skins were all pale, but covered with black markings. The swirls and designs looked like script. Two tall men stood on either side, a shorter man and a woman in the center. The shorter man shouted something I couldn't make out. Midian yelped and bolted for the back of the apartment. Four pairs of eyes turned on me. Behind the elaborate tattoos, they looked surprised. Both of the tall men were holding pistols.

Fear shrilled through my veins. I should have been skittering away from them; I should have been mewling. Instead, I slipped off the wrought iron stool and spun my plate like a Frisbee. It shattered against the short man's temple, but by then the stool was already flying through the air toward them. They dodged it as I jumped, rolling over the counter on my back and landing, on my fingertips and the balls of my feet, on the kitchen floor.

The woman shrieked, and the crack of a pistol came at the same moment the countertop I'd been on burst apart. A bullet made a sound as it passed over me, a little exhalation of death.

The woman came around the corner, and as if I'd been

expecting her, I launched forward, my shoulder slamming against the side of her knee. I felt something in her joint give, but her hands came down on me like thrown bricks. We struggled on the floor. I couldn't tell if she was screaming or I was, but seconds later, we were both on our feet. She had Midian's cutting knife in her hand. I could still see where the onion juice had dried on the blade.

'Who are you?' she said. She had a Slavic accent. Her eyes were the blue of gas flame. Her face was written like a Chinese scroll, columns of esoteric characters from her hairline to her neck.

I didn't know I intended to move until the skillet was in my hand. She leaped forward, the knifepoint moving for my body. I caught the blade with the skillet and spun, more gracefully than I had ever moved before, throwing the woman to one side, and then coming around to land the skillet hard on the back of her head. I heard the report of a pistol again and the refrigerator door over my shoulder puckered. I dropped and rolled, pressing my back against the cabinet, where I could neither see the front room nor be seen from it.

The woman groaned. Blood pooled beneath her head.

'Drop your guns,' I shouted. 'Do it now.'

It was an idiotic thing to say, but I felt them hesitate. I jumped forward, grabbing a drawer at random, and, twisting from my belly, pulled. It broke free, silverware arcing through the air toward my attackers. They fired, but the shots weren't aimed. I dove out toward them.

The fear vanished. I moved as if my body simply knew

what to do. I just had to stand back and let things follow their course. I rose to my feet, pushing the coffee table hard into one man's shins as I did. As he stumbled, I stepped onto the table. His descending head met my rising knee, and he spun back.

'Stop!'

The last man stood across the room from me, his legs braced, both hands on his gun, steadying it. His eyes were wide. There was no way I could get to him before he pulled the trigger. No way I could get to cover before the bullet hit me. To my surprise, I smiled.

The pistol shot startled me, and I waited for the pain. Nothing came. Shock, I thought. It's the shock. I'll die in a minute here. But then a second bullet slammed into the man, and he slumped. Blood flushed the thick pale cloth of his gi, making it look like skinned meat. Midian stood in the hallway leading to the bedroom, what looked like a World War I Luger in his hand.

He looked at me. His expression was cool and appraising.

'You're pretty good at that,' he said. 'Close the door, kid.'

For the space of a long breath, I didn't understand what he meant. When the trembling came, I felt like I was perfectly steady and the building was rattling. I crossed the four steps to the apartment's door and pushed it closed. The wood was splintered and white where they'd kicked it in. The earthquake in my body got worse. I felt it in the soles of my feet, like the floor was tapping on my shoes. I wasn't sure I was going to be able to remain standing.

When I turned back to the room, the woman had risen to her hands and knees. Midian, behind her, leveled his Luger at the back of her head.

'No!' I screamed.

He looked up as he pulled the trigger. The woman pitched forward, her skull split open. I dropped to my knees.

'You don't need to look at me like that,' Midian said as he stepped over her body and toward the small man crumpled in the middle of the floor. The attacker had shards of the plate in his hair, his legs bent under him. His eyes were closed. I could see him breathing. 'These aren't people. They're qliphoth. Shells. They're what's left after a rider's taken over.'

'Please stop,' I said.

Midian fired twice into the small man's head. I closed my eyes. The euphoria of the fight was gone, as if it had never been there. Tears ran down my cheeks, but I felt too sick to move. I heard Midian walk to the last man, the tall one I'd kicked.

'Don't,' I breathed. 'Please. Please don't.'

The gun barked. My body spasmed. I doubled over, vomiting up the eggs and onions and brandy. I was crying with the same sense of illness, the same violence. Soft footsteps came toward me, and I was suddenly sure that he was going to kill me too. I put up a hand, thinking somehow I could push away the gun.

Midian knelt beside me. Skeletal hands slid under my arms, and he lifted me. Together, we stumbled toward the bathroom. I puked again as we passed the kitchen, but he kept pushing me on. Soon, I was on my knees in front of the toilet curled in fetal position. There was blood and sick on my sleeve. Midian sat on the edge of the bathtub, watching me collapse.

'Please,' I said. 'Please.' I didn't even know what I meant by it.

'The first time's the worst, kid,' he said in his industrial ruin of a voice. 'Killing someone isn't like an action movie. You don't just go bang real loud and they fall down. It does something to you. I understand that.'

My eyes were shut tight. I could feel my mouth open wide enough to ache at the jaw, like I was screaming. Only a whine came out. My heart felt as if something precious had died. Some tiny part of my mind, cool and observant, was surprised to see all the rest of me coming unhinged.

'They came in here, kid. They came after you. You did what you had to do. They weren't even human, no matter what they looked like. Remember that. They're just shells. All those folks were already dead.'

For the first time, I wanted to believe him. All the bullshit about Eric and the Invisible College and unclean spirits. I wanted it all to be true. I wanted to believe it.

I remembered the woman's blue eyes. Whoever she was, she'd been a baby once. Her mother had held her in her arms. She'd had a first kiss. Someone had looked into those eyes with love. I saw her skull open under Midian's bullets.

For a moment, I couldn't breathe.

'Take your time,' Midian said. 'It's gonna be okay. Just take your time.'

It wasn't okay for a very long time. It felt like food poisoning, or worse. But eventually my strength gave out a little, and the violence of my reactions calmed. Midian had left me alone, so I locked myself in the bathroom and took a long, cold shower. The water seemed to ground me and pull me back to myself. When I stepped out and picked up a towel, I felt fragile, but I could function.

In the apartment, I could hear Midian grunting and talking to himself. The sweet, harsh smell of his cigarettes covered anything else. I was grateful for that. I sat on the floor and dug through the puddle of my clothes until I found my cell. I looked at it for a long time before I could bring myself to make the call.

Aubrey picked up on the second ring.

'Jayné?' he said, pronouncing it wrong.

'Hey,' I said. 'I need to ask you something.'

'Sure,' he said. 'Anything. What's up?'

I could hear something in the background. Voices. Traffic. The real world. I took a deep breath.

'What do you know about the Invisible College?'

There was a pause that lasted years.

'Oh, thank God,' he said. 'I was afraid Eric hadn't told you about any of it. I was going to bring it up when I got you from the airport, but I thought if he hadn't, I'd sound like a schizophrenic. Eric's murder. It was about Randolph Coin, wasn't it? Was he actually trying to take Coin on?'

I leaned forward, hunched over the cell. Mostly what I felt was relief. Even if it wasn't true, if it was all stories and deceptions and madness, at least there was someone I could talk to. I almost started crying again.

'Jayné? Are you there? Are you all right?'

'You remember how you said I should call if I needed any help?' I asked.

'Yes. Absolutely.'

'I need help.'

4

The bodies were lined up on the wooden floor of the front room. Midian had erected a levee of towels around them and draped black plastic trash bags over their heads. I was grateful for that. The curtains were closed, cutting us off from the street and the city. With the windows covered, I realized how small the apartment was. Aubrey was leaning against the interior brick wall. Midian sat on the couch beside a rough pile of history books and loose papers, his cigarette filling the air with a dim haze. His clothes were streaked with blood. I perched on the remaining kitchen stool. The one I'd thrown in the fight had bent enough that it wobbled now. I knew how it felt.

'O-kay,' Aubrey said. Then, 'Wow.'

'The upside is no cops,' Midian said. 'I figure they set up some kind of sound-dampening cantrip before they broke in, or else . . .'

'Or else?' Aubrey asked.

'Brick walls,' Midian replied with a shrug.

Aubrey nodded. His expression was grave, but there was a businesslike quality to how he took the whole thing in. I scratched my arm. I'd found a sweatshirt in the back. It smelled like Midian's cigarettes, but the white shirt I'd worn here was ruined. I tried not to look at the bodies.

'Well, we've got two issues,' Aubrey said. 'We need to get rid of these guys, and we need to make sure you and Jayné are someplace safe.'

Midian smirked at the mispronunciation of my name, but didn't correct him.

'My guess is we've got a little time,' Midian said. 'Coin throws his ninja strike team at us and they don't come home, he's going to get careful for a while. But I wouldn't want to wait until morning.'

Aubrey nodded. I wanted to say that I was sorry, but I wasn't sure who I wanted to say it to. My mind felt like it had been sandblasted. Aubrey pulled out his cell phone.

'Hey, hey, hey,' Midian said, standing up. 'I wasn't keen on it when the kid invited you in. Who the fuck are you calling?'

'Friends,' Aubrey said. 'We've all worked with Eric one time or another. They know the score.'

Midian frowned but didn't stop him. I felt a rush of profound relief that Aubrey knew what to do next. I didn't have a clue.

When I'd come out of the bathroom half an hour earlier and told Midian that Aubrey was on his way, the cursed man had almost lost his temper. He'd asked me everything I knew about Aubrey—who was he, who did he work for, how did he know Eric, why did I trust him—and it became clear that I didn't actually know anything. Only that when I'd asked for help, he'd said yes.

After he'd arrived, there had been a brief dancing back and forth between them. Midian had given a *Reader's Digest* condensation of the story he'd told me, and Aubrey had accepted it. Aubrey had explained that he and Eric had worked together before, and that he knew a little bit about Coin and the Invisible College, but that Eric had warned him off. Both men had seemed satisfied, at least provisionally. I watched it all like it was a television show.

Aubrey's clean-up crew arrived twenty minutes later. There were two of them, both Aubrey's age, both men, both unfazed by the corpses on the floor. The first looked vaguely Japanese, his head shaved to stubble, in a sand-colored shirt and pale, worn jeans. He said his name was Chogyi, but to call him Jake. The second, with white-blond shoulder-length hair and black clothes, only nodded to me. Chogyi Jake said his name was Ex.

'Ex?' I said. 'Like in ex–football player?'

'Ex-priest,' Chogyi Jake said.

'Ex for xylophone,' Ex said, stooping by the bodies. He had lifted the plastic trash bags. 'The birth certificate says Xavier. What killed them?'

'I did,' Midian said. 'The kid there kept them busy while I got the gun.'

'They were armed too,' Ex said. 'You let a twenty-year-old girl fight four riders sent to kill her while you rummaged around for a pistol?'

'Twenty-two,' I said.

'She was doing a pretty good job,' Midian said.

'Adrenaline,' I said. 'It was the adrenaline.'

'Must have been pretty good adrenaline to give you that much precision and control,' Ex said dryly.

'The kid's got some kind of mojo on her,' Midian said. 'She didn't trip the alarms when she came in either. I've been trying to figure that out.'

'Wait a minute,' I said. 'What?'

Midian shrugged. 'You shouldn't have been able to hold those bastards off,' he said. There was a little apology in his voice. 'They're pros. They should have cleaned your clock. But they didn't.'

'No,' I said. 'It wasn't like that. I was just scared. It was fight or flight. I don't even know how . . .'

I waved my hands at the room, the corpses, the four men who I barely knew.

'It doesn't work like that,' Ex said. 'You think Eric put some kind of protection on her?'

Midian looked at the newcomer with distrust, then shrugged.

'He left her the whole joint,' Midian said. 'Be all kinds of stupid not to watch out for her too.'

'I don't have powers,' I said, louder than I'd meant to. My hands were on my knees, the knuckles bloodless and white.

'Can we get back to the issue at hand?' Aubrey said. 'We've got a rider cult in town. They took out Eric, and now it looks like they're after Jayné. We have four shells that we need to get rid of, and Jayné and Midian here to get to shelter. Whatever else is going on, that's where we're starting, okay?'

'Right,' Chogyi Jake said. 'I've got the van downstairs. I'll go get the dolly and the drop cloths, and we can get them out of here.'

Ex stood up. There was blood on his fingers. There was blood everywhere.

'The door isn't as bad as it looks,' he said. 'A couple long wood screws will hold it together well enough that no one will notice unless they're looking for it. I can take care of that while Chogyi Jake loads them up.'

'Good thing you boys are on the side of the angels,' Midian said. 'A serial killer would pay a lot for those kinds of services.'

'You can come with us,' Ex said. 'Help dig.'

'What about getting me to shelter?' Midian asked.

'We can keep you covered,' Ex said.

Midian shrugged. Aubrey nodded his approval.

'I'll get Jayné back to Eric's place. When you're done, you can bring Midian too.'

'You think that's safe?' Chogyi Jake asked.

'Eric has more wards and protections on that house than anyplace else,' Aubrey said. 'It's not perfect, but it's the best I can think of. And we're a little short on time.'

They all took his point. I let him lead me out of the apartment and down to the street. Night had fallen while I'd been inside. It was a shock to see the cars and the low iron fence, to smell the exhaust, the distant suggestion of rain. I'd only been in the apartment for a few hours. It had been a lifetime.

He drove the same car he'd had at the airport the day before. I strapped on the seat belt and leaned against the window as he pulled into traffic. The moon looked more or less the way it had before I'd been attacked, before I'd been part of killing someone. The city lights obscured the stars. Aubrey didn't speak, and neither did I, but I was sensitive to all the small movements and sounds he made. Shifting his weight as he accelerated or touched the brakes, clearing his throat. My body felt heavy, like I'd had the flu and was still recovering. A police siren wailed but Aubrey didn't seem worried by it, so I let myself ignore it too.

Back at Eric's house—my house—Aubrey took my keys and opened the door so that I could shamble into the living room and sit on the couch. He sat beside me, his hand on the cushion above and behind me; close, but careful not to touch. I leaned toward him, my fingers reaching out like roots on a seedling. His physical presence was more comforting than I could have imagined.

'Are you okay?' he asked.

'No,' I said. 'I'm pretty fucked up. I've never . . . I've never been part of anything like that.'

'It's hard,' he agreed.

'I don't have powers. Whatever they said, I'm just a normal girl who—'

'Don't worry about it,' Aubrey said. 'We'll make sense of the loose ends later.'

I didn't know why I hated Midian's suggestion that I was anything more than I seemed. Maybe because I was frightened that it might be true, and one more world-shifting change was set to pop my brain. One question kept pushing through the confusion, and even though I more than half didn't want to hear the answer, it came out. I ran my hand through my hair, trying to pull myself together.

'They really are the ones who killed Eric, aren't they?'

Aubrey sighed. His arm behind me shifted. I wanted it to come down around my shoulders, but it didn't.

'I think so. The Invisible College . . . Eric's talked about them before. I didn't know that he was going up against them now. They're not good.'

'What are they, then? I mean, not good. No cookies. Check.'

Aubrey leaned in. I could smell the detergent on his shirt, the salt and musk under it like a perfume made from freshly washed boy. Something was making my throat a little dry, and I didn't know if it was his body close to mine or another aftereffect of the shock. Or if there was a difference.

'There was a story Eric told me one time. He said Coin had been part of a scheme that took orphans from Eastern Europe and . . . hollowed them out. Put other things in them. Riders. And then the kids were adopted out. People would think they were adopting children, and instead, they'd get . . . monsters. Families would be broken apart. The riders would have a safe place to grow until they were ready to move on or spawn daughter organisms.'

'And Coin did it all for shits and giggles?'

'Coin did it in trade,' Aubrey said. 'For the favors those riders could do him later. Eric stopped it. The Invisible College has hated him ever since. So yes, I think he'd be wise to try and break Coin. And I know they'd want Eric dead.'

'Okay,' I said.

He looked over at me. I couldn't quite read his expression. I tilted my head, asking the question without asking.

'You're like him,' he said. 'You're . . . impressive in the same way.'

I felt a flush in my skin, and I caught my breath like he'd asked me to freaking prom. I was acting like a sixteen-year-old on her first date. It embarrassed me. I tried to stop.

'What way's that?' I asked.

'Well, you didn't even know about Eric's work until today, right? Now you've found out about him, and about riders and magic. You've been attacked. You've seen people die. Any one of those would have been enough to spin you. All of them together . . . I'm surprised you aren't in a puddle on the floor.'

'I feel like I am,' I said with a great big adult, non-sexually charged sigh. 'I feel like I'm floating off somewhere about three feet to the left of me.'

'Well, it doesn't show. And food and sleep can't hurt, right?'

He shifted, preparing to rise, and I reached out. I put my hand on his arm. From his eyes, I thought he felt the plea in the motion.

'It's going to be all right,' he said. 'I know it doesn't seem like it, but it will. You've been six different women in the last twenty-four hours. You're just a little dizzy. But it'll be all right.'

I was aware of how badly I wanted to kiss him. I could feel his arms around me, my face against his shoulder as if it had already happened.

'Jane,' he said.

I corrected him. He looked embarrassed and tried out my name a couple of times, finally getting it right. Before he could get back to his thought, I leaned over toward him. I could feel the warmth of his body, hear the shushing of his shirt against his skin as he moved. I'd heard stories about people hooking up after something terrible. Emergency room doctors falling into bed together, soldiers after a firefight, strangers who'd survived some life-threatening disaster. I'd never understood it, but now it made sense.

I wanted. I wanted him to touch me. I wanted his body to reassure mine. I wanted something that would take away everything I'd seen and touched and done, something bright and good and true. Something that would hold off death. I wanted him to say my name again, and not in the tone he'd just used.

The voice, when it came, wasn't his. It came from the back of the house, and it was Uncle Eric's.

'Hey,' it said, 'you've got a call.'

I yelped and jumped back, my heart thumping like a pair of sneakers in a dryer. Aubrey looked at me, and then back at the dark hallway.

'Hey,' the voice came again. It was tinny, like someone talking through a computer. 'You've got a call.'

Aubrey walked back into the darkness. I followed. Eric's voice led us to the bedroom. A huge, elaborate cell phone glowed on the bedside table, its screen the size of my palm. The voice was Eric's ringtone. I picked it up. The incoming call wasn't a number I recognized. Aubrey shook his head; he didn't know either.

'Let it drop to voice mail,' he said. I did, and when the icon appeared saying that there was a message waiting, I thumbed through the menu system until I found it. The cell dialed. I put it on speaker.

'Um,' the cell said. 'Hi. I'm looking for Eric Heller? My name's Candace Dorn? A friend of mine told me that you were in Denver right now and you could help people with . . . um . . . weird problems? I know this sounds really odd, but I think there's something wrong with my dog. He wanted me to call you.'

The voice sighed, as if giving up something. When she spoke again, she sounded resigned.

'My dog wanted me to call you. If you don't think I'm a complete nutcase, could you please call me back?'

She left her number, said thanks, and hung up. I looked over at Aubrey.

'Her dog?' I said.

'It's possible,' Aubrey said. 'Sometimes dogs can pick up on things. If there's a rider trying to cross over from Next Door, or if someone is being ridden. I've heard weirder things. And that's what Eric does. Well, did.'

'Helped people with their dogs?'

Aubrey chuckled, then smiled, then sobered.

'Eric did what needed doing,' he said. 'It kept him busy. There are probably going to be a lot of people looking for him. For a while, at least.'

'I should call her back,' I said, 'and tell her that we can't help.'

Before I could press the button, he reached out, putting his hand over mine.

'Let's hold off,' he said. 'Just in case she's really with the Invisible College.'

'Right,' I said. 'I should have thought of that.'

I looked into his eyes. The desire I'd felt was still there, and I thought maybe I could also see a little of it in him. But the moment had passed. He felt it too, because he sighed.

'I'm going to try to scare up some food,' he said. 'Then you should sleep, if you can.'

'What about you?' I asked.

'I'll be here,' he said. 'Don't worry.'

We ate grilled cheese sandwiches with the crusts cut off and ginger ale from bottles he found in a dusty back cabinet. We didn't talk much, and when we did, it wasn't about anything. When I made my way back to the bedroom, he didn't follow me.

I expected to fall asleep quickly, but as tired as I was, I couldn't wind down. Instead, I punched the pillows into new shapes. I shifted to my back or my belly or my side. I got up and did sit-ups to tire myself out. I looked out the windows. I wondered what my parents would think.

The thought alone evoked my father's glowering disapproval and my mother's rabbitlike fear. Uncle Eric had been rich beyond any of our dreams. He'd spent his days fighting against spirits that invade the world and possess human bodies. No wonder Dad freaked out. Anything that didn't fit into his neatly packaged worldview was evil by definition. Mom would have just made some tea and ignored the idea that anything was happening anywhere. It wasn't really something I'd been thinking of majoring in either, for that matter. The question was, now that it had all fallen into my lap, what was I going to do about it?

Just after midnight, I gave up, put on my same blue jeans and liberated another one of Eric's white button-down shirts. The living room was silent, the flickering blue of the television the only light. Aubrey lay on the couch, his arm tucked under his head, his eyes closed. I stood there for a few seconds, watching him breathe, then went back and got a blanket to put over him. The television was on a news station and muted. I turned it off.

The sane thing would have been to get a boatload of money, sell all the properties just in case there were two-hundred-year-old curse victims hanging out in them, and begin again someplace new. Start from scratch and forget the last twelve hours, like they'd never happened.

I wondered if they would let me. The Invisible College. I remembered the blue-eyed woman. I saw her die again, and if my heart sped up and my throat closed down, it wasn't as bad as it had been before. She'd been dead before she walked in. She'd been possessed by something from outside the real world and sent to finish the job they'd started when they killed my uncle. She was a victim, not of me but of Randolph Coin. Or whatever evil spirit had taken over Coin's body.

I wanted to believe it, and I halfway did. But only halfway. Faith and I had always had a difficult relationship, and we were talking about killing people—killing *more* people—based on nothing but faith. Sitting in the dark at the kitchen table listening to the air conditioner hum, my mind kept circling back to prod at things.

Was it more likely that spirits from outside reality snuck in and took people over, or that people went nuts sometimes? Or got involved with cults? Was it more likely that I had magic superpowers I'd never known about, or that I'd had a hellish adrenaline rush and the people I was fighting weren't actually all that competent? Was it more likely that Midian was two-hundred-plus years old, or that he was a disfigured guy in his fifties with a lousy set of coping skills? Aubrey seemed kind and sane and good, but I'd known a lot of men who seemed just the same and believed in things that I didn't. God, for instance.

I looked at the window, and the darkness had made it a mirror. Here was a woman on the trailing edge of twenty-two with no friends left. No family left. A shitload of money from nowhere, and the man who'd given it to her—who, judging from the way he'd put her name on everything, had always meant for her to have it—had been murdered.

I looked the same. Same dark eyes. Same black hair. Same mole I'd always told myself I'd have taken off as soon as I had the tattoo removal done. But I wasn't the same. And if everyone I'd met that day—Midian, Aubrey, Jake, Ex—was insane or deluded, I wasn't sure it changed anything. Uncle Eric was dead. Someone had killed him. And I was going to find out who. Randolph Coin was the best lead I had. So that was the lead I'd follow.

A sound caught my attention. The click of metal against metal in a slow, almost meditative rhythm. It was me. Without even noticing, I'd taken the key ring out of my pocket and was tapping it against my thigh. The key to the doomed apartment, and two others. Storage facilities. I lifted the keys, running my fingers over their teeth.

'Yes, little tomato,' I said to the key ring. 'I'll check you out too.'

5

I was asleep when the others arrived. I woke up to the sound of voices and the smell of fresh coffee. I pulled myself together: quick shower, fresh clothes, and out to the kitchen. Midian, his ruined face seeming oddly comforting only because it was familiar, stood at the stove wearing a buff-colored apron. Ex and Aubrey were sitting at the table where the lawyer and I had been just the day before. Chogyi Jake smiled at me in greeting while he poured coffee into a black mug.

It was like walking into someone else's home. The four of them all seemed perfectly at ease. It was like they all belonged there and I was the intruder, awkward and out of place. I hadn't bothered with shoes. The kitchen tile was cool against my soles, and the coffee almost too hot to drink.

'I was wondering if you were going to get up,' Midian said. 'You aren't Jewish or Muslim or anything fucked up like that, are you?'

'*Excuse* me?' I said.

In answer, he held up a package of bacon, his desiccated face taking on a querying expression.

'Yes, I'd love some bacon,' I said. 'Thanks.'

'We were just going over strategy,' Aubrey said. 'How to proceed from here.'

'The . . . um . . .' I said, gesturing vaguely with the coffee.

'No one's finding those bodies,' Midian said, slapping several slices of bacon onto a hot skillet. He raised his voice over the sudden violent sizzling. 'Say what you will about these boys' moral systems, they're effective when it comes to hiding evidence.'

Ex shot an angry look at Midian. Chogyi Jake seemed more amused. I had the sense from Aubrey that the morning had been going pretty much along these lines. I hopped up on the counter. It was the sort of thing that would have made my father crazy, and even in these surreal circumstances, I felt a little rebellious doing it. None of the men present had any objection.

'Well, I have some things I need to do,' I said. 'I have to take Eric's death certificate to a couple banks and fill out signature cards and things, unless you guys plan to buy all my food and stuff.'

'Everything does go better with money,' Midian said, nodding his approval in my general direction. 'Eggs with that?'

'Sure,' I said.

He moved the still-frying bacon to one side of the skillet and cracked two eggs into the grease in the cleared space while Ex shook his head and said, 'I don't like it. We're under siege here. We need to take precautions.'

'Not siege,' Chogyi Jake said. 'Attack, yes, but to say siege presupposes that our movements are limited.'

'And it's not really you,' I said. I hadn't thought about the words, they just came out. Four pairs of eyes turned to me. I shrugged. 'They came after me. Well, me and Midian. I pulled Aubrey into it, and he pulled you guys.'

'She's right,' Ex said. 'Coin doesn't have a lock on the three of us. If there's legwork to be done, it should be—'

Midian coughed out his derision.

'Don't be a schmuck, Ex. The girl's cutting you loose. Over easy all right? I can do over medium if you really want, but I'm not feeding you a hard yolk.'

'It's fine,' I said, trying not to look at Ex or Aubrey. I was sure my embarrassment was showing, and it only made me more embarrassed. 'And I'm not . . . I don't see how I'm in a position to cut anyone loose or keep anyone on, for that matter. But I am a big girl. All grown up. I don't want any of you in trouble over me.'

Somehow saying it out loud lent me the confidence to meet Aubrey's eyes. He looked sympathetic but also resolute.

'Eric was a friend of ours,' Aubrey said. 'Of all of ours. This isn't just your fight.'

'We know the risks,' Chogyi Jake said.

'Better than you do,' Ex finished.

'Three fucking musketeers. That makes you d'Artagnan,' Midian said, handing me a plate. The eggs were touched with rosemary, two strips of crisped bacon at the side, a slice of golden-brown toast with an almost subliminal layer of butter, and a sprig of parsley to set the whole thing off.

'Thank you,' I said. I actually meant about the food, but Ex was the one who replied.

'Not needed,' he said. It was the kindest tone he'd taken all morning. 'This is what we do.'

The conversation barreled ahead as I ate. By the time I used the last crust of the toast to sop up the last golden trail of egg, Aubrey had a game plan in place. He would take me to run my errands—bank and Eric's storage facilities both—while Ex went back to the apartment on Inca to make sure everything that needed cleaning was cleaned and also to retrieve the books and whiteboard I'd seen when I was there. Chogyi Jake and Midian were going to stay at the house and go over Eric's wards and protections, including digging up any information that would explain why I'd suddenly gotten good at fighting and hadn't set off Midian's alarms. We would reconvene that evening with any new information in hand and decide what we were going to do.

Going out to Aubrey's minivan, I saw the van Chogyi Jake had talked about last night, its paint a faded noncolor and windowless in a way that would have made me nervous if I was walking alone. A black, almost chitinous sports car was parked beside it.

'Ex?' I asked, nodding at the sports car.

'Ex,' Aubrey agreed. 'You've got the directions to your banks?'

I held up three MapQuest printouts.

'And the storage joints besides,' I said as he pulled out. The air conditioner hummed, cranking out a cool breeze to fight the August heat. I watched the house in the side mirror as we drove away. It could have been anyone's. There was nothing about it that gave any hint that Eric Heller had been anything particularly special. We turned at the intersection of a bigger, busier street, and the house vanished.

'I've got one thing I need to do when we're done,' Aubrey said. 'It's just a quick stop to pick up some things.'

'Your place?'

'My work, actually,' he said.

'Oh,' I said, then laughed. 'You know, I never really thought of you as having a job. What do you do when you aren't fighting the forces of darkness?'

'I'm a research biologist,' he said. 'I've got a grant from the NIH, and I'm based at the University of Denver. It's how I met Eric.'

'Seriously? And you're studying what? The biomechanics of ghosts?'

He laughed. I liked the way he laughed. I had the sudden physical memory of leaning in last night, almost kissing him. It was disorienting.

'Parasitology,' he said. 'Did you say Seventeenth Street?'

'And Stout, yeah. So you work with . . . what, stomach worms?'

'My dissertation was on behavior modification of mammals by single-cell parasites. Eric read it and tracked me down. Have you ever heard of *Toxoplasma gondii*?'

'I was an English major, when I was anything,' I said. 'If Shakespeare wrote a sonnet about it, I might have run into it. Otherwise, no.'

'It's a really cool organism,' he said. 'Pretty much the classic example of parasitic mind control.'

'Parasitic *mind control*?' I said. My flesh crawled a little.

'In mammals at least. There are some pretty great ones for insects and mollusks too, but if you want to play with hosts that have spinal cords, *T. gondii* is the best game in town.'

Aubrey's eyes were bright, and he leaned forward over the steering wheel as he spoke. Enthusiasm made him seem younger than he was. I kind of wished he was getting jazzed about something with a lower ick factor, but as he went on, the urge to wash my hands lessened a little and I found myself getting interested.

'It usually lives in a cat's intestinal tract,' he said. 'We call the cat the final host. It's where the organism really wants to be.'

'So what does it do to the cat's mind?' I asked.

'Nothing. Zip. Nada. But there's a middle part. In order to get from one cat to another, it passes through mice. So the first step is to go from the inside of a cat to the inside of a mouse.'

'And you do that by . . . ?' I asked just a heartbeat before I figured it out. I made a face. 'We're about to talk about mice eating cat poop, aren't we?'

'Well, yeah,' he said. I weighed whether to change the subject back to mystical assassins and my recent slaughter thereof, and reluctantly decided to stay with the poop-eating mice. We paused at a red light. Two homeless men passed beside the car, faces flushed with the heat.

'The thing that's interesting is what happens once it's inside the mouse,' Aubrey continued. 'Normally, mice avoid anyplace that smells like a cat's living there. Just good sense. But infect a mouse with *T. gondii,* and it isn't afraid anymore. In fact, it starts liking the smell. The infected mouse starts hanging out where cats are more likely to be. Good for the cat, because it's more likely to get a meal. Good for the parasite. It can get into a fresh host. Lousy for the mouse.'

'Okay, that's the creepiest thing ever,' I said. 'I think I get it, though. That's like riders. The things that are inside Coin? And the ones we killed last night?'

The light turned green. Traffic started moving.

'Some riders can be like that, yeah,' Aubrey said. 'I don't think the Invisible College ones are quite that flavor. But there are also a lot of riders that will just hang out in the back of someone's mind and . . . *change* them. You know?'

'The way your amoeba thing changes mice,' I said.

'Actually, the way it changes people. *T. gondii* infects humans too. People with the cysts in their brain suffer mild disinhibitions. Men become more prone to violence.'

'And women?'

Aubrey glanced over at me and then back at the road.

'Sex,' he said. 'It makes women more affectionate and prone to . . . ah . . .'

'Get prone?' I suggested. A green sedan cut in front of us. Aubrey swore, hitting the brakes and his horn at the same time. I took the opportunity to switch subjects.

'So Eric read your paper and tracked you down?'

'Yeah,' Aubrey said. He seemed relieved not to be talking about sex. I wasn't sure whether I was or not. 'He was working on an idea about riders. See, there are some things about riders that look a lot like biological agents. And then there are things that really just don't. What we were doing was sort of reverse-engineering riders. Figuring out what kinds of constraints are on them from the way they act.'

'Hey, that was Stout,' I said, pointing back at the street sign we'd just passed.

'It's a one-way. They all are downtown. We'll go down Champa and turn around.'

'Okay,' I said. 'Sorry. You were saying? Reverse-engineering something?'

'Yeah, like cicadas. Did you know cicadas have prime-numbered cycles?'

'I did hear about that, yeah,' I said. 'Something about staying away from things that eat them, right?'

'That's the theory. If the cicadas are trying to avoid a predator with a five-year cycle, they develop a thirteen-year period and only coincide with the predator every sixty-five years.'

'Okay,' I said. I was getting a little lost, but I didn't want Aubrey to think I was stupid. 'So what's the five-year predator?'

'There isn't one,' he said. 'At least not now. But that the prime numbers show up suggests that there *was* one, even if it's already gone extinct. So when primes show up in riders, maybe it's because there's something out there that *they're* avoiding. The Invisible College is actually a good example of that. They have this ceremony every seven years. Why seven?'

'Because it's a prime, and they're avoiding something?' I said.

'Maybe, yeah. Or then again, maybe because there are seven wandering stars,' Aubrey said. 'Or because God made the world in seven days. Or there are supposed to be seven categories of the soul. It's hard to know what kinds of rules actually apply. Eric wasn't about to let any good hypothesis go untested, though. Here, this is Seventeenth Street. I'm going to grab that space and we can walk from here.'

'Sounds good,' I said, noticing for no good reason that seventeen was a prime. I got out of the minivan, stepping into the beating sun. I felt a little light-headed, but whether it was the conversation or the altitude or just the spiritual jet lag that my utterly transformed life brought on, I couldn't say. Aubrey came up at my side, his fingertips brushing my arm. I let him lead me across the street.

'Eric thought if we could figure out how riders changed people, we could make a better guess at what they wanted. What their agenda was.'

'Midian said they're an infection,' I said.

'Midian has some simplistic ideas about infection,' Aubrey said.

The bank was down a very short block. As if we'd agreed on it, Aubrey and I dropped the subjects of parasites and spirits when we entered the dry, cool desert of the financial world. The lawyer had given me the name of the woman to ask for when I got to the desk. I expected to be put in one of the little wood-grain cubicle offices that competed for space with the line of tellers, but instead Aubrey and I were escorted to an elevator, and then up to a plush private office where I presented my paperwork, signed theirs, and was given access to the first of Eric's cash accounts. They promised me an ATM card in about a week. Just to see if I could, I withdrew ten thousand dollars in cash. The woman didn't blink.

'Dinner's on me,' I said as we walked back out onto the street. Aubrey looked stunned.

'It *really* is,' he said.

There were other banks and more paperwork, but I put them aside. My hands kept finding their way to the keys for the storage units, fidgeting with them. Whatever I was getting into, I now had enough money in my name to do whatever needed doing. Aubrey was oddly quiet as we walked, and I took the chance to pull out the MapQuest printouts and see which of my next stops looked closest. I didn't realize how much the August heat had been pressing on me until Aubrey started up the car and the first blast of the air conditioner hit my skin.

'Okay,' I said. 'This one's on Eighteenth Street. That should be pretty close, right?'

'What? Oh. Yeah, that's over by the Children's Hospital. We could almost walk to that.'

'Let's drive anyway,' I said. And then, 'Hey, are you all right?'

'I'm fine,' Aubrey said. 'I just . . . Eric and I never talked about money. I didn't know that he was in that kind of tax bracket.'

'Me either,' I said as we pulled out into traffic. 'Turns out there was a whole lot I didn't know.'

Aubrey smiled, but his brows didn't quite lose their

furrow. It was only a few minutes before we pulled into the storage facility. The gate code was written on the key chain. I read it to Aubrey, and he leaned out and punched the buttons. The bar rose, and we headed into the asphalt rat maze that was the storage joint.

I didn't know quite what I'd expected, but this place wasn't it. It was too prosaic. White stucco buildings with green garage doors lined a dozen tight alleyways. A family was loading boxes into the back of a big orange U-Haul truck, a girl maybe eight years old waving to us as we passed.

Aubrey cruised down two alleys, struggling to make the turns before I saw the numbers for Eric's unit. We came to a halt just outside it. I fit the key into the padlock. The click as it came free was soft and deep. The lock was heavier in my hand than I'd expected. I took hold of the rolling door, prepared to lift it up, but I hesitated. Despite the heat, I shivered.

'The people who have the thing,' I said. 'They don't know it, do they?'

'The people who have what?'

'The *T.* whatever. The parasite,' I said.

'No. I mean, you could test for antibodies and find out, but generally there aren't many symptoms.'

'Except that it changes who they are,' I said.

Aubrey wiped the sweat off his forehead with the back of one hand. A few alleys over, the U-Haul truck started up with a loud rattle. I kept my fingertips on the shaped metal handle of the garage door, hesitating.

'Is something wrong?' he asked.

Yes, I wanted to say. I fought four people with guns to a standstill yesterday. I walked through Midian's magic alarms like they weren't there. I have more money in my backpack right now than I've ever had in my bank account. And what if whatever's in here changes things *again*? I didn't particularly like who I was last week, but at least I *knew* who I was.

'No,' I said. 'It's nothing.'

'You're cool?'

'Cucumberesque,' I said.

I tightened my grip on the handle and pulled. The garage door shrieked in metallic complaint and rose up. Daylight spilled into a concrete cube behind it, smaller than an actual garage. White cardboard boxes were stacked three deep against the walls, and an industrial-looking set of steel shelves at the back supported a collection of odd objects. A violin case, a duffel bag, two translucent bowling balls, a stuffed bear with a wide pink heart embroidered on its chest.

It looked like a secondhand store, but it felt like a puzzle. I picked up the stuffed bear. The nap of the fake fur was worn, the thread that made its mouth was loose and thin with use. A child had loved this bear once. I wondered who that had been, and what had brought the beloved object here.

'I've got something,' Aubrey said.

He was standing beside the stack of boxes, the top one open. Looking over his shoulder, I saw a stack of three-ring

binders with words stenciled on the spines: INVISIBLE
COLLEGE — 1970–1976. INVISIBLE COLLEGE — 1977–1981.
There were easily a dozen of them. Aubrey lifted one out
and opened it.

'What is it?'

'Newspaper clippings. Lists of names and places,' he said
with a sigh. 'I don't know what it all means.'

'Let's get it in the car,' I said. I suddenly wanted very
badly to just leave. 'Let's get as much of this out of here as
we can and we'll make sense of it later.'

He grunted in agreement and hauled the box out toward
his car. I grabbed the next box and followed him. It wasn't
until we picked the duffel bag up off the shelf that we
found the guns.

6

'This is nice,' Midian said, chambering a round with the rolling sound that only shotguns make. He looked down the barrel and nodded his appreciation. 'Good workmanship.'

Chogyi Jake and Aubrey were squatting by the coffee table. Three empty shells lay on the table's edge, two small piles of debris in the center. Ex stood by the kitchen table, copying the diagrams from the Inca Street whiteboard onto a legal pad.

'They're all loaded the same way,' Aubrey said. 'Silver shot, rock salt, and I'm not sure what this is.'

'Iron filings,' Ex said. 'According to this, he loaded them with silver, salt, and iron.'

'If he wasn't sure precisely what form the rider took, that would cover a very broad range,' Chogyi Jake said.

'Or if he was loading for more than one,' Midian said. 'You gotta remember, he was hiring on a *loupine* for muscle. They're tough bastards, but not the last word in reliable.'

I sat on the couch, my knees drawn up to my chest, watching and listening. Through the evening, the four men had decoded Eric's plan, details unfolding like petals falling open.

According to the calendar Eric had left us, the Invisible

College was scheduled to begin the rituals that would summon riders and inject them into the new crop of initiates within the next day or two. As the ceremonies continued, the gap between the real world and what Eric called the Pleroma and Aubrey referred to as Next Door would turn permeable. Randolph Coin would be at his most vulnerable just before the final ceremony, scheduled for just after dawn on August 11, one week from today.

So now we had a countdown. Seven days.

In seven days, we were going to kill someone. The thought made my skin crawl. Or we were going to get the rat bastard who'd killed Eric, which felt better. My head kept bouncing between anxiety and wrath, like I was two different people.

'This is all from the one storage unit, right?' Ex asked, walking into the main room. 'You didn't make it to the other one?'

'No room in the car,' Aubrey said.

'We need to get to that other one,' Ex said. 'I think it has props for the invocation to draw Coin out. We'll need to inventory those.'

'I've got to . . .' I said, standing and heading for the back door. 'Excuse me.'

I heard the silence behind me as I walked out into the backyard. I could feel their eyes on my back even after I closed the door. The yard was immaculate: the grass green as emeralds and freshly cut, mums in the flower beds threatening to bloom, a cherry tree with a little overripe fruit still on the branches making the air heavy with sweetness and corruption. I sat in the darkness and stared up at the moon. I saw the inked face of the blue-eyed woman.

The door slid open behind me, and then just as quietly shut.

'Hey. Are you all right?'

Aubrey looked uncertain in the dim light. He was wearing blue jeans and a T-shirt with the logo of an old science fiction show, long since off the air. His hair was mussed. It occurred to me that we'd forgotten to stop by his labs at the university.

'I can't do this,' I said. 'We're talking about murdering someone.'

He came to my side and lowered himself to the ground, legs crossed.

'I thought you understood,' he said. 'These aren't people. Not anymore. They're—'

'Riders,' I said. 'Spiritual parasites that have magic powers and take over people's bodies. I understand that. I just . . .'

I closed my eyes and saw Midian fire his Luger into the back of the woman's head.

'Jayné?'

'I just don't believe it,' I said. 'I want to. But I don't.'

'You think we're lying?' he asked. The idea seemed to surprise him. I didn't laugh, partly because it wasn't funny.

'It isn't about trust. I believe that *you* think it's true,' I said. 'That's not the same. I grew up with a father who knew how the world worked. Who knew how God worked, and what was right and what was wrong. And I believed everything he said because he was sure. And then when it turned out that I *wasn't* sure . . .'

I spread my hands.

'Knowing that *you* all believe it isn't the same as believing it myself,' I said. 'And I can't do this if it isn't true. I can go to the police. I can hire a bodyguard. I can do a lot of different things, but I can't kill someone.'

Aubrey was quiet. I wanted to brush the hair away from his eyes. I wanted to ask him to forgive me.

'If you knew that riders were real,' he said. 'If you had evidence that the world really does work the way we all say it does, could you trust me about Coin and the Invisible College?'

'I don't know,' I said. 'Probably.'

He was silent for a moment, then sighed and looked up at the moon with me. I could feel the subtle warmth of his body. Somewhere nearby, a police siren rose and faded away. My stomach felt like I swallowed a bowlful of lead shot.

'You're angry?' I asked.

'What? No! No, I'm not mad. I'm just thinking.'

'Did *you* believe it? When Eric came to you and told you all about this . . . this stuff. Did you believe it?'

'No,' Aubrey said. 'He had to prove it to me.'

A minute later, he rose and walked slowly back into the house. I heard voices raised in conversation. Midian, Ex. I didn't think Chogyi Jake ever raised his voice, so if he was talking I might never know. He reminded me of my mother that way.

I had ten thousand dollars in my pocket, less forty that

I'd spent on pizza and beer for the bunch of them. I could Google private investigators tonight, make a half-dozen calls in the morning, and set hounds on Randolph Coin's heels. If he was really the person who'd killed Eric, I could get the evidence and have the bastard thrown in jail for the rest of his life. I didn't know why that seemed to make less sense than magical vigilantes taking on a society of evil wizards.

I thought of the three small stones dropping at the apartment, one-two-three. It could have been some kind of magical alarm system. It could have been something else.

I put my head in my hands and hoped that my mind would clear. It didn't.

I heard Aubrey come back out. When I looked over, something was glowing white and blue in the palm of his hand. It said something about my state of mind that I thought it was a ball of witch fire or some other tiny miracle. Then he stepped a little closer, and it was just the screen of Eric's cell phone. He held it out to me.

'Call her,' he said.

'Who?' I asked, taking the phone. It was warm.

'The woman that called. The one with the dog.'

I looked down at the phone. The icon for voice mail was still there.

'What if she's with the Invisible College?' I said.

'I'll take one of the shotguns,' Aubrey said, and something in his voice was light, even though I knew he was serious. I thumbed through the logs, found the most recent missed call, and selected the menu option that returned it.

Aubrey sat next to me. The branches of the cherry tree shifted in the breeze.

'Hello?' a woman said. I thought the voice was the same, but it seemed tighter.

'Hi,' I said. 'This is Jayné Heller. I think you called my uncle Eric?'

'Oh, thank God,' the woman said. She sounded like she was crying. 'Oh, thank God.'

I'd expected that, at the soonest, we'd arrange to meet the woman and her dog sometime in the morning. But ten minutes after I ended the call, Aubrey and I were in his minivan headed north for Boulder.

'It used to be left-wing hippie central, kind of the way Colorado Springs is the home port of all the right-wing nut jobs,' Aubrey said. 'There were a lot of people dabbling in alternative spiritualities and magic and drugs and things. These days, it's mostly people who feel like they're saving the planet because they're buying groceries from Whole Foods.'

'Okay,' I said.

'Did she tell you anything about what was going on?'

'Just that her dog wanted her to call us,' I said. 'I think it has to do with her boyfriend too, but I'm not sure.'

'She was pretty upset, sounds like.'

'Yeah,' I said. Ahead of us, taillights tracked off into the darkness, lines of red in the black. 'Yeah, she was pretty messed up. I don't know what we're doing, though. I don't know anything about what Eric used to do.'

'I know enough to start,' Aubrey said. 'Hopefully it'll be simple.'

We turned onto Highway 36, and then, sooner than I'd expected, we were pulling onto the South Boulder Road exit. A knot was tying itself in my belly, embarrassment and fear.

I was embarrassed because I was about to go talk to a stranger—a desperate one—about supernatural ghosties slipping into her dog's mind, and only half of me thought it was possible. The fear was because the other half thought it was.

Candace Dorn's house was a pretty bungalow with a wide porch, complete with swing. A huge tree commanded the yard, choking out all competition. Even the grass looked thin and unlikely where the tree's shadow would have fallen in daylight. All the lights were on, the windows blazing, like the woman was trying to push back night itself. Aubrey killed the engine, then reached into the backseat for the leather satchel he'd packed before we left. I grabbed my backpack.

One of the shotguns was back there too. He didn't take it out, and as we headed up the root-cracked concrete walk to the house, I wasn't sure if I was relieved at that or worried.

The woman who answered the door reminded me of my high school art teacher. She had dark, curly hair and skin that had tanned too many times, now permanently dark and leathery. She had a dieter's figure and a pianist's hands. Something in the way she held herself caught my attention, but I couldn't put my finger on it.

'Candace Dorn? I'm Jayné,' I said. 'This is Aubrey. He's here to help.'

'Please come in,' she said, standing back. I wondered whether she'd have done the same thing if we'd had a shotgun. Something made me think she would. 'Thank you for coming out. I don't . . . I just don't know what to do. I don't believe any of this is really happening.'

'Can you tell us what exactly is going on?' Aubrey asked.

The house had hardwood floors and pale patterned rugs. Tin Mexican wall sconces threw white light up the walls, and clunky, colorful paintings struggled to give individuality to furniture that all came from IKEA. I noticed that there was a wicker basket by the fireplace cradling a crushed pillow slicked with white and brown dog hair.

'It started maybe a week ago,' Candace Dorn said. 'Charlie—that's my dog—woke up acting really strange. He was biting himself and barking at my fiancé, who he always just loved before. He wouldn't eat, he wouldn't let me go out of the house. He's never been like that before.'

'What did the vet say?' I asked.

Candace paced the length of her living room without answering me. Aubrey sat on the arm of an overstuffed chair.

'I don't believe in . . . voodoo or whatever,' Candace said at last.

'What makes you think this is voodoo?' I asked. 'Or, you know, whatever?'

Candace opened her mouth, closed it, then walked back

toward the rear of the house. Aubrey met my eyes with an unspoken question. I followed her.

The kitchen showed some signs of disarray. One of the cabinet doors was resting against the wall, its hinges broken. The wooden table had a long, fresh gouge white as a scar against the dark varnish. Candace walked to the back door, and I realized what about her stance bothered me. My first semester at college, I'd agreed to play tackle football with some friends even though they'd been drinking. I'd broken one rib and cracked another. For a month afterward, I'd walked just like Candace did now.

When she opened the door, a German shepherd was waiting. He froze when he saw us, his gaze shifting from Aubrey to me and back again. This was Charlie.

'These are the people I called,' Candace said. Her voice was unsteady. 'They're the ones who can help.'

I had never watched an animal's expression change before. Charlie's unease became something else. He nodded to me and then to Aubrey. If he'd been human, it would have been a perfect gesture of masculine greeting.

'Charlie,' I said, acting on a hunch, 'could you go to Aubrey's right hand and touch it with your left forepaw?'

Charlie barked once, and then did exactly as I'd asked. Aubrey's brows rose. Candace Dorn touched her hand to her mouth. There were tears in her eyes.

'That isn't Charlie in there, is it?' I asked.

She shook her head. The dog looked up at me with an intelligence that I could only think of as human. *You wanted proof*, I told myself. *You wanted to be sure.*

'Before this happened,' Aubrey asked, 'had anything else changed? A new piece of art or some new person coming into your home? Was anything different?'

'No,' she said. 'Nothing happened. It was just one day . . .'

'And when did your fiancé start beating you up?' I asked.

The silence was total. When Candace spoke again, she sounded defeated.

'After I called you,' she said. 'After he found out that I'd called.'

Aubrey let out his breath like someone had punched him. Charlie the dog looked up at me, brown eyes fearful and resolute. When I knelt and put my hand on his ruff, he whimpered once.

'There are some things that can displace people,' Aubrey said. 'Move into a body and cast the former owner out.'

'Like into an animal,' I said. 'Unclean spirits. So when you said that you could handle the easy ones, this wasn't what you had in mind, was it?'

'Not so much, no,' Aubrey said. 'I think we'll need Ex. If any of us can fix this, it'll be him. He used to be a Jesuit. Casting out spirits was one part of the coursework.'

Candace Dorn stepped forward, her hand out as if she was stopping us. The unease in her expression made perfect sense to me. We'd just come into this sudden surreal hell that her life had become and started talking like we understood it.

'What are you saying?' she demanded. 'What's going on here?'

'There are things called riders,' I said, surprised by how informed and competent I sounded given that I only knew what I'd been told in the last day or so. 'They're spirits. Our best guess is that one of them took over your fiancé's body and pushed his soul, or whatever you want to call it . . .'

I pointed at the dog. Charlie whined again. Candace didn't kneel down so much as melt. Her spun, emptied expression was perfectly familiar. I'd felt exactly like that since my first visit with Eric's lawyer.

'Aaron?' she said.

The dog—Charlie or Aaron or some combination of the two—stood up and walked over to her. The movement had a dignity that spoke as eloquently as words. *I would never have done this to you.* Candace started crying in earnest now, confusion and fear and relief. Aubrey already had his cell phone out. His face was gray and serious. I motioned him to come out to the front room with me.

Candace and her dog needed a moment alone.

Aubrey sat on the couch, explaining the situation in fast, telegraphic sentences. I could hear Ex's voice compressed to a thin, synthesized version of itself coming from the phone. I stood with my arms crossed, looked out the window into the hot August night, and tried to make sense of my own heart.

My sense of doubt and confusion was gone, and in its place, something richer and stranger was growing. The tattooed assassins, Midian's curse, Eric's death. My alleged powers. None of those had been as convincing as the expression in the dog's eyes.

So, okay, riders existed. Aubrey and Chogyi Jake and Ex and Midian weren't suffering a group delusion. They were telling the truth. I'd seen the evidence now, and so at last I could really believe.

And Eric. I was standing now where he would have been, doing—however poorly, however uncertainly, with my near total ignorance intact—what he would have done. I was proud of him, and sad beyond words that I hadn't known what he was when I could still have asked him about it.

There had to be a reason he hadn't told me. All the things he'd done for me over the years, all the little intercessions that kept me out of trouble with my dad. He'd been watching out for me then, and so maybe he'd been watching out for me in this too. One thing was certain: there were more kinds of danger in this than I had ever imagined.

But he'd also left it to me. He'd left me the keys to the kingdom. So he hadn't thought there were more kinds of danger than I could handle.

And that, oddly, was the answer I'd been looking for. The warmth in my heart was pride that he'd chosen me to take up his work. To step into lives like Candace's. It beat the crap out of being a college dropout with a bad reputation and no family. And maybe he'd known that too.

Still lost in speculation, I didn't notice the police cruiser slowing down until it pulled in behind Aubrey's minivan. I watched the cop get out, consider the house and the back of the minivan, then turn on the flashing lights and mutter into a radio strapped to his lapel. Aubrey cut the connection with Ex and looked out with me. He muttered something obscene.

'He must have seen the shotgun. We can't have this guy around when Ex shows up,' Aubrey said. 'Let me go see what's the trouble.'

He'd started walking past me toward the door, then stopped, his weight tugging at me. He turned to look at me, and I realized that I'd grabbed his arm. I hadn't meant to, but having done it, I knew why I had.

'Don't. Don't go,' I said. Then, louder, 'Candace? Hey, Candace. Your fiancé wouldn't be a cop, would he?'

7

He came up the same path I'd walked with Aubrey half an hour before, the palm of his hand resting on the butt of his pistol. The flashing lights silhouetted him and hid his face. At my side, Candace was staring out the window and murmuring a constant string of syllables equal parts prayer and vulgarity. The dog stood between her and the door, still and silent and thoroughly undoglike.

From my glimpses through the window, I guessed the man was around two hundred pounds. He had a Taser, Mace, a pistol. He had a badge. For all I knew his murmured conversation on his lapel radio had been calling more police to his cause. Plus which, he was a supernatural beastie capable of God only knew what.

We had Aubrey, me, Candace Dorn, and a very intelligent dog. I didn't like our chances.

'Okay,' Aubrey said nervously. 'We're going to be okay. We'll just . . . we have to just . . .'

The man reached the door and pounded on it. The house itself seemed to tremble.

'Candace!' the man shouted. 'Open the door!'

It was the voice—the anger and power and implicit violence in it—that snapped me into action. I took Candace by the arm, shaking her until her eyes shifted to mine. Her face was pale.

'You need to get out of here,' I said. 'You and Charlie head out the back. Go to a neighbor's or a friend's. Anyplace it'll take him a while to find you.'

'That isn't Aaron,' she said. 'It's his body, but that isn't Aaron.'

'I know,' I said. 'Leave this part to us. Just get out. Do it now.'

The dog nuzzled her hand, whining slightly, then jerked its muzzle toward the kitchen. *Let's go.* Candace drew a long, shaking breath while the thing in her fiancé's body hammered the door again. She nodded, pulled me into an embrace as sudden as it was brief, and then she and Charlie the dog were gone.

'How long until Ex gets here?' I asked, trying hard to keep my voice from shaking.

'Half an hour if there's no traffic and he's speeding,' Aubrey said. 'An hour if there is and he isn't. Did you have a plan besides getting those two out of harm's way?'

'Nope,' I said.

'Then we'll probably want to keep his attention on us until they're clear,' he said, as if this was all perfectly sane and acceptable. I saw then how someone could love Aubrey. 'Hold on a minute!' he yelled. 'We're coming!'

The thing at the door paused, surprised (I guessed) by a man's voice and the unhurried, casual tone Aubrey had taken. Aubrey pulled a cloth bag from his pocket and pressed it into my hand.

79

'Ashes and salt,' he said. 'It may help block or absorb anything it tries to do.'

'You mean besides shoot us,' I said. The bag was heavier than I expected.

'Besides that,' Aubrey agreed.

'Open this fucking door and do it now!' the cop shouted.

'Who is it?' Aubrey asked, his voice loud enough to carry through the door. 'Can I see some identification, please?'

The shots weren't like the ones you hear on TV or in the movies. Two dry cracks, quieter than the pounding of the thing's fists, and the wood around the doorknob bloomed into splinters. The ridden policeman kicked the door open so hard it almost came off its hinges. Aubrey leaped back, diving for cover. I stepped around the corner, the cloth bag gripped tight in my hand.

'Where is she?' the thing in the cop's body demanded. The voice had lost any vestige of humanity now; the words were flies and saw blades. 'Give her over, and I might let you live.'

'She's upstairs,' Aubrey lied. 'Just leave me out of it.'

It surged into the room. I hadn't been prepared for the change. Its skin was darker than a bad bruise and tinted blue as a storm cloud; the head that canted forward from the shoulders was long-jawed and carnivorous, the eyes the yellow of cat piss. Its chest worked like a bellows, ripping the police uniform and popping the Velcro fastenings of the bulletproof vest. I wasn't afraid of being shot anymore. I was just afraid.

Aubrey was on his knees, struggling to stand. The

creature raised a hand, points of metal or chitin glittering on its fingertips. With a sense of being in a dream, I watched myself swing forward, grab those powerful fingers, and twist from my waist. Something in its wrist popped, and it let out a yell that seemed like it would break glass.

The impact when it slammed me against the wall drove my breath out. Its eyes were fixed on me. I saw Aubrey diving toward it, saw its leg lash out, saw Aubrey fall again. Its good hand was around my throat. The air was getting thin. I scratched at its eyes, my arms faster than I would have thought possible but still not fast enough. I didn't see its wounded hand cut into my side; I only felt it.

The cut was cold. My blood spilling down my ribs felt like ice water. And then something pushed in under my skin, something slick and cool and ancient beyond words. Instinctively, I knew the rider was entering me, trying to take my body as its own. I felt an answering warmth rise from the base of my spine to my heart to my throat. It felt like a fireball, and I shouted as I used it to push the invader out.

The creature stumbled back, dropping me to the ground. Its eyes were wide and uncomprehending. I thought I saw a flicker of fear before it launched itself at me again. I leaped toward it, inside its swing, and brought my fist up into the soft place under its jaw. The bag of ashes and salt burst like a water balloon. The thing choked and stumbled back. Aubrey appeared from nowhere swinging a fire poker like it was a machete. The beast raised its arms to protect its head against the assault, and for five or six seconds I thought we stood a chance.

'Jayné! Stay back!' Aubrey shouted, but I was already in motion. It caught my leg as I tried to kick it, lifting me up like a twig. My knee shifted, and I shrieked with pain. I caught a glimpse of Aubrey—red-faced, his teeth bared in rage—flailing at the thing's back with the poker. I was airborne. The plaster and lath wall gave when I hit it, but the sound of the fight was muffled now. Aubrey's yelling was distant and soft, the beast's answering howl no more than unpleasant. I tried to rise to my knees, but it didn't go as well as I'd hoped.

I opted for sitting, and when I looked up, the thing was squatting before me. It didn't look even vaguely human now. Its clothes were in ribbons, and the small glimmering badge that hung from one strip of shattered cloth seemed like an insult. The boots were strips of leather clinging to wide hooves. His belt . . .

I blinked, trying to gather myself. His belt was on the floor behind him. The gun was still in its holster.

'What are you?' it buzzed. I had the impression there was a light inside its mouth, like something was burning in there.

'My mother's daughter,' I said blearily; I'd meant Eric when I said it. My brain was clearly getting scrambled. I dropped to my belly and kicked off from the wall, scooping up the belt, drawing the gun, and twisting back to face the thing almost before it could react. Almost, but not quite. Its fist came down on the bridge of my nose and the world turned monochrome and quiet.

I almost didn't see the dog attack.

I wavered there on the edge of consciousness, and when I came back, the beast was grabbing at the German shepherd, whose teeth were buried in its neck. I raised the gun, but Aubrey put his hand over mine, pushing the barrel away.

'Can't kill the body,' he grunted. 'Need the body. Aaron! Close your eyes.'

I couldn't tell if the dog complied, but Aubrey staggered to his feet, a small black cylinder in his fist. There was a hissing sound, and the beast howled, scrabbling at its eyes with fingers that gouged great strips of flesh from its face. The dog leaped back, whining, and my own eyes started to water. Mace. I really didn't think that was going to stop it. I raised the gun again, but Aubrey had his arms spread wide, like he was gathering in the air itself. I saw his ribs flex as he breathed in, and I realized his shirt had been ripped apart somewhere in the violence. When he shouted, it wasn't a human sound. It rang like a bell, like there was music in it, like there was an angel speaking my name in a voice so low it deafened.

The beast twisted, shuddered, and sat. Its skin grew pale, its head thin, its face human. Aaron the fiancé lay on the splinters of a couch, his body slack. Aubrey staggered and fell to his knees.

I crawled over, putting my hand on Aubrey's thigh. He was trembling.

'Is it dead?' I managed to croak.

'Bound,' he said. 'Sleeping. Should be okay until Ex gets here.'

'Good trick.'

'Eric showed me.'

'Could have tried it a little earlier, though,' I said.

'Yeah, I was thinking that myself,' he said, then smiled. There was blood on his teeth. I smiled back, and the dog came to us, licking Aubrey's face nervously. I wanted to sleep, but instead I staggered to my feet and closed the blinds and the front door. The place was a ruin. Couch, coffee table, overstuffed chairs—all of them were broken. The walls were shattered in three places, and the glass shutters guarding the fireplace were shards clinging to strips of warped copper. I walked back to the kitchen, almost surprised to see it intact. I washed my hands until the shaking got too bad, and then I just stood there, leaning against the counter.

'You're hurt,' Aubrey said from the doorway.

'No. I'm . . .' I looked down at my blood-soaked side. 'Oh. Hey, yeah. I'm hurt.'

I laughed, and the pain shot out from my side to the base of my skull. Somehow that seemed hilarious, and I sank to the floor in a feedback loop of laughter and pain. I watched Aubrey's feet come across the tile floor, felt his hands lift me up to sitting. When he pulled off my shirt, I didn't stop him. I felt wrung out and quiet now. Through the door to the ruined front room, I saw the dog sitting, its eyes fixed, I assumed, on the newly human body resting in the wreckage. Aubrey's left eye was swelling shut, and I could see a bruise darkening at his collarbone. His hands shook. He touched a warm cloth to my side and I winced.

'I'm sorry,' he said.

'It's okay,' I said.

'No, I mean I'm sorry I brought you here. This was way more than I expected. It was stupid of me.'

'It's okay,' I repeated.

'You could have been killed.' I was a little surprised by the distress in his voice. Maybe I shouldn't have been. I took his hand in mine and drew his eyes up to meet my own.

'What would have happened to her if we hadn't come?' I asked. Aubrey nodded as if accepting my point, but when he tried to look away, I squeezed his hand. 'Really. What?'

'I don't know,' he said. 'In the short term, I don't know. It would have tried to protect itself while it grew to maturity. Then probably it would have taken her over too.'

'The rider,' I said.

'Or its daughter organism, yeah,' Aubrey said. 'This is how they breed. Or . . . well. I think it is. This is all coming from the parasitology filter. Ex would probably couch it in terms of souls and salvation.'

'I'll take your filter, thanks. This is what Eric wanted you for,' I said. 'To understand how parasites breed. And to stop them. And we did, right? So go us. Nice job.'

'I think this is going to need stitches,' he said.

I looked down at the ruined flesh where the rider's claws had cut me. When I got dizzy, I looked away.

'Yeah,' I said. 'I think you're right.'

The dog yipped once and rose to its feet. I heard the front door swing open then closed, and Ex came in, his pale eyes wide. Aubrey raised a hand in greeting, and Ex mirrored the gesture with an autonomic air.

'Turned out it was a little hairier than we thought,' I said. 'Who knew?'

'The guy out front has a rider,' Aubrey said. 'Probably *jaette* or *haugtrold*. The original soul's in the dog. The house belongs to Candace Dorn. The horse is her fiancé, Aaron. He's a cop. Since there isn't a SWAT team outside right now, I'm guessing the rider did something to keep the law away while he killed us.'

'And I need to go to a hospital, get stitched up,' I said. I thought I sounded very calm.

'Right,' Ex said, then a moment later, 'Okay. I'm on it.'

And that, more or less, was that. Aubrey got me a loose blouse from Candace's closet to preserve my modesty on the drive. I pressed a towel to my side and tried not to bleed on his minivan. On the way to the emergency room, we concocted a story that we'd been out on a date and got jumped by three muggers. Since it was Boulder, I suggested making them a band of roving neocons, and Aubrey laughed. By the time we staggered into the ER and plopped down to tell our story to the intake nurse, I almost felt human again. Parts of my body ached that I hadn't known existed, the doctor who looked me over called for about eight different X-rays to see how many of my bones were broken, and the blouse we took from Candace wound up balled into the biohazard can.

When they asked about my health insurance, I took the money out of my pocket. Nine thousand nine hundred and

change after pizza and beer. It was enough to cover treat-
ment and a night's observation. Barely. Even though he was
falling down exhausted, Aubrey took point talking to the
cops while I drifted in and out of consciousness. The hard,
narrow hospital bed was the most comfortable place I'd
ever been. Monitors strapped to my chest and arm let out
low pongs and chimes.

When I let my eyes close, my watch said it was one in
the morning. When I opened them a minute later, the
morning sun was pouring in the windows, heating up the
walls. Chogyi Jake was curled in the chair at the foot of my
bed, a paper coffee cup forgotten in his dozing hand. My
body ached badly, just lying there. But I was all right. I'd
lived through it.

The sun tracked its slow way up the sky, and I let my
mind wander. It was Sunday. Somewhere out there, far to
the east, my mother and father were going to church in
their starched clothes, ready to watch their preacher sweat
and exclaim and witness to the power of a god I didn't
believe in. West, in Arizona, a new semester would have
started at ASU. The dorms and apartments would be filled
with men and women sleeping off Saturday night, just the
way I had done this time last year.

Closer by, Randolph Coin—or the thing inside him—
had already started leading its seven-year swarm into a
dance that would take more bodies away from people like
Aaron the German shepherd and Candace Dorn and give
them over to these unclean spirits. At Eric's house, Midian
was probably frying up steak and eggs, with Aubrey and Ex

either at his side drinking coffee or sleeping off the night's exhaustion. Chogyi Jake murmured something and shifted his weight without spilling his coffee. I smiled at the man's sleep-peaceful face and let myself sink back down into my amazingly expensive, thin, uncomfortable pillow. I had expected to greet this particular morning with a sense of despair and isolation, and instead I felt at home in my life for the first time I could remember.

It was Sunday, the fifth of August, and it was my birthday. I was twenty-three.

8

The doctors in Boulder released me that afternoon with precautions about not doing anything to pop my stitches or aggravate my knee. Chogyi Jake took me home in his van, but I was already fading. I fell asleep almost as soon as I got back home, and when I woke up Monday morning, the house was silent.

I slipped out of bed, careful of my various wounds, pulled on a thick wool robe that was a little too large for me, and padded out into the hallway. The door of the guest bedroom was ajar, and Aubrey was in the bed, his eyes closed and his mouth hanging open. I watched him sleep, watched his chest rise and fall and rise again. Part of me wanted to step in, slip into the bed, and curl up beside him. Before I could act on the impulse, I heard the front door open and familiar voices fill the space. Ex and Chogyi Jake. And then Midian, welcoming them.

'The one thing we know for absolute certain is that it didn't work,' Ex said.

Midian coughed once and shrugged his shoulders. He nodded to me as I walked through the doorway.

'Hey. The resident skeptic rises,' he said, and I shuddered at the sound of his voice. Every morning, it seemed a

M. L. N. HANOVER

little worse than I'd remembered it. 'I figured you for sleeping in through noon.'

'Got hungry,' I said.

'Can we stay on point here?' Ex snapped. 'We can't hold to Eric's plan. It already *failed*.'

'It was discovered,' Chogyi Jake said. 'But the core of it was never tried, so we can't really say it wouldn't have worked.'

'Coin's a smug little cocksucker,' Midian said. 'Even after we took out his little ninja squad, I don't know that he'd be on *high* alert. He knows we got away, but he has to assume that he broke the plan's back. Plus which, little old herself here does have some superpowers. You want a donut? The guys brought back a dozen, and the coffee'll be ready in a minute.'

'I'd take a jelly. And I don't have any superpowers,' I said, but it didn't have the force of conviction anymore.

'Your priest buddy, Ex, has been doing some research,' Midian said, ignoring my protest. 'Looks like there's protective mojo on you that makes you hard to see, magically speaking, which might be why you got in past the alarms. Could also have something to do with how you kicked all the ass back at the apartment and then with that nasty up in Boulder. Did Eric ever give you anything that had writing on it you couldn't actually read? Like a ring or something? Or take you to a hot spring? Natural hot springs are good too.'

Before I could say no, he hadn't, Ex broke in.

'But we don't know the details yet, and the point still stands that Eric got killed.'

'I'm not saying it isn't a risk,' Midian replied calmly as he handed me a jelly donut. The powdered sugar was white as snow, a splash of red at the side. 'I'm just saying it's a calculated one.'

Ex's face went pale, his jaw hard. For an instant, I was sure he was going to hit Midian. Instead, he muttered something obscene, turned, and stormed out the front door, slamming it behind him. Chogyi Jake sighed and picked a cake donut out of the box on the counter.

'No offense, Jake,' Midian said, sitting at the table. 'Your friend there? He's a prick.'

'He's angry with himself,' Chogyi Jake said. 'He deals with it poorly. Give him time to work it through. He'll be back.'

'What's he pissed off about?' I asked around a mouthful of sugar.

'He failed to protect Aubrey and you from the *haugtrold*,' Chogyi Jake said. 'You could have been killed. Both of you. He didn't insulate you from that danger.'

'It wasn't his job,' I said.

'He feels otherwise,' Chogyi Jake said.

'Since we're talking about stupid, though,' Midian croaked as he poured three cups of coffee, 'walking in on an unknown situation like that *haugtrold* when this whole thing with Coin is still hanging fire? That was dumb.'

'We didn't know it was going to blow up on us,' I said, accepting one of the cups. The coffee smelled rich and tasted just bitter enough to forgive the donut. 'Aubrey knew I wouldn't be able to kill Coin unless I was sure that all this talk about riders and magic was true. He didn't think this thing with the dog was going to be dangerous.'

'Well, he's paying the price of that little fuckup,' Midian said.

Something in the way the dead man spoke made my gut clench, suspicion suddenly burning through me like a cold fire. I put down the coffee cup and wiped the sugar off my lips with the back of one hand. Midian raised his ruined eyebrows.

'What do you mean?' I asked. 'What price?'

The pair were silent for a moment, some unspoken calculation passing between them. Chogyi spoke first.

'Riders are very powerful. Magic—violating the rules of the world—it comes easily to them. For humans, using your will or qi or whichever name you put to it . . . is more difficult,' Chogyi Jake said slowly, as if choosing his words carefully. 'Even of the people who learn about magic, few ever do more than small cantrips. Changing how you perceive things, for example. Making yourself charismatic or more difficult to remember. They're things that are very much like what we all do anyway, every day. We focus our will to it, and it becomes more *effective*. When you start to do things that affect objects or violate the customs of nature—the sorts of things that riders manage by nature—those are more difficult.'

'The alarms at the apartment, for instance,' Midian said. 'Those were a sweet sonofabitch to set up. If it wasn't me and Eric doing it together, wouldn't have been possible.'

'Okay,' I said.

'Eric knew more than any man I've ever met, and he taught things to some of us that are . . . advanced. Possibly optimistic. Aubrey bound the *haugtrold* with a very powerful magic. It is called the Voice of the Abyss. Or Calling Da'ath. There are other names for it. It . . . it isn't something that is invoked lightly.'

'I don't understand,' I said.

'Jesus wept,' Midian said. 'He used a tool that was stronger than he was, and it smacked him one. It's no worse than smoking a few thousand cigarettes. That's as much as you need to worry about, okay?'

'How badly did it hurt him?' I asked, my eyes on Chogyi. He didn't look away.

'Every time he makes that invocation, it becomes easier for his soul to come free of his flesh,' he said. 'Easier for him to die. Illness will be harder to recover from. Wounds slower to heal. There is no simple way to measure it, but at a guess, stunning the *haugtrold* cost him a year of his life.'

I closed my eyes and pressed my hand to my mouth. I felt like I was going to be ill. The coffee I'd drunk haunted the back of my tongue.

'I've got to . . . I'm going to be right . . .' I said as I walked away. Neither of them tried to follow me. I found my way back to my bedroom—Eric's bedroom—and then the little bathroom. I turned up the shower until the steam was billowing out, then took off the robe and stood under the near-scalding water.

I had thought the adventure was only that: a scrape with danger that had netted us a few cuts and bruises and

93

restored an innocent victim of these parasites to his own body again. We'd saved Candace Dorn from whatever violence and misery the rider had intended. Go us.

Go me.

Now it turned out Aubrey had done himself permanent damage saving me, and I was furious with myself because of it. Furious and guilty and a little frightened. I'd brought him into the situation. My need to understand, my need for proof that had seemed so important before seemed petty now. If I'd just had faith, he wouldn't have been hurt . . .

I soaped up as best I could with a still-swollen knee and a shoulder that didn't bend as well as I was used to. The hot water made my stitches ache, and when I finally got out, the towel came away slightly red when I patted the wound dry. It hurt, but I figured I deserved a little pain.

I dressed slowly, in my own clothes this time. Somehow putting on another of Eric's shirts seemed wrong at the moment. Old blue jeans. Pink Martini T-shirt. Just me. Just Jayné. No demon hunting, no magic, nothing that would put anyone in danger on my account.

The bedroom door was still ajar. The sound of conversation had moved from the kitchen to the couch, but I didn't go out to join them. Instead, I slipped into the guest room and closed the door behind me.

Aubrey was still asleep. Now that I knew to look for it, I noticed his skin had a gray tinge I didn't remember. His breathing was deep and slow. I sat on the edge of the mattress, my weight pulling Aubrey toward me. He looked younger when he was asleep. None of the small lines that time was starting to etch in the corners of his eyes or mouth showed. I could see what he'd looked like when he was a child. I drew a lock of hair back from his face with my finger. The swelling around his left eye had gone down, but there was still the darkness of a deep bruise like a shadow inside his skin. A scab ran from his collarbone to hide under the sheet.

His eyelids opened a fraction, hazel eyes looking up at me through sand-colored lashes. He didn't seem at all surprised to see me.

'Hey,' I said softly.

'Hey,' he said. He drew an arm free of the sheet and I took his hand in mine. I could feel my heartbeat ramping up, the adrenaline flushing into my blood as I leaned forward and kissed him. His lips were rougher than I expected, stronger. I sat back up and his smile had a soft humor in it, like he was amused by something that was also a little sad.

'I'm still dreaming, right?'

'Yeah,' I said. 'You totally are.'

'Thought so,' he said, and closed his eyes again. I held his hand for a moment, then stood up and made my way back out to the living room.

'All I'm saying is that we can sound out how worried Coin is by his actions,' Ex, returned, said from a perch on the couch's armrest. 'If he's moved the ceremony someplace else, then we can say for sure that he's still on high alert.'

'And if he hasn't?' Midian asked, gesturing with a lit cigarette, an arc of blue smoke trailing the movement.

'Then we know he's not worried enough to move it,' Chogyi Jake said. He was sitting cross-legged on the floor.

'A little reconnaissance,' Ex said. 'Once we have more information, we can make a better judgment on how to go forward.'

'Could someone get me up to speed here?' I asked, sitting down carefully.

'Eric's notes,' Midian said. 'He knew where Coin's little party was supposed to be. A warehouse up north. The bare bones of the plan were pretty simple, but timing's an issue.'

'After a certain point in the ceremony itself, riders under Coin's dominion are committed,' Chogyi Jake said. 'They can't break off until their invocation is complete. Even if Coin suddenly walks out, they won't be able to disengage quickly enough to follow him.'

'They'd lose the whole crop,' Midian said. 'Thing is, I can pull Coin out. Well, I can't, but someone else can, using me as a focus.'

'I'm lost,' I said.

'There's a kind of connection that's made when you curse someone,' Ex said, 'so by cursing Midian, Coin also made a connection between them. Eric was planning to exploit that connection to pull Coin out beyond his protections, so that someone could kill him.'

'I don't want to do something that's going to hurt anyone. I mean any of us,' I said.

'I'll be badly tired,' Chogyi Jake said, 'but I'll recover. It doesn't require violating any laws of physics.'

'I think that sounds good,' I said. 'But first I think I'd

like to know a little more about how this spirit magic stuff works. You guys mind running me through the tutorial?'

'Thought you'd never ask,' Ex said, his tone more angry than welcoming. I forgave him. I knew where it was coming from. I was more than a little pissed off at me too.

'That's him,' Ex said.

I wanted to sink down into the car seat or else strain forward to see better. The binoculars pressed against my eyes shortened the space and blurred the chain-link fencing. It was as if there was no barrier between us and the two men far away down the street who were getting out of a car just humble enough to not call itself a limousine. They weren't what I'd expected. The larger was broad as a linebacker and easily a head taller than his companion. His Hawaiian shirt blared red and blue and green, and his tree-trunk arms swirled with complex designs and patterns that made my eyes ache. Ex didn't have to tell me that he wasn't the one.

The smaller man—Randolph Coin—closed the passenger door and said something, nodding toward the warehouse and then to the train tracks beyond it. His face was wide and round, heavy at the jowls, and sparkling with a bright animation. When the big man answered, Coin laughed. He looked like a successful businessman, only without the soul-crushing grayness. Even with the pounding heat of the afternoon, he wore a dark jacket. The big one wiped an arm across his inscribed forehead, and I realized that Coin wasn't sweating.

'He isn't marked,' I said. 'I don't see any tattoos on him.'

'It's a glamour,' Ex said. 'Changes how people perceive him.'

'Rider magic?'

'Normal people can do it too, if you train them enough. Takes a few years. Right now, you should just focus your qi in your belly and bring it up to your eyes. Don't push past that, though. We don't want them to notice us.'

It was Tuesday, and we were in the northern suburb called Commerce City. The train tracks angled southwest to northeast, just north of where we were parked. The warehouse was to the south, exactly where Uncle Eric's notes and plans said it would be, and Coin and his sheriff walked toward it now with unhurried calm. I closed my eyes and tried to remember what Ex and Chogyi Jake had taught me the day before. I pictured a warm ball of smoke just a few inches south of my navel and on an inward breath took energy into it from all around my body. Then I imagined the smoke glowing blue and white with flickers in it like lightning as it traveled up my spine, through the back of my head, and into my closed eyes.

There was a physical sensation that went with it that reminded me of watching a cat slink along under a bedspread. I opened my eyes again, and Randolph Coin was transformed. Swirls of ink eddied at the corners of his eyes. Black marks darkened his lips. At the warehouse door, he paused, turning back toward the car like he'd heard something. Startled, I let the smoke dissipate. My eyes became my eyes again, and his face was only flesh-colored. I put down the binoculars.

'All right,' I said. 'That's good. Let's get out of here.'

Ex slipped the car into gear, the purring motor lowering its voice as we slid out onto the street. The highway was south of us, but we'd have to loop around to reach it. The gray-blue industrial warehouse vanished as we made the first corner. The dog track loomed up on our left, and I let out a breath.

Randolph Coin, evil mage who had killed my uncle and tried to kill me and Midian. Who trafficked with the things that lived in the Pleroma and took over bodies like Aaron the Boulder cop's. Who *hadn't* moved the induction ceremony from its rented warehouse by the greyhound racing track.

Randolph Coin, who wasn't afraid of us.

I watched Ex's face as he pulled the car onto I-270, merging with the traffic like a fish with water. His pale blond hair was pulled back into a tight ponytail, his expression focused and serious, his grip on the steering wheel hard. He leaned forward as he drove, as if he was controlling the car by the direct force of his will as much as by the wheel in his hands.

'I screwed up,' I said.

He glanced over at me, no more than a flicker, then his ice-blue eyes were back on the road.

'If you say so,' he said.

'I shouldn't have let Aubrey leave the shotgun in the car,' I said. 'If we were going into something that we thought might require protection, it was stupid of me to leave the weapon outside. And I should have brought you and Chogyi Jake as backup. It was my fault.'

The lines around his mouth softened a little bit. Not much.

'It was an easy mistake to make. Don't let it bother you. You'll do better next time,' he said. And then a few moments later, 'Eric should never have taught him that. It's like giving live ammunition to a ten-year-old. It doesn't matter how good his intentions were, it's too much power to have control over it.'

'It worked,' I said. 'The thing would have killed us if Aubrey hadn't done what he did.'

'Yeah,' Ex said, and gunned the engine, passing a semi and cutting back into traffic in front of it.

'We'll do better next time,' I said.

'Yeah.'

At the house, Midian was waiting on the couch, a soccer game playing on the television. His sleeves were rolled up to expose the blackened beef jerky of his forearms and he was smoking another cigarette. The house was starting to reek of them. He stood as we came in the room.

'Well?' he asked.

'Coin's still where he was. One bodyguard. No one watching from the roof, no wards on the perimeter past what Eric was expecting. He thinks we've gone to ground,' Ex said.

'We're on, then?' Midian asked. Ex hesitated for a moment. I knew what he was thinking. *We'll do better next time.*

'Yeah,' Ex said. 'We're on.'

Midian grinned, smoke curling between his ruined teeth.

9

The plan was simple, and even easier because it was already laid out. Instead of Eric luring Coin free of his hive, Chogyi Jake would do the work. Instead of Eric's hired muscle attacking Coin, Ex and Aubrey and I would do the honors with sniper rifles and custom ammunition designed to disrupt riders. I pulled up satellite photos of the warehouse and everything around it from Google Earth and printed out copies for everyone. Ex diagrammed where each of us would be and worked out the timetable. I kept expecting him to tell us to synchronize our watches, but since all of our cell phones pulled the data from the same satellites, that part was really covered already. I'd just been watching too many old movies.

Aubrey joined in just before sundown, looking like a man only half recovered from the flu. He moved slowly, and I tried to tell myself it was mostly just the wounds. The physical ones.

When we'd done everything there was to do, Aubrey crawled back into bed. Chogyi Jake left, going off to run some normal human errand—feed his cats, check his mail, something mundane and reassuring like that. Ex set himself on the couch like a guard, turned on the television, turned it off again, and pulled a book of essays by Bertrand Russell out of his things. He read it with a constant sneer. Midian sat in the kitchen, a cup of coffee in one hand, a cigarette in the other.

Back in the bedroom, my laptop open on the bed, it struck me that the hardest thing was going to be waiting the three days before our moment came. I got online and against my better judgment, I checked the blogs of everyone I'd known from before I'd come to Denver. My old boyfriend was still bitching about the band he was in that never quite got it together to practice. My dorm mate from last year had apparently just noticed that feminism existed and couldn't decide whether she thought it was a good thing. The girl I'd once considered my best friend hadn't posted anything since she'd gone off to Portland with her boyfriend in June.

It was a depressing exercise. When I'd gone to college, all bridges to my parents and church reduced to cinders and ash behind me, I'd thought I was starting my real life at last. I'd thought that everything I did, every person I met or hated or fell in love with, *mattered*. And now that I'd left that behind too, I could see that I'd been wrong. The drama and the experiments and the passionate lack of direction were all doing just fine without me. It was like pulling my finger out of water. My absence hadn't left a hole.

I thought about leaving a comment. *Inherited more money than God, fighting forces of darkness. Think I'm in love with my dead uncle's not-boyfriend. L8R.* I didn't. For one thing, they wouldn't have believed me, and for another, it turned out I didn't care if they did. Or if that wasn't true, at least I didn't want to care. I told myself that they'd left as little mark on me as I'd left on them, and I was even able to convince myself a little.

I spent the rest of the evening Googling the terms that Ex and Aubrey and Chogyi Jake kept tossing around. *Riders, possession, daughter organism.* By the time I fell asleep, I was reading long essays about the difference between a therian and a werewolf, and I'd learned the term *otherkin.* Things that a month ago would have seemed like schizophrenic ravings were making sense to me now, and I didn't know whether I found that reassuring or scary.

When the sunlight streaming through the windows woke me, I felt like crap. I made my way out to the main part of the house to find Ex and Aubrey had gone. Midian lay on the couch, hands folded corpselike on his chest. Only Chogyi Jake was there and awake, working on a crossword puzzle and drinking green tea.

'Hey,' I said.

'Good morning,' he said. His smile was one of the most genuine things I'd ever seen. 'Ex is out getting the rifles. Aubrey said he had to see to his lab. He debated waking you before he went, but he wanted to let you rest.'

'Probably a good call,' I said, hiding a pang of disappointment. 'So. What are you up to?'

'Nothing in particular. Why?' he asked. And then, with a conspiratorial lowered voice, 'Getting stir-crazy?'

'I was thinking. We know that all the Invisible College guys are busy, right? It's not like they're going to send out any more hit squads to just wander the streets in case they bump into us.'

'That's certainly the assumption, yes,' he said, folding the half-finished puzzle.

'So. There's no real *reason* we couldn't go shopping?'

Chogyi Jake's van smelled like a mechanic's shop: motor oil and WD-40 and the cold, subtle scent of steel tools. The windows all had a thin coating of old grease that made the world outside seem like a movie with the focus just barely off. The bucket seats were cracked, the foam stuffing peeking through. The back compartment was dark as a cave. Perfect for moving corpses. The dead woman's face—the blue of her eyes, the black marks inscribed on her skin, the surprise on her face—flickered in my mind for a moment. I shook myself, hoping movement could dislodge the image.

'There used to be a really good bookstore just across the street,' Chogyi Jake said as he pulled into a parking space. A California Pizza Kitchen cowered under the looming weight of Saks Fifth Avenue and I felt something in my belly starting to uncoil. 'It's over on Colfax now. We can go there after this if you'd like.'

'Pretty clothes first,' I said. 'Mind-improving literature later.'

'As you wish,' he said, with a smile. I had the feeling he was amused by me, and that he took some joy in my self-indulgence. I liked him for it.

I had another ten thousand dollars in my pocket, freshly drawn from the bank without a word or a whisper from anyone. We walked through the growing heat of the August morning and into the air-conditioned artificial cool of the mall, like walking into another world. I breathed in deeply and felt the smile come across my face.

Saks Fifth Avenue. Neiman Marcus. Abercrombie & Fitch. None of them was safe from me. Victoria's Secret gave up a half dozen of the great-looking bras I had never been able to afford. I got blue jeans, I got suits, I got the little black evening dress that my mother had said every girl needs, but said quietly so my father couldn't hear. I bought a black leather overcoat that I wouldn't be able to wear for months and steel-toed work boots I didn't need. I got a new swimsuit—a one-piece, because halfway through trying on the bikini, I got irrationally embarrassed about the stitches. I bought four hundred dollars' worth of makeup even though I never wore any.

It was an orgy. It was a binge. It was glorious excess, my lowest consumerist impulses turned up to eleven. Chogyi Jake made two trips to the van without me, carrying away the bags and boxes rather than letting them build up to an unmanageable bulk. I saw it in the eyes of the clerks: the crazy rich girl was on a roll.

When it dawned on me that I hadn't eaten breakfast and lunchtime was a couple hours past, I went from fine to ravenous in about twenty seconds. Chogyi Jake led me back toward the van and the pizza joint, a dozen more bags digging into our hands. My stomach growled, and in my low-blood-sugar condition, I was starting to feel a little light-headed and ill. I still had two thousand and change in my pocket, and I didn't think I'd go back to the mall after we ate. Maybe we'd hit the bookstore he'd talked about. I wondered if there was something I could buy for Aubrey.

'Well,' I said after we'd taken our seats and placed our orders, 'I think you've seen me at my worst.'

'Really?' Chogyi Jake said, scratching idly at the stubble on his scalp. 'That wasn't so terrible, then.'

'You don't think so? I just spent over seven thousand dollars on a shopping spree. My father would lose his shit, wasting money like that.'

'We all have ways to distract ourselves from fear. You have this. Ex has his religion. Aubrey has his work,' Chogyi Jake said. 'I don't see that any of them is more or less a vice than another. Certainly, there are worse.'

'I'm not really like this,' I said. 'I mean, I never do this kind of thing.'

'Well, almost never,' Chogyi Jake said, laughter in his eyes.

'Yeah,' I said. And then, 'Why do you think it's about fear, though? Why not just greed?'

'It would only be greed if you wanted more money. This would have been gluttony. But even if it is that, it is still about wrestling your anxiety. Addictions are the same. Drinking to excess. Sexual expression without love or joy. Abuse of cocaine or hash or heroin.'

'Drugs do the same thing as religion? Don't let Ex hear you say that,' I said. I'd meant it as a joke, but it didn't quite come out that way.

'He knows,' Chogyi Jake said. 'He knows what he does and why he does it.'

'You knew Eric, right? You worked with him before. What did he do?'

Chogyi Jake smiled and leaned forward. The chrome and mirrors of the restaurant seemed too hard and bright for an expression as gentle and compassionate as that.

'Eric carried a heavy burden. Much of it he held to himself. I believe he sacrificed many things to the work he undertook, and I don't know all of the prices he paid. He cultivated a kind of solitude that kept people away from him.'

'To protect them,' I said.

'Or himself.'

The waiter came by before I could follow up on that, two pizzas literally piping on his tray. The smell of hot cheese and tomatoes derailed any train of thought I'd had, and I descended into making yum-yum noises for the next fifteen minutes. When the calories started to cross into my blood, where I could use them, I began to turn what Chogyi Jake had said over in my mind. Something bothered me like a rock in my shoe. It was in the way he'd spoken, in the calm that seemed to come off him in waves. I was down to two slices and starting to feel a little bloated before I spoke again.

'What do you do?'

He raised his eyebrows in a question.

'For fear. The anxiety,' I said. 'What do *you* do?'

'These days, I meditate,' he said. 'Before that, it was heroin.'

I didn't know that it was what I'd expected until he said

it, and then it was perfectly clear. I smiled at him, and he smiled back. We didn't say anything more about it. I paid the bill, shouldered the burden of my purchases, and we went out to the van. The sun was blazing down on us now, the light like a physical pressure on my face. He opened the back door of the van. The compartment was almost full of shining bags, plastic wrap, boxes. Clothes hung from hooks in the roof like a little mobile dry cleaner's. I ran a hand through my hair, a little stunned to see it all at once this way. Chogyi Jake was silent.

'If this is all about fear, I must really be effing scared,' I said, gesturing toward the back of the van. I was surprised to hear my voice break a little on the last word. He didn't move either toward me or away. I started weeping and pushed my tears away with the back of my hand. It was half a minute before I could speak again. 'I'm really, really scared.'

'I know,' he said. His voice was comforting as warm flannel in winter. 'You've changed a lot in a very short time. It will take time before you can really be still again. It's normal.'

'I don't have any friends. I don't have a family. I'm afraid if I do this wrong, I won't have any of you guys anymore either. Isn't that stupid? I've got a bunch of evil wizards who want me dead, and that's what I'm afraid of?'

'No,' Chogyi Jake said. 'If it's true, it isn't stupid. It's just who you are right now.'

I started crying harder, but somehow I wasn't ashamed. He didn't put his arm around me. He didn't touch me. He only stood witness. It was the kindest thing anyone had ever done.

'I don't want . . . I don't want them to see all this. I don't want them to think I'm like this,' I said.

'I know a shelter,' he said. 'They'll be grateful for whatever you want to give.'

'Okay,' I said, nodding. 'Okay, good.'

'Eight hours for that?' Midian said as Chogyi Jake closed the door. 'Fuck *me*, sister. Did you have to try on the whole store before you picked something?'

'I got what I needed,' I said lightly. Chogyi Jake smiled as I walked back toward my room. I was beginning to see how he could use the same expression to mean a lot of different things.

I'd kept seven outfits with associated footwear, a small purse for occasions when the leather backpack was insufficiently formal, two lipsticks, some eyeliner, the swimsuit, three of the good-looking bras, a bag for my laptop, and, after some wavering back and forth, the steel-toed boots. Somewhere in south Denver, there were going to be some victims of domestic violence hiding from their boyfriends and husbands in very nice clothes. Put that way, it didn't seem like enough.

By the time I'd showered and changed, Ex and Aubrey were back. I walked into the living room to see three unfamiliar rifles on the coffee table. They weren't from the stash at the storage facility. Ex, squatting beside them, nodded to me. Aubrey was leaning against the wall. He looked better,

I thought. Still tired and bruised, but there was color in his cheeks. The time at his lab seemed to have done him more good than sleeping had, and I remembered what Chogyi Jake had said about using his work to cope with fear. I went to stand beside him.

'Okay,' Ex said. 'These are all thirty aught six, and they're all bolt action. At four hundred yards, the round is going to drop about fifty inches, so these have scopes that I set to take that into account, okay? Don't try to make the adjustment yourself. It's already in the equipment.'

Aubrey folded his arms and nodded seriously. I found myself mirroring him without meaning to. Midian breezed in from the backyard, ruined yellow eyes taking us all in with something equally amused and curious.

'Where did you *get* these?' I asked.

'Wal-Mart,' Chogyi Jake said.

'They're usually used for elk hunting,' Ex continued. 'A couple of standard rounds from one of these can drop a thousand-pound animal. That won't make a damn bit of difference with Coin. So that's where the custom ammunition comes in.'

I hadn't noticed the box until he pulled it out from under the coffee table and put it in between the rifles. It was carved rosewood with a finish so rich and subtle it seemed to reflect the light of a nearby fire. Ex opened it and let the cartridges spill out. The bullets were all black and engraved with script that looked like Arabic. I stepped closer, putting out my hand, but hesitated before I touched them. They were beautiful, but the prospect of holding one made my flesh crawl. They smelled like fire, and I had the uncanny sense that they were aware of me.

'These are the big trick,' Ex said. 'They all have the Mark of Ya'la ibn Murah and the sigil of St. Francis of the Desert both. They're like the wards and alarms that protect this place and the alarms at the apartment. If things go well, they'll ground out the rider. Now, these are pretty heavy work for a human being to do. Eric put a lot of work into getting them, so it's not like we can whistle up some more if we run out. We have to make these count.'

'Check,' I said.

'For this to work, these have to break skin. Rubbing them up against him won't make him happy, but if the round doesn't penetrate, we might as well not have tried. That means keeping him outside his wards and distracted. Okay?'

We all nodded together, even Midian. Ex looked pleased.

'I've arranged some time at the practice range for you two,' he said, nodding at me and Aubrey. 'You don't want the first time you use this to be in the field. That's tomorrow morning. We'll leave from here at noon. It's going to take five or six hours, so don't plan anything for the afternoon.'

Aubrey's eyes flickered, recalculating something, but he nodded his agreement.

'Good,' Ex said. He put the engraved bullets back in their box, and I relaxed a little, just having them out of sight. 'We're up to speed, folks. This was Wednesday. Tomorrow's practice. Friday, we're making another on-site visit to be sure we all know what the place looks like when you aren't looking down from orbit. Saturday morning, we end this.'

'Nice work,' Midian said. 'All this in place, I think we've got half a chance.'

We sat around for a few more minutes. Ex and Midian started talking about occult issues like frat boys talking football. Under Chogyi Jake's prompting, the rest of us split off into a conversation about Aubrey's lab and the experiments he was conducting. As Aubrey got into it, I could see his shoulders loosen and the lines of pleasure and laughter start to come out around his eyes. I remembered what it had felt like, kissing him.

Chogyi Jake excused himself for the bathroom and left the two of us alone. Ex and Midian were talking about the wards on the Inca Street apartment and whether the protections on Eric's house were more effective. I tried not to listen, not wanting to remember any of that. Instead, I focused on Aubrey.

It's just fear, I told myself. *This is only fear. You can deal with it.*

'Hey,' I said, heart in throat, 'after the practice range tomorrow, can I take you out to dinner?'

'Sure. We should check with the guys and see what they want, but I know a great Indian place that—'

'You singular,' I said. 'Ixnay on the uralplay.'

Aubrey turned a little, looking at me square on. He hadn't shaved today, and the stubble on his cheeks made me think of Sunday mornings and tangled sheets. Aubrey was blushing and pretending that he wasn't.

'Um, well. I mean, sure.'

'Just to clarify,' I said. 'This is a date. I'm asking you on a date. We're going to do this insanely dangerous thing in three days, and I'd like to carpe some diem before it goes down.'

The blush was rising up from his neck, brightening his cheeks. Even his earlobes were getting in on the action. He took a deep breath and let it out slowly.

'Count me in,' he said.

I was quietly thrilled for the rest of the evening. Midian roasted a chicken in lemon and salt that tasted like heaven, we all stayed up talking about things that weren't ghosties and ghoulies and long-legged parasites that suck your soul out the back of your head. Aubrey sat beside me. When he passed the rice pilaf to me, our fingers touched a fraction of a second longer than strictly necessary, and it felt like an electric jolt. But in a good way.

I went to bed feeling like I'd conquered the world, even though all I'd really managed was to ask Aubrey out. That was, in all fairness, pretty good, given my track record. I spent an hour on the Internet reading what I could find about the uncomforting sigils on Eric's ammunition, and then fell asleep to the soft sounds of Chogyi Jake and Aubrey talking in the guest room, and beneath that the drone and chuckle of the television in the living room, where Ex and Midian were, I assumed, doing something deep and mystical that only to the uninitiated looked like watching late night talk shows.

The nightmare was like being assaulted.

I was in darkness. The world around me was a salad of familiar objects—couch, folding chair, desk lamp—and arcane brass sculpture. I was naked, and powerfully aware that there had been a sound just a moment before. Something in the darkness with me. Something that wasn't supposed to be there.

Something big.

In the logic of dreams, I knew that if I could just get the key to my old dorm room, I could get out before it found me. I started moving through constantly shifting rooms and courtyards, trying to find where I'd hidden it.

The sound came again. A deep rushing, like beating wings the size of mountains. When I looked up, the sky was a single eye, staring back down. The pupil was a terrible blue, and the blood vessels in the white spelled out words and phrases that made me want to scream. The massive eye darted this way and that, searching for me. I huddled under a filthy blanket, trying not to breathe. Slow footsteps, echoing like something from a hospital corridor, came slowly closer and closer. My hands were balled in fists so tightly I knew I was breaking bones, and if he heard them snap, he'd find me. But I couldn't unclasp them. My hands wouldn't respond to me.

I woke with a start, still trying not to scream. The clock said it was three in the morning. I was covered with a slick, cold sweat. I got up, opening and closing my hands just to prove to myself that I could. In the dim light of city nighttime, the bed looked gray. I pulled on my robe. I was totally awake, but the dream felt like it had been worked into my skin. I stood there for long minutes, trying to talk myself into going back to sleep, then I scooped up the pillow and threw it in the wastebasket. I thought that if I was quiet, I could make myself some tea without disturbing the others.

But they were already in the kitchen. All of them. Aubrey sat at the table, his hair still wild from the bed, and his expression was tight and angry. Chogyi Jake leaned against the table, his arms crossed. Ex was in a black T-shirt and sweats, his face pale and haunted.

'You too, eh?' Midian asked as I stood there, staring at them.

'I had a rough dream,' I said.

'Caught in the dark, sound of huge wings?' Aubrey asked.

'God's eye looking down,' Ex said. His voice was bleak.

'How did . . .' I began, then let the question die. They'd all had the same dream. At the same time. I could see the dread in their faces.

'Wasn't God,' Midian said. 'That, ladies and germs, was Randolph Coin. He's looking for us.'

10

When dawn finally came, I was surprised that it woke me. I hadn't expected to sleep again that night. The others were all moving a little slower too, the weight of Coin's presence still lingering in the backs of our minds. As the day grew bright and hot, the sun commanding the profound blue sky, the oppressive sense of threat faded a little. It didn't ever quite go away. We got on with the work at hand.

I'd never really thought about fighting supernatural evil as a lifestyle choice. Still, I was surprised that it felt so much like planning a crime. The range Ex had in mind was less a formal police-style building with individual runs and paper targets than an open field down a dirt track halfway between Denver and Colorado Springs. Aubrey's minivan looked out of place in the wide, rough terrain.

We were just setting up the targets—bales of hay with Robin Hood–esque bull's-eyes strapped to them—when Eric's voice spoke again.

'Hey. You've got a call.'

Aubrey and Ex both looked over at me as I dug the cell phone out of my pocket. The number on the ID was familiar. Candace Dorn again.

'I wish you'd change that ringtone,' Ex said as I answered it.

'Hello?' I said, putting my free hand against my other ear and walking to the back of the minivan.

'Hi,' Candace said. 'I'm sorry I didn't call back earlier. Is this Jayné?'

'Yeah. It's me. Is everything okay? I'm really sorry about your living room, by the way. I didn't mean to trash the place.'

'I don't care about it,' she said. 'Really. It's fine. Everything's fine. Aaron is back from the hospital, and he's going to be fine.'

I hadn't realized he'd been in, though in retrospect it made sense. Dog bites, the *haugtrold* cutting its own face, whatever damage Aubrey and I had managed to inflict. I glanced over at Ex as he laid out the rifles and two boxes of less arcane ammunition on a blue tarp. I wondered what exactly the exorcism process entailed.

'Good,' I said. 'I'm glad to hear that. And Charlie?'

'Charlie's doing all right too. I think he's a little confused by the whole thing. Needy. Dogs, you know.'

I didn't, but I made appropriate social noises. There was a pause on the line, the kind of silence where no one is bringing up the difficult issue. I would have taken the lead if I'd known what was up.

'I was . . .' Candace said, and then stopped. When she started again, she sounded grim. 'My friend. The one who gave me your number. He said that I should have talked about all this before. He's right, I know that. It was just

117

with Charlie and Aaron and all the rest, I was focused on the situation at hand.'

'Sure, of course,' I said, not knowing what she meant. There was another pause on the line. 'Candace. If there's something we should be talking about, we should maybe talk about it? What's up?'

'I needed to talk to you about the price,' she said. I could tell from the way she said it that she was past uneasy and into scared.

It was the first time the thought had even crossed my mind. Eric's money had to have come from somewhere; that was true. And since this was what he did, I supposed it followed that whatever he'd charged for his work had to have been pretty astronomical. I didn't know what to say. From the little empire that I'd inherited, I had to think the money had been huge. On the other hand, I hadn't talked to the lawyer about it. Maybe the money had come from someplace else. Maybe Eric had some sort of sliding scale. I was caught flat-footed, and I felt stupid for not knowing the answer.

But then, the question wasn't really what Eric would have done so much as what I was going to do. That made it easier.

'Don't worry about it,' I said. 'It's on the house.'

Whatever Candace had expected to hear, it wasn't that.

'Are you . . . do you mean that?'

'Look, I'm actually kind of new at this,' I said. 'My uncle was the expert. You didn't get the high-powered guy, and I got some on-the-job training I needed anyway. Besides. We trashed your place.'

There was a sound I couldn't make out. Ex, still over at the tarp, gestured to me impatiently. I held up my hand in a 'one minute' gesture before I realized that what I was hearing was Candace in tears.

'I owe you,' she said. 'If you ever need anything, please call me. You saved my life. You saved me.'

'I was glad we could help. Seriously. Look, Candace, I've got to go. But you tell Aaron to get well soon, okay? Take care.'

I dropped the call and shoved the cell back into my pocket. Ex frowned down at the rifles as I came back. Aubrey raised an eyebrow, asking wordlessly what the call had been.

'Follow-up,' I said. 'Nothing important. What did I miss?'

For the next hour, Ex talked us through the workings of the rifles. It wasn't as complex as I'd expected in theory, but the practice was tricky. I knew that the gun would kick when I fired, but I underestimated how much my sore shoulder would object. The first four shots I tried missed the target completely. The fifth got on the paper, but outside the concentric rings of the bull's-eye. Ex walked me through the whole process, his voice serious and low. I got better until I started getting worse, and he decided I'd had enough and turned his attention to Aubrey.

It turned out Aubrey had a much better eye for the thing than I did. His second shot hit the paper target. His fourth was in the center circle. I tried to figure out what he was doing differently, but as I watched him, my mind kept wandering. The afternoon was sweltering hot, and we drank through our bottles of water long before we fired the last round. I tried a couple parting shorts and kicked out bits of hay from the bales, but nothing better than that.

I had the sense that Ex was confused that my uncanny ability to fight didn't translate to being able to hit the broad side of a barn with firearms. I felt a little ashamed of my lack of talent, but he tried to keep my confidence up.

'It doesn't really matter how good a hit you get on Coin,' he said as we broke down the rifles and folded up the tarp. 'We aren't trying to kill him with the shot. Graze his pinky finger, and as long as it breaks skin, we're fine.'

'It's going to be hard,' Aubrey said. 'I mean, this was fun, but looking at a real person is going to be different.'

'He's not a real person, though,' I said. 'He's just a rider in a stolen body.'

'It's still going to be hard,' Ex said. His voice didn't leave room for discussion.

I didn't realize how hot and tired I was until we had loaded everything back into the minivan and turned back toward civilization. The first blast of air-conditioning was like standing in front of an open refrigerator, and I think I must have sighed, because Aubrey glanced over at me and grinned. Then his smile faded.

'Jayné,' he said. 'Look, if you want to postpone . . . well, postpone tonight. I absolutely understand.'

'No,' I said, surprised by how much I meant it. 'I really don't.'

We spent the ride into Denver listening to the radio.

Twice, I turned to look into the backseat. Ex was staring out the window, his face etched in a frown. We hit the tech center on the south side of the city right around rush hour, and the traffic slowed to a crawl. Long rows of red brake lights beaded I-25 like a Christmas tree. I propped my legs on the dashboard and looked out as the buildings slid slowly by.

A small knot of tension was building in my gut. I wanted to get back to the house, get out of my sweat-soaked clothes and into something clean. I wanted to go out with Aubrey and drink and dance and show the world that I wasn't scared. I wanted Saturday to be over, and the thing that lived inside Randolph Coin's body defeated. The traffic moved languidly, shifting forward, pausing, then shifting again. My mind moved between unease at the still not quite faded memory of the monstrous eye looking down at me and a deep, slow-rising desire that came from the immediate, distracting presence of Aubrey's body and breath. We reached our exit, and Aubrey pulled us off the highway and onto surface streets that easily went twice as fast.

He pulled into the carport that we'd left empty specifically to allow the transfer of firearms without alarming the neighbors. Chogyi Jake met us at the door and helped Ex with the equipment while I headed to the back to fulfill the first of my fantasies.

I was glad I'd donated most of yesterday's purchases. The debate over the handful of outfits I had kept was painful enough. If I'd had the full wardrobe, I would have melted down completely. I settled on a red skirt with a white scoop top that showed off a little cleavage without screaming slut. A little lipstick and eyeliner. Nice leather shoes with a heel low enough I could still run in them if something happened. I considered taking Eric's cell phone, but decided against it for the small, petty reason that it was too bulky for the purse I wanted to carry and I sure as hell wasn't taking my leather backpack on a date. Besides, Aubrey would have his cell.

I looked at myself in the bathroom mirror and told myself I looked beautiful. I didn't look like a high school kid trying on her older sister's outfits. I didn't look desperate. I didn't look out of my depth.

I tried putting my hair up, just to see if it helped. I decided it made me seem like I was trying too hard, so I left it down. I hoped that the others wouldn't be around, and that Aubrey and I could head out without any comments. While I was at it, I might as well have asked for a pony.

'Well, now,' Midian said. 'Our little girl cleans up pretty nice.'

'You don't have to sound surprised,' I said, willing myself not to blush.

Aubrey, sitting on the couch, looked much better than I did. While I'd been dithering, he'd clearly run home, transformed, and come back the best version of himself. His honey-colored hair was just ruffled enough to look at ease. His clothes were half a notch more formal than mine— slacks, jacket, and a deep blue shirt that worked for his complexion. And when he saw me, his eyes went a little wider, which was exactly what I needed just then.

'You shouldn't go,' Ex said. He was leaning against the back wall, his arms crossed. 'Both of you. After what happened last night, you should see this isn't the time for fun and games—'

'Save your breath, preacher,' Midian said. 'They made up their minds. Besides, Coin's just looking. He didn't *find* us.'

'Leaving the warded house is a mistake,' Ex said.

'It's their mistake to make,' Midian said. 'And your subtext's starting to show.'

Ex turned a venomous gaze on Midian, but the cursed man either didn't notice or didn't care. Chogyi Jake appeared from the kitchen and nodded silently with his usual beatific smile.

'You kids have a good time, now,' Midian said. 'Play safe, and don't come back early. I'm going to teach these boys a little bit about how you play poker. If you get back before I've cleaned them out, I'll be disappointed.'

'We'll do what we can,' Aubrey said, and then, directly to Ex, 'We'll be careful.' Ex grunted and turned away. Aubrey offered me his arm. It was the cheesiest thing a guy had ever done with me. I liked it.

The summer sun was just pushing its way down to the western horizon, the light turning bloody in the pollution and heat. Far to the east, the sky was dipped in indigo, a few stars struggling to find themselves in the gloom. Aubrey held my hand as I got into his car, and then we were off.

'I know this Cuban place,' he said.

'Anything,' I said. 'You're driving.'

'Jayné?'

'Yeah?'

'Thanks for not postponing,' he said.

'Welcome,' I replied, smiling to myself.

Growing up at home, boyfriends had been clandestine by nature. There wasn't any going out without a chaperone. There were church group parties, there were occasional get-togethers with girls from school, and very, very rarely I would go out of town for a track meet or a speech competition. My first kiss had been at the state qualifiers my sophomore year with a guy I'd met that night and never saw again. The next year, I'd arranged a plan with three of my friends that let me slip out to a movie with a guy from French class when my parents thought I was at one of their houses. I did it four times before we got caught, and I was grounded for a month. My mother had wept for days, and my father made me go talk to the pastor at our church about the sin of lust, a conversation that neither the pastor nor I enjoyed.

When I opted for a secular college, my father lost all perspective. In fairness, I'd known he would and that expectation had been part of what made the decision easy for me. He made it clear that I would do as he said, or I wouldn't be welcome in his house. I called the bluff. I can still remember the look in his eyes when I left. It was like he was watching someone he loved walk off a cliff.

When I got to ASU, I didn't have any idea how to deal with men. I didn't have any experience or any friends. All I could do was fake it and hope. My first lover had been a graduate student who was the teacher's assistant in my biology class. I found out later he'd been going through the roll in alphabetical order, and made it through the early Ns before the end of the semester.

His name was Gianni, and he'd had a gentle touch and a quick smile. He'd been an attentive lover. When he left, I was glad to have known him and profoundly less than devastated that he was gone. My second lover was named Cary. His jacket was back at the house. We hadn't ended so gracefully.

The restaurant looked like a frame house, pale blue siding with yellow pastel trim. Aubrey parked on the street and we walked across the low, well-cut lawn like we were going to a friend's house. His hand brushed mine as we walked through the door, and I took it. We sat at a small table, and I let him order wine for us both. I smiled at him across the table and he smiled back.

Gianni, Cary, Aubrey. It seemed like I had a thing for guys whose names ended in a vowel sound. I shook my head, trying to dislodge the thought before I said it or anything equally asinine out loud.

I ordered the black tiger shrimp. Aubrey got something called ropa vieja. I sipped the wine, feeling the warmth of the alcohol in my throat. Aubrey smiled. I smiled back. We didn't say anything.

'This feels a little awkward, doesn't it?' I said.

Aubrey shook his head, denying it, and then said, 'Well. A little, maybe. First dates.'

'I guess,' I said. 'Not just that, though. I feel like I'm

looking over my shoulder all the time. Like *they* are going to be there.'

'Tell you what,' Aubrey said, 'you keep watch behind me, I'll keep watch behind you.'

The anxiety in my belly softened a little.

'Sounds like a plan,' I said. 'Is it always like this? When you and Eric were working on things before, was it always this . . .'

I raised my hands, trying to make a gesture that would express what I couldn't find words for.

'No,' Aubrey said. 'This is the most intense thing I've ever done. It's intimidating. I keep wanting to call Eric and ask him what to do, and then I remember that he's . . .'

'Yeah,' I said. 'I know what you mean.'

'I'm sorry,' he said. 'That's not very good first-date chatter, is it?'

'It's weird,' I said.

'In all kinds of ways,' Aubrey said. 'Apart from all the rest of it, I keep trying to wrap my head around the idea that you're the girl Eric talked about. You aren't what I expected.'

'How so?' I asked. 'I mean, what kinds of things did he say about me?'

Aubrey thought about that for a second.

'He wasn't wrong about any of it. It's just the person he was talking about was a kid, and you aren't. He said you were smart. Mouthy. That his brother was about the worst match for you as a father that he could imagine,' Aubrey said. 'I didn't get the feeling that they particularly got along, Eric and your dad.'

'Cats. Dogs,' I said. 'Our family has had its Jerry Springer moments.'

'I heard a little bit about that. There was some static when you stopped believing in God.'

'It didn't start out that way,' I said. 'It's where it ended up. Maybe it's where it had to end up.'

'How'd it start, then?'

'I stopped believing in hell,' I said. 'I kept thinking about it, and I just couldn't make it square up. My dad and the pastor and everyone, they kept talking about a god that loves people and wants us to be well and happy, and then they'd talk about all the terrible things that would happen to me forever if I pissed him off. It just didn't make sense, you know? Why would someone that loves you make it so that you could be tortured forever just because you didn't do what he said? So I figured they were wrong. I figured that there wasn't really a hell, because God loved us and he wouldn't do that to us.'

'How old were you?'

'About twelve, I think,' I said. 'I tried to explain it to my dad, but he didn't think much of it. Eventually, I figured out that I shouldn't talk about it. But then I started thinking about other things that didn't make sense. I looked at the world, and it just seemed . . . I don't know . . . bigger than what they were telling me. And somewhere in there, I woke up and thought, you know, if Jesus died for my sins, that's not really something I asked him to do.'

Aubrey laughed. It was a warm sound, and I relaxed a little, just hearing it.

'It sounds like you didn't lose faith in God as much as in your church,' Aubrey said.

'When you stop believing in someone who's been telling you stories, you stop believing in the stories too,' I said. 'I *wanted* to believe, just for tactical reasons. It would have made my life a lot easier. But there you go.'

The food came, and it was better than I'd expected. It turned out ropa vieja meant 'old clothes' but was really shredded beef with some genuinely wonderful spices. We talked a lot about my family and Eric and behavior-changing brain cysts, which should have been gross but was actually really interesting. The background fear faded if it never quite went away. I had flan for dessert. Aubrey just drank coffee.

'So,' he said when I put down my fork, 'you think Midian's cleaned them out yet?'

'Probably not yet,' I said.

He smiled.

'Yeah,' he said. 'Me neither.'

We went to a nightclub in an old church that played well-mixed techno. Despite my expectations, the Goth contingent was in the minority. Most of the people seemed like young-professional types and college students. I danced for a while, Aubrey near me, but not so close that we were really dancing together. Then the floor began to get crowded, the bodies of strangers pushing us closer. My anxiety about the Invisible College and Coin and the nightmare was all still there, but instead of spoiling the night, it made things sharper. More real. I could see how someone could wind up addicted to danger.

I took a break, drank a martini, and went back out determined to put the uncertainty behind me. When we started dancing again, I took Aubrey's arms and put them around me. He went awkward and unsure for maybe two minutes, and then we were leaning into each other. The music didn't stop, and I didn't want it to.

The high Gothic vault above us glittered with mirror balls and glowed with blue and orange lights just bright enough to give us our shadows. Stained-glass windows looked down on us. Aubrey's body was warm under my hands, and his face had a seriousness that suited it even more than his smiles. He was a good dancer once he relaxed, and it turned out so was I.

I had a second martini, and then another drink that I couldn't quite identify. When I started feeling light-headed, I went up to the rooftop deck for some air. The city lay spread out before me in the darkness, glittering black and orange. The night had cooled down to comfortable, the breeze warm against my skin like Denver itself exhaling gently against me. I heard Aubrey come up behind me; I could already recognize his footsteps. When he put his hand on my shoulder, I leaned back against him.

'It's beautiful,' he said.

'Yeah.'

'You are too.'

I turned, lifting my mouth to his. He tasted like good whiskey and fresh coffee. He smelled like musk and spice. I rested my head against him and tried to catch my breath.

'You know,' I said softly, 'you never did show me your apartment.'

It was a small place near the university. A low counter separated the kitchen from a living room hardly wide enough to hold the couch. The bedroom was small, a queen-size bed pressed into a corner to leave a path. But the floors were wood and had been polished until they glowed, and every spare surface was piled with books and unlit candles. When we got there, he started to say something, but I stopped him for fear of losing the moment.

There had been times I'd seen a naked man and thought it was exciting or funny or weird. Lying on Aubrey's half-made bed and seeing him lit only by the soft light that filtered in from the street was the first time I'd thought a man was beautiful. My body had a warm, relaxed feeling, the bruises and cracked ribs only a seasoning on a rising tide of pleasure. Aubrey's skin against mine was rough and sweet and perfect. His fingers were gentle, and even with stitches holding my side together, I felt beautiful. I came once before he was in me. He had a three-pack of condoms in his bedside table in an unopened box. We went through two of them.

In the aftermath, sweat drying on my back and neck, my body still twitching, I listened to his breath as he fought against sleep. The clock at the bedside said it was a little after three in the morning. I was awake and as alert as I'd ever been. I slid out from under the bunched sheet and paused in the doorway to look at Aubrey stretched out, naked and spent, his eyes closed, one arm raised over his head. He looked strong and vulnerable both. He didn't know who I was. Not really. There were only stories that Eric had told him, a few shared days, and the fact that when I'd needed someone, I'd called him.

And when I'd called him, he'd been there. It was about as much as I knew of him too. So maybe it was enough.

My clothes were in knots on the floor, and I didn't bother trying to untangle them. I took myself to his bathroom, had a quick shower, and wrapped myself in his robe—soft green terry cloth that smelled like him. When I went to the kitchen, I didn't turn on the lights for fear of waking him. Between the shower and the deepest part of the night, it was cool enough that a cup of tea sounded good. I boiled some water, found a cup and a box of tea bags by the light of the gas flame, and took myself out to the couch while the tea steeped.

Aubrey's computer was an old laptop perched on the couch's armrest. I booted it up, found wireless service, and pulled up Firefox. I figured that if there was something in his work that had caught Eric's attention, it would be good for me to know. Besides which, I wanted to be able to talk to Aubrey about the things that were important to him without sounding like an idiot. I Googled *Toxoplasma gondii* and his name.

That's how I found out about his wife.

11

Her name was Kimberly. She had her PhD from UC Berkeley, several papers listed in the indexes of things like *Clinical Microbiology* and *The Journal of Parasitology*. From what I could tell, she was presently on staff with a research project out of Grace Memorial Hospital in Chicago. And she had cowritten at least two papers with Aubrey. One was called 'Patterns in Parasitic Modification of Host Behavior,' and the whole thing was posted on a newsgroup, ripped off from a magazine called *Nature*. The other one I found was 'Cystic Extent as Behavioral Metric in *T. gondii* Infection.'

In the pictures of her that I found online, she had shoulder-length auburn hair and surprisingly blue eyes. When she smiled, she looked a little like Nicole Kidman. I found a website with pictures of a rafting trip that she and Aubrey both went on a few years before. There were four other couples, but I kept staring at Aubrey, who was laughing, his arms around his wife. In the photograph, his wedding ring seemed to glow.

She was beautiful. She was well educated. She was married to the man I'd just fucked. I felt like someone had punched me in the stomach. I sat in the darkness, the robe catching on my stitches when I breathed. The right thing to do was wake him up and ask him. Talk to him. Let him explain.

Instead, I pulled up Thunderbird and went through his e-mail. A quick search of his inbox listed a dozen messages from her in the last weeks. I read the last four, hoping they were talking about divorce. They weren't. The best thing I could say was they weren't love letters. The tone between them was intimate and friendly, talking about old friends and shared sources. The last one was from only two days ago. It was a short note saying that she was sorry to hear about Eric's death, and telling him to be careful. When I pulled up a copy of his previous year's tax returns, it listed his status as married.

I left the laptop on the couch. I managed to get all of my clothes up off his floor without waking him. I dressed in the bathroom with shaking hands. I thought I might cry or throw up, but I just pulled on my underwear and my skirt. The scoop top was badly wrinkled, but I wasn't going back in to steal one of Aubrey's shirts. If I looked like I was on the walk of shame, that was pretty much dead accurate. I pulled the top on, put my feet in my low, comfortable heels, and grabbed my purse on the way out.

The university district came to life slowly as the black night sky paled to blue. I found a coffee shop, where I ordered a cappuccino with two extra shots and a lousy pastry that I looked at more than actually ate. The fatigue of a sleepless night had started to wear on me. My side ached, my ribs ached, my knee was swelling again where the *haugtrold* had wrenched it. I'd been dancing on it. How stupid was that? I'd been hurt, almost killed, and I'd numbed the wounds with martinis and techno-pop in an all-out effort to get myself seduced by Aubrey, the married guy. Nice going, Jayné.

I wanted the coffee to be as bad as the pastry. I wanted bitter, tasteless blackness and half-soured cream, but it was actually pretty good. The barista was maybe a year younger than me, with a pierced tongue and nose. She put on a Ray Charles CD, raised her eyebrows at me to ask if I needed anything, and left me alone when I shook my head. I cupped the cappuccino in my hands and let the music and the dawn change the moment for me.

Okay, I felt stupid. Okay, I'd been humiliated. It wasn't the first time. It probably wouldn't be the last. I'd let myself fall for a guy who had lied to me, or at least omitted a great big honking truth that pretty much anyone would have seen as worthy of mention. I wondered whether I would have done anything different if I'd known he was married. I was fairly certain I would have.

On the upside, I still had the money and property Eric had left me. Midian and Ex and Chogyi Jake were all probably at my house right now, working on the plan to avenge Eric and break the Invisible College. I'd helped save Candace and Aaron from a rider. I just had to stop the bullshit, decide what was actually important to me, and take care of business. Going to bed with Aubrey had been a mistake. Mistakes happen. It was time to move on.

I thought back to my post-shopping breakdown with Chogyi Jake. It was possible that I was a little more vulnerable and raw than I wanted to admit. Going for Aubrey—going for anyone—was a normal kind of screwup to make. Lonely little girl reaches out to the first kind face that wanders by. Pathetic? Okay, I could accept that. I just wouldn't let it happen again.

I wondered if Ex and Chogyi Jake knew about Kimberly. Ex, maybe. It would explain why he'd seemed so pissed off at the two of us going out. I thought Chogyi Jake would have warned me. Maybe. Or maybe not. They were quick enough to hide the bodies of the people I'd helped kill, but maybe that didn't really put them on my side.

Whatever my side was.

'Fuck you, Aubrey,' I said to myself. 'I needed a stand-up guy, and I got you instead. How fair is that?'

People came in and out of the coffee shop, mostly students, I guessed. The barista worked her machine in bursts of steam and the gurgling of espresso. Ray Charles calling his friend to go get stoned segued to a cover of 'Yesterday' that pointed out how clean and soulless Paul McCartney really sounded. It was nice sharing a little morning pain with Ray, if only because he put me in perspective. I finished my coffee, left the pastry half eaten, and headed out to the street. It took a while to find a taxi, but I managed, and twenty minutes later I was home.

'Sweet fucking Jesus,' Midian said as soon as I walked in. 'I figured you for dead.'

'Not dead,' I said, and tossed my purse on the couch. 'Where is everyone?'

'Out looking for you,' Midian said. 'Aubrey came by a

couple hours ago looking like someone stole his dick and said you'd gone missing.'

'Well, you can tell him I'm back,' I said. 'I need to get into some clean clothes.'

'Not such a good date, eh?' Midian asked. It was hard to tell with his ruin of a voice, but I thought he was a little amused. I didn't answer.

I'd changed into jeans and one of Eric's white button-down shirts when I heard Aubrey and Ex arrive. Their voices were harsh, like they'd been fighting. I stretched, summoned up my righteous anger, and headed out to take the bull by the horns.

Ex was livid. He wheeled on me as soon as I appeared in the living room.

'What exactly was that little stunt supposed to—'

'Jayné,' Aubrey said at the same time, 'we need to talk about—'

I put my palm out toward Ex, shutting him down, and turned to Aubrey.

'We need to talk?' I asked.

'Yes,' he said. 'Please, I understand what happened, and I know what it seems like, but—'

'Are you and Kimberly divorced?' I asked.

Aubrey blushed and looked down at his feet. Ex's jaw actually dropped. I'd always thought that was just a figure of speech. Apparently he hadn't known.

'Aubrey?' I said.

'We're separated,' he said.

'Not divorced,' I said.

136

'No.'

'So then still married.'

'Yes.'

'And you didn't tell me,' I said.

'No,' Aubrey said. 'I should have.'

'Okay,' I said. 'We've talked.'

I brushed past Ex and into the kitchen. It was probably only my own embarrassment and humiliation that made me read Ex's expression as delight. When he and Aubrey followed me in a moment later, they were both perfectly sober. Midian was sitting at the kitchen table, the telephone handset to his ear.

'Jake,' he said, pointing at it. 'He put me on hold. It's okay, though. You two were loud enough back there I followed everything.'

'Good,' I said. 'It's Friday morning, almost ten o'clock. This time tomorrow, Randolph Coin's going to be dead. Let's try to focus on that, okay?'

'Fine by me,' Midian said, and then, into the handset, 'Yeah. She's back. Everything's fine, or, well . . . fuck it, it's close enough. Get your ass back to the ranch here, and we'll finish up. Yeah, what?'

He paused, frowned, and shook his head.

'No. If they don't have yellow onions, I'll think of something else. Just bring me the rest of it,' he said, and then put the handset back in its cradle. 'Since he was out anyway, I asked him to pick up some stuff. Didn't figure we'd be going out for dinner.'

'Yeah, probably not,' I said. 'Let's go over the plan again.'

No one suggested anything else. I took out the maps and schematics, and Ex walked through the whole thing again, quizzing the three of us. Aubrey answered his questions in a clipped, hard voice and sat with his arms crossed. When Chogyi Jake appeared with a bag of groceries, Ex made him go through the whole thing by himself while Midian made ham sandwiches with fresh tomatoes and hot mustard for lunch. My brain was a storm of anger, betrayal, and humiliation, but I forced myself to follow the details of the plan. Midian and Chogyi Jake at the southeast edge of the property. Ex in his car to the north, me in among the railroad tracks to the west, and Aubrey in his minivan to the south. Three different angles, so that no matter where Coin stood, at least one of us would have a clear shot. When Chogyi Jake and Midian had drawn Coin out past his protections, Midian would give the signal by raising both hands. If for any reason he couldn't do that, Chogyi Jake would drop to the ground. The plan to go out and look at the place physically seemed to have fallen by the wayside in the day's drama. I didn't bring it up.

The air between me and Aubrey should have bent with the tension, but Chogyi Jake either didn't notice anything or, more likely, dedicated himself to ignoring it. Anything that Ex felt was covered by his drill sergeant attitude.

I felt my mind starting to get fuzzy at about one o'clock. I'd been up since eight in the morning the day before, too excited by the twin prospects of going shooting and my ill-fated date to sleep in. That put me at about twenty-nine hours awake.

'I'm going to crash for a while,' I said. 'Knock if something happens.'

The silence that accompanied me out of the kitchen told me that the house would have to be on fire before anyone disturbed me. That suited me just fine.

I stripped and crawled into bed, one pillow under my head, one over it to block out light and sound. My muscles seemed to vibrate with fatigue. This time tomorrow, it'll all be over, I told myself. I'll be safe and rich and, God as my witness, I'll be straight the fuck out of this city. I could go back to ASU. Paying tuition out of pocket would be easy. I could get my degree. I could transfer to some other university. Hell, I could probably buy my way into the Ivy League with a few weighty donations here and there.

It was a strange thought. In a way, everything was ending tomorrow. The shot that took out Coin and broke the Invisible College also freed me. No more tattooed ninja hit squads breaking down my doors. No more need for bodyguards like Ex and Chogyi Jake. Or Aubrey.

I imagined myself going back. Driving up to the dorms in a chauffeured Rolls-Royce, maybe. I pictured Cary's reaction, seeing me rising like a phoenix from the ashes and salted earth I'd left behind me. I slid from that to going home, paying off the mortgage on my parents' house, buying my mother a car, telling my father that I wouldn't go to church on Sunday if I didn't want to, and watching him realize that his power over me was gone. Even his power to drive me away. Somewhere in it, I had become the primary funding behind the hospital in Chicago, dressed in a good Armani suit with Nicole Kidman–esque Kimberly asking my permission to go ahead with her work. I didn't notice the shift between daydream and dream until I found myself in the nightmare of wings and Coin's massive eye and woke with a shout.

The door thumped, someone throwing a shoulder against it. Someone was calling my name. Ex, I thought, the last shreds of dream fading. Ex was screaming my name. But at least he was pronouncing it right.

'I'm okay!' I shouted back. 'Leave the door alone. I'm fine.'

'What the *fuck* is going on in there?'

'Bad dream,' I said. 'I'm fine. I'll be out in a minute. Just calm down.'

I'd been asleep almost four hours. I hauled myself up out of bed, vague and hungover. My skin felt sticky with rank sweat. My period had started a week early. I needed a shower.

'You're all right?' Ex's voice sounded like he was expecting me to lie. 'Was it Coin again?'

'I don't know. Maybe,' I said, the details of the dream already out of reach. 'I'm fine. I'm just still waking up. I'll be out.'

Ex's silence seemed untrusting, but I ignored it and pulled myself into the bathroom. If he broke the door down to rescue me from a bad dream, I'd throw him out of my house. I was deeply weary of dealing with male bullshit. I felt tired and sluggish. Happily, I had my old leather backpack in the bedroom with me. Going out to hunt for tampons wasn't something I particularly wanted to deal with at the moment.

The water helped. I washed my hair three times just for the pleasure of feeling the warmth running down my back. I prodded the wound in my side. It itched and felt odd when I tugged at the stitches, but it didn't particularly hurt. The bruises on my knee and back were also starting to heal, going from storm-cloud blue to a deep green with yellow and brown at the margins. I got a glimpse of the tattoo, a remnant of my sixteenth birthday's drunken binge, on the small of my back. In the mirror, it looked like oriental script, though I'd been assured by several people back at ASU that it wasn't. I felt a sudden nostalgia for the days when keeping my parents from knowing I had a tattoo was the biggest risk I had to deal with.

I put on my own T-shirt, my old jeans, and pulled my hair back into a ponytail. I considered myself in the mirror, then without thinking, my hand reached out for the eyeliner. I didn't give a damn what any of them thought, but looking decent made me feel better. When I came down the hall, the smell of steak, wine, and grilled onions greeted me like a friend. The windows were ruddy with the warm light of sunset. I had a momentary image, the memory of a dream I'd almost forgotten. A black disk like a sun that radiated like light, but different.

'Jayné.'

Ex was sitting alone on the couch. His blond hair was unbound and flowing over his shoulders. His expression was grim.

'Ex,' I said, folding my arms.

'I need you to make peace with Aubrey,' he said softly.

'I really don't see how that's any of your business,' I said.

He held up a hand, and his expression made it a request for silence instead of a command. I nodded my permission for him to go on. He stood up, his hands clasped in front of him in a way that made me think of prayer. He was taller than I was under normal circumstances, and I hadn't put on shoes. I felt like a kid at the principal's office.

'We're going into something tomorrow that is already profoundly difficult,' he said. 'We've gone over everything often enough that I know it starts to seem easy or certain. That's why I keep going over it. But the truth is we're taking a huge risk. We can't be divided or distracted.'

'We can't?' I said. I had been through about as much condescension as I was in the mood for, and Ex saw that.

'I'm not asking you to do this for him or yourself. I'm asking for me,' he said. 'If something goes wrong, if someone gets hurt or killed, and it's because I didn't say the right thing or do what I needed to, then it's going to be my fault. Right now, I'm afraid that you and Aubrey are going to be distracted. And I don't want to see either of you hurt again.'

'Not on your watch,' I said. I'd meant to say it with contempt, but it didn't come out that way. I felt myself soften a little. 'So you want me to just blow it off?'

'Not especially, no,' Ex said. 'But I want you two at peace with each other.'

I took a deep breath and let it out slowly. We looked at

each other in the warm light of evening. He was a hard-faced man, and he didn't look away from me.

'Where is he?' I asked.

'They're all out back. The kitchen's too hot to eat in. And I wanted to talk to you first, so I sent them out.'

'Okay,' I said. 'I'll do the olive branch thing. But I'm not looking to forgive and forget.'

'And I'm damned glad of that too,' Ex said with a rare smile. It crossed my mind briefly that I should ask what he meant by the comment. But he was already walking toward the backyard, and with everything that changed in the course of the evening, by the time we spoke again I'd forgotten what he'd said.

12

I waited until I'd eaten dinner. Midian had cooked steaks in red wine and black pepper. The onions were sweet and tart, and he'd done something with butter and garlic that made broccoli taste good. We sat on the back porch, drinking wine and watching the stars come out. Aubrey sat a little apart, his smile tight and restrained. Chogyi Jake and Midian were both taking up the slack in the conversation by trading jokes and stories, cajoling Aubrey out of his funk and me out of my rage. I was almost feeling human by the end. Ex kept looking over at me, prompting me to make a move. I'd promised to make peace, but I still resented it. It wouldn't have killed Aubrey to open the discussion. He could start by apologizing again.

I knew I wasn't being fair or even particularly rational. I tried to suck it up.

'Aubrey,' I said, and his head came up like he'd heard a gunshot. 'You got a minute?'

'Sure,' he said. I led the way back into the house. I was pretty sure the others weren't going to come anywhere near us until this was over. I sat on the couch, legs folded up beneath me, arms crossed. Aubrey took the hearth, watching me with his best poker face. We sat there in silence for a few seconds.

'Why don't you tell me about your wife,' I said.

'Okay, fine,' he said, then took a breath, gathering himself. 'Kim and I met when I'd just been accepted into the doctoral program. We were looking into some of the same questions, so we had a lot to talk about. It worked. For a while.'

Something changed in his expression, softening it. Nostalgia, I thought. He looked down at his hands as if the story was written on his skin.

'We'd been married for about two years when Eric showed up,' Aubrey said. 'She was still here back then. We were both at the university, and she was doing some work on a study at the medical center. The money wasn't great, but we were doing all right. Eric sent us both e-mail at first. He said he'd read our work and had some questions about the logical structures of parasitism. How parasite-host systems worked, what kinds of patterns you'd see in host behavior modification. He was really interested in reverse-engineering things.'

'But Kim wasn't interested,' I said.

'She *was*. At first. Eric took us both out to dinner to talk things over, and it was great. Kim and I had both been swimming in the problems for so long, it was like we talked in code. Just having Eric there to explain things to made us look at everything with fresh eyes. I think both of us were pretty excited afterward. It turned into a weekly thing. There were probably five or six months that everything was great. And then the riders came up.'

He smiled, still not looking at me. He was seeing Eric and Kim, hearing conversations from years before. I might almost not have been there.

'I was amazed,' he said, as if confessing something. 'I was delighted. Riders and hosts and the idea of a universe next door that worked in a totally different way from ours, but with common strategies . . . it felt like revelation. Kim didn't believe it at first. I think it was just too weird for her. That it offended the scientist in her.

'Eric trained us both. It took a while to believe what we were seeing. I think I bought in before she did. And then Kim just sort of turned off. She didn't want anything to do with it. We started fighting. I said some things that I shouldn't have.'

'Indulge me,' I said. My voice was harsher than I'd meant it to be, but I was still pissed off. He looked up at me and the calm and nostalgia vanished.

'I told her it was wrong to ignore evidence,' he said. 'I told her that she was being narrow-minded and parochial because she'd come across something that didn't fit in her worldview. Instead of rethinking how the world is, she was shutting her eyes and pretending it wasn't true.'

'You told her she was being religious,' I said.

He chuckled, but there wasn't any mirth in the sound.

'I guess so,' he said. 'She didn't see it that way. She said I was being stupid. Arrogant. Either riders were a fraud and Eric was a con man with his own agenda or they were real and Eric was dangerously irresponsible for having anything to do with them without more information. The last fight

146

we had, she told me that the work with riders had made me either a dupe or an idiot, and she wasn't going to live with either one.'

'You had to choose between Eric and her,' I said.

'Sort of,' he said. 'Anyway. She moved out, got a job in Chicago. It was one of those situations where you had to still work together, because so many of our studies were interlinked. Things cooled off, and we stayed on decent terms. About a year and a half ago, she told me she was seeing someone else. I agreed that it was over, and we had a kind of agreement in principle to finalize the divorce. File the paperwork, all that. But she's insanely busy, and I was spending half my time working on my research and the other half helping Eric.'

'And seeing other people?'

'In principle,' Aubrey said. 'It never actually happened, but I got used to thinking of myself as unattached. If I'd thought there was any chance of Kim and me patching things up, I would never have . . .'

Aubrey took a deep breath and let it out slowly. He looked up at me. He was tired.

'Look, Jayné,' he said. 'The truth is that Kim and I have both moved on from who we were together. I didn't expect things to happen so quickly with you, and Kim honestly didn't enter my mind. It's something I've been resigned to for so long, it just felt like history.'

'You could have told me all this over dinner,' I said.

'Actually, I'm not sure I could have,' he said. 'I think talking about your ex on a first date is sort of a party foul.'

'Finding out about the wife online isn't better,' I said.

'How about finding out by snooping through my e-mail?' Aubrey said. 'That's all fine and dandy?'

'What?'

'I said how about going through my e-mail? While I was asleep. My taxes. Or, if you'd like, how about cruising the Internet looking for scraps of my life to pass judgment on? Or, when you get upset, running off without even bothering to leave me—any of us—so much as a note to say you're okay? All of those are perfectly fine, adult behaviors?'

'That's not what I'm here to talk about,' I said, feeling the moral high ground shifting under my feet.

'Well, I've brought it up,' Aubrey said.

I opened my mouth, a thousand practiced zingers suddenly falling apart before I could deliver them. Aubrey shook his head, something between sorrow and disgust in his eyes.

'I don't deserve this, Jayné,' he said. 'Kim and I aren't together. We haven't been for a long time. And as far as I can tell, you're treating me like I've somehow betrayed you personally because I haven't filed all the paperwork in a timely fashion.'

'I think being married is more than that,' I said.

'Have you ever been married?'

'No,' I said, 'but . . .'

I knew the next words. I could feel the syllables against my tongue. *Marriage is sacred.* And I could hear the voice that was saying them. It was my mother's. It all fit together with a click that was nearly physical.

I had rejected my parents and their parochial, small, restrictive ideas. I had broken off with my family and allowed myself the kind of experiences they were always tacitly afraid I'd have—sex, beer, R-rated movies—and I'd pretended that I had remade myself. But Aubrey's history took me by surprise, and I'd reacted like I was still sitting in the fourth pew. My liberal, broad-minded tolerance could still be scratched off with a fingernail.

'Fuck,' I said, anger and embarrassment giving the word weight. Aubrey waited. The silence went on. I had to say something else.

'You're right. I shouldn't have dug through your computer,' I said. 'I shouldn't have freaked out and bolted. But here's the thing. I don't have a great track record with . . . trusting people. Especially when it comes to sex. You're still married to this woman I've never met, and okay, maybe it's all just paperwork. But you are, and I found out right after we'd slept together. I'd love to pretend it was all okay with me, but it's not. I'm sorry it's not. I really, really want it to be. But it's just . . .'

Outside, Midian laughed. Ex said something I couldn't make out. Aubrey sucked in his breath. I felt like we were breaking up. There was a knot in my throat. I wanted to cry. Because that one last level of humiliation would have just put the cap on the whole conversation.

'I understand,' he said.

'We need to be able to work together,' I said, leaning forward on the couch. 'Coin's a badass. He killed my uncle. He's kept Midian under a curse for two hundred some years.

And I'm taking him on. *We're* taking him on. Knowing someone close to me, someone important, is holding back information is hard. I know I shouldn't pass that kind of judgment, but when I . . . um. Aubrey? What is it?'

His body had gone tense, the color drained from his face. When he spoke, his voice was very steady and controlled.

'*How* long has Midian been under a curse?'

'Two hundred something years,' I said. 'He said he was born at the end of the French Revolution. Why?'

'He's two hundred years old?'

'A little more than that, but yeah.'

Aubrey stood up carefully and walked to the kitchen. I looked at the empty doorway, then unfolded myself from the couch and followed. The duffel bag of guns we'd found in the storage facility was still there on the floor. Aubrey knelt beside it.

'Aubrey?'

'Curses don't make people live indefinitely, Jayné. Outliving your life span is something people *try* for. Living two hundred years isn't a curse. It's something else.'

He took out one of the shotguns, checked to be sure it was loaded, and handed it to me. I took the wood stock and cold steel barrel in my hands, my mind still back on Kim and sex and Ray Charles singing over coffee. The gun seemed out of place.

'Midian?' I said. 'This is about Midian?'

Aubrey took out another shotgun, chambered a round, and looked up at me.

'If he's lying about the curse, we need to know why,'

Aubrey said. 'If he's not lying about the curse, he's not a human.'

'Oh,' I said. The air seemed to have gone out of the room. I was having a hard time catching my breath.

'Are you ready?' he asked.

I looked down at the shotgun in my hands. Salt, silver, and iron. Defense against a wide variety of riders. I felt like I'd woken up and found a rat crawling on my leg. I nodded.

'Follow me,' Aubrey said.

We stepped onto the back porch with the guns already drawn. Chogyi Jake, the first to notice us, cocked his head in something that seemed no more than mild curiosity. Ex leaped up, his chair tipping backward and onto the grass. Midian's ruined head was toward us, wisps of hair clinging to it like trails of fungus. When he turned to look over his shoulder at us, his yellowed eyes were expressionless. He picked up his cigarette, took a deep breath, and let the smoke seep out his nostrils.

'Aubrey. Jayné,' Ex said. 'Put down the guns.'

Midian lifted a hand and waved Ex's words away. He shifted his chair to face us, two shotgun barrels pointing at his head. The ruined man sighed.

'It was the Bastille Day crack, wasn't it?' he asked.

'Yeah,' I said.

'I was kind of hoping you wouldn't remember that,' he said, and wheezed out a laugh. 'I always talk before I think. It's a vice.'

'What the fuck is going on?' Ex demanded, his face

flushing red. Midian gestured toward me and Aubrey with his cigarette, the smoke leaving a trail behind it.

'The kids here just figured out I'm a vampire,' he said.

'But I've seen you in daylight,' I said.

'That's *nosferatu*,' Midian said. 'I'm *vârkolak*. Don't let it bug you. Taxonomy's always a bitch.'

We'd moved into the living room, each of us keeping Midian covered as we'd left the backyard behind. Midian sat in the overstuffed chair, a cigarette still between his thin, fleshless fingers. Ex and Chogyi Jake had grabbed guns too, but Midian's casual air—legs crossed, black-toothed smile more amusement than chagrin—made me feel like we were being silly somehow. After all, he'd been with us for days. He'd been cooking our food, taking his turn at guard duty. If he'd wanted to kill us, we'd all be dead by now.

'I don't believe it,' Ex said. His face was blank as a mask, but I could guess at the rage behind it. 'Eric fought against riders, not next to them.'

'Eric did whatever he needed to do,' Midian said. 'If he needed to get his hands dirty along the way, he wasn't the guy to hesitate.'

'What else were you lying about?' I asked.

Midian looked at me with disappointment in his eyes. It was like seeing a teacher's reaction when a student asked a particularly stupid question. The ruined man sighed.

'Well,' he said, 'first off, I sort of let you think Eric was doing me a favor with this whole Invisible College thing. Not quite true. Eric came to me.'

'Why would he think you'd fight against one of your own kind?' Ex asked.

'Jesus Christ, padre,' Midian said. '*My own kind.* Shit. Would you say that to a black guy? Or a Jew? I'm a rider, Coin's a rider, that doesn't make us buddies. Look around the room here. You've got the girl here who can't figure out if she's a kick-ass superhero or a college dropout loser. The biologist guy who can't stop feeling guilty for getting in her pants. Which, I'll point out, was not exactly just his idea, but they don't remember that. Tofu boy over there, who's showing his dedication to nonviolence by helping to shoot Coin in the head, but it's okay because he's not the one pulling the trigger and anyway Coin's not human. Shakyamuni'd be real proud of him for that doublethink. And *you* caught between a bunch of promises you've made to some great big Nobodaddy in the sky, a lifelong apology for fucking up when you were a kid, and a perfectly natural jealousy—'

'Drop it,' Ex said. 'You can't split us apart.'

'That's the point, dumbfuck. You *are* split apart,' Midian said, sitting forward. His contempt ignored the shotgun Ex pointed at his chest. 'You've got four people here, and six different sides. It's no different Next Door. The *loupine* fight the *ifrit*, who ally with the *zombii*, unless they're at war with them. The *orisha* undermine everything the *noppera-bō* try to do. The Graveyard Child works against Father Ba'al, and they both hate the Black Sun. It's a fucking mess over there.'

'So Eric was set against the Invisible College and felt he

could use you because you hated Coin too,' Chogyi Jake said. 'The enemy of my enemy is my friend.'

I shifted my shotgun to rest on my leg. My arms were getting tired.

'Coin fucked me,' Midian said philosophically. 'That part was always true. I was in Rome back then, and Coin and his buddies were just getting a foothold in the south. They'd been bopping around Finland eating lutefisk and making candles or something. Anyway, I took over this body. It used to belong to a fella named Porfirio de la Vega. Well, it turns out the Invisible College had been going after the poor bastard too, but I got him first. Coin got a hair crosswise over it and broke me. I can't feed. For two hundred years, I can't feed and I can't get out of the body. I just sit in here. But the curse connects us, me and Coin. So when Eric decided it was time to take the bastard out, he came looking for me.'

'I don't believe you,' Aubrey said. 'Eric would never make an alliance with something like you.'

Midian dug in his pocket and extracted a fresh cigarette, lighting it off the butt of the old one. The cherry glowed red, the smoke came off gray. His yellowed eyes were fixed on Aubrey.

'You never heard of the lesser evil?' he asked. 'Well, that's me. Didn't you ever wonder why he didn't pull any of you boys into this? It's a dirty operation. Messy. Morally impure. But he thought it needed doing, so he was going to do it. He left you poor fuckers out to protect you from it.'

We were silent for a moment. I could see the other three—Aubrey, Ex, Chogyi Jake—weighing the idea. They all seemed to think it was plausible.

'He didn't need to do that,' Ex said, but his voice sounded less sure now.

'Yeah, well,' Midian said with a shrug. 'Take it up with him.'

'This changes things,' Aubrey said.

'Does it?' Midian asked. 'You can't pull Coin out without me as the focus. I mean, maybe if you find someone else he's cursed between now and sunup, but even if you do, so what? It's not going to make any difference.'

'What do you mean?' I asked.

'Look. You get some random Suzie Sunshine who Coin put some ugly mojo on, haul her ass out there, and use her to break him, it's still going to lift my curse. What we're doing isn't just for me. Everyone Coin's acted against gets helped out, whether you like us or not.'

'It's just that on balance, that's more good than bad,' Ex said.

'Don't trust me on it,' Midian said. 'Trust Eric.'

'I have to think about this,' Ex said. 'We need to set guard on him.'

Midian made an impatient sound, but Aubrey was already shifting position. Chogyi Jake walked into the kitchen and came back with a length of rope. I pressed back against the wall to let him pass. Midian rolled his eyes but held out his wrists like a man waiting for the police to cuff him. As Chogyi Jake bound the thin, frail-looking wrists,

Aubrey looked over to me. This time last night, I'd been dancing with my hands around him. It seemed like longer ago.

He nodded to me and then toward the kitchen, where Ex had gone. I hesitated for a moment, then pointed my own shotgun toward the ground and walked away.

The remains of the meal preparation hadn't been cleared away yet. The cutting board was still bloody from the steak, and knives lay in the sink, their edges catching the light. The air was rich with wine and garlic. Ex was sitting at the table, his head in his hands. I leaned the gun against the side of the refrigerator and pulled out the chair across from him. The clock on the wall above him showed we were coming in on midnight.

'So,' I said softly. 'What do you think?'

'I should have seen it,' Ex said angrily.

'Well, you didn't,' I said. 'What else do you think?'

Ex looked up at me through his eyebrows. For a few seconds, he looked on the verge of doing something violent, but he shook his head and the impression went away. He pulled back his hair, tying it with a rubber band, then squared his shoulders.

'It makes sense,' he said. 'The curse, the divisions between forms of riders, Eric's willingness to use that to his advantage. Everything it said makes sense, but . . .'

'But,' I prompted.

'I don't trust him. He's a rider, and he has his own agenda.'

'Do you still think Coin killed Eric?' I asked.

Ex weighed the question for a moment, resting his chin against one knuckle. He nodded.

'Those people he sent to kill me and Midian? Those were part of the Invisible College?'

'Yes.'

'Okay, then,' I said. 'Nothing's changed. Coin's still going to be at his weakest in a few hours. We still have everything we need to go up against him.'

'I know,' Ex said. 'I don't think you can be safe when the Invisible College is hunting you, and killing Coin will break their power. I can't think of a reason not to go forward. It's just . . .'

'You trusted someone. And then you found out they didn't actually deserve it,' I said. 'Now you have to suck it up and work with them no matter how you feel, just to get the job done. Kind of like what you were saying to me earlier tonight.'

'Aubrey,' he said.

'I'm not saying he's a body-stealing vampire or anything,' I said, feeling a twinge of distress left over from my interrupted talk with Aubrey. Had we broken up? Had we ever really been together? I wasn't totally sure. I pulled myself back to Ex. 'I'm just saying there's kind of a parallel. But we can't be divided or distracted. That was you talking.'

'And after?'

I tilted my head.

'After we kill Coin. What do we do about Midian?' Ex said, his voice almost a whisper. 'If we're allies now, that's going to be over by this time tomorrow. As soon as Coin goes down, the thing inside that body will be free to do whatever it wants. He will go out into the world, and he'll hurt people. Maybe kill them. He's a rider, it's what he does.'

I gazed out the window, or tried to. With the darkness outside and the light in the kitchen, the glass was more like a black mirror. I looked tired. The kitchen behind me, reversed left for right, seemed alien. My body felt heavy and weak, my mind a little dizzy from too many changes too close together. Ex waited, his silence pushing me to answer, and I thought it was deeply unfair of him. I hadn't planned any of this. Picking up Eric's plan had all been Midian and Ex, Aubrey and Chogyi Jake. Even the encounter with Candace Dorn's *haugtrold* had been Aubrey's insistence more than mine. Making me decide what to do now, just when things got hard, seemed vaguely monstrous.

'We give him a head start,' I said. 'A day, maybe.'

'He'll vanish,' Ex said. 'We might never find him again.'

'It's a risk,' I agreed. 'But the alternative is we kill him tomorrow morning. Use him for what we need, and then stab him in the back when we're through with him.'

'It could be the best thing,' Ex said.

'Maybe. But we can't do it.'

Ex didn't speak, but his expression was clear enough. *Why not?*

'We're the good guys,' I said.

13

We split the night into four hour-and-a-half shifts to guard Midian. Mine was three to four thirty, which slated me for a longish nap before and a short one after. Midian, his hands still tied, ignored the situation except to sigh theatrically, stretch out on the couch, and get more sleep than the rest of us. I sat in the facing chair, Eric's shotgun across my thighs, and listened to the small sounds of the night.

The clock in the kitchen ticked quietly to itself. Sirens rose and fell in the distance. Once, a helicopter chopped the air so far away I could barely make it out. And Midian—Midian the vampire, or *vârkolak*, whatever that was—breathed slowly in and out in the rhythm of deep sleep. In a few hours, I was going to be looking down a rifle at the thing that had killed Eric, but just now, the world was silent and still, and my mind was clearer than I had expected it to be.

The mystery that Midian's revelation had left me with was this: if Eric wasn't doing this to help Midian, who was he helping? There was, I assumed, someone out there who he'd intended to benefit. Someone like Candace Dorn. I wondered how I would find those people and let them know that the thing had been done, or if they'd just know when it happened. Ex and Aubrey and Chogyi Jake hadn't found anything in the old notebooks that explained how this whole thing had started, but there had to be more books, more records. Somewhere there had to be something about how he'd found Midian, and what came before that, and before that. Or maybe he'd kept it all in his head.

I thought about the list of properties the lawyer had shown me. And those had been the tricky ones. There were others. More. I could have spent months going through all that. Years. And if I didn't find some master record, I'd still wonder if it existed somewhere I just hadn't thought to look. I was out of my depth. I'd known it from the moment Uncle Eric's fortune fell out of the sky like something from an old Looney Tunes cartoon, and sitting alone in the dead of night, I felt it deeply. I was scared, I was faking it, I was probably in gut-wrenching danger that I didn't understand. I'd spent the last few days as disoriented and dizzy as someone on her eighth time on the roller coaster.

But there was also a small, secret joy way down deep that surprised me. I was rich beyond my wildest dreams. Things hadn't gone the way I wanted with Aubrey, but they'd still left me feeling wanted in a way that was almost more reassuring than actually having a boyfriend would have been. And regardless of why Eric had gone after the Invisible College in the first place, I knew why *I* was doing it.

I was doing it for Eric.

I heard the low beeping of Aubrey's cell phone alarm and checked the time. Four thirty. My turn at guard duty was over. I listened to the soft, shoeless footsteps as he walked down the hall toward me, and I nodded to him as he stepped into the living room.

'Everything okay?' he asked, his voice hushed.

I handed him the shotgun.

'It'll do,' I said, and then, 'Hey. About . . . what happened at your apartment? Midian wasn't wrong. It was my idea too, and it's not like I told you all about everything in my history either. So. The Kim thing was a shock, and I'm a little easier to spin right now than usual. But . . .'

I shrugged.

'So we're good?' Aubrey asked.

'We're working on it,' I said. 'I mean, you're still married.'

Halfway down to my bedroom, I stopped, considered, and then turned back. I was too wound up to sleep. I headed to the kitchen, turned on the light over the sink, and brewed up a pot of coffee that wasn't as good as Midian's. A little before six, the windows were bright with the coming dawn. Ex and Chogyi Jake walked in quietly. Ex looked tired but focused. Chogyi Jake might have just woken up from eight solid hours, except that his smile didn't reach his eyes as much as usual. Without a word, Ex put the rifles on the kitchen table. The black ammunition seemed to writhe in my peripheral vision.

'Well, hey,' Midian said from the living room. 'Nice day to kill someone. Is that coffee? Because if it is, you over-brewed it.'

'Good to know,' I said, and heard his wheezing chuckle.

'Okay,' Ex said, his voice cutting through the morning

like a drill sergeant's. 'We've got one more run-through on this, and then we go.'

Midian and Aubrey came into the kitchen. Midian's hands were free, and he was rubbing his wrists. I noticed that he kept his distance from the bullets. We went through everything again for the last time, then Ex loaded the rifles and handed one to me and one to Aubrey. Ex offered the shotgun to Chogyi Jake, but he refused it.

'When we get this done, who's gonna want pancakes?' Midian asked, his ruined lips in a leer. I wondered how I could have imagined he was really alive.

'Let's go,' Ex said.

We went.

The first difference I noticed was the air.

We drove north toward Commerce City, Ex in the windowless van, Chogyi and Midian in Ex's sports car, Aubrey and I sitting silently in his minivan. The warehouses along the railroad tracks came slowly nearer, the rising sun flooded the still relatively empty highway and turned the asphalt to gold, and the air around us seemed to grow less substantial. The light moved through it differently. I put it down to my own nerves until I felt something bump against me, tapping at the base of my spine. I had the sudden physical memory of being eight years old and swimming in a lake where fish would sometimes blunder into me.

Aubrey saw me shudder.

'Yeah,' he said. 'I can feel it too.'

'This is them?' I said, gesturing at the world in general. 'This is the Invisible College doing whatever they're doing?'

'It's Next Door getting close,' Aubrey said. 'I've felt something like this before. The riders are about to move into their new bodies.'

Something unreal moved past my legs. I felt its wake.

'I really want this over with,' I said.

By the time we got to the warehouse, I felt like the old high school science class movie of an ovum surrounded by a million flailing sperm. The air was full of unseen creatures bumping and pressing and shifting against me. There were so many, I stopped being able to tell one from another, my body just registering them as a constant, repulsive crawling. There was nothing in the early morning light to show that any of it was happening. If anything, the strangeness of the light made the world seem static, like we'd driven into a still frame from a movie. Aubrey dropped me by the train tracks. We didn't speak, but as I lifted the rifle out of the back, his hand touched mine. The double sensation of real, human contact and the press of riders just outside reality moved me, and I was tempted to kiss him. He pulled back and I hefted the weapon, already loaded with its unpleasant black bullets. I made my way to the corner of the little building we'd picked, looking down on Google maps like God and angels. I leaned against the masonry block, the blue paint flaking away. The boxcars loomed to my left like great, blind, industrial cows. Nothing moved.

Fifty or sixty cars filled the parking lot, and three huge

silver buses were parked against the side of the building. A chain-link fence surrounded the whole place. Two gates opened to the street—one wide enough for semis to negotiate with ease, one no wider than a door. The second was closer to me, chained shut. When I lifted the scope to my eye, I could read the numbers on the combination lock.

Aubrey's minivan appeared on the street, coming down from the north, then passed out of sight, making its way toward his assassination post. I wouldn't be able to see Aubrey or Ex and the windowless van from where I was. I sat crouched in the long, blue shadows of morning, my back against the wall, invisible creatures pressing against me.

'Hey,' Uncle Eric said. 'You've got a call.'

I plucked the cell phone out of my pocket, cursing myself quietly for not putting the phone on vibrate, and let the barrel of the rifle lower toward the ground. The display only told me that it was a conference call. I picked up before Eric spoke again.

'Hey,' I said.

'Are you in place?' Ex asked.

'Yes,' I said.

'Okay,' Aubrey said with a small, coughing sigh. There was a rustling on the line and something clanked. 'I'm set.'

'Midian and I are heading in,' Chogyi said. 'You'll see us in just a moment.'

His voice was calm. Just hearing him sound like that loosened the knot in my belly a little bit. I almost smiled.

'Okay,' Ex said. 'Focus on drawing Coin out. Don't worry about us. We'll be watching for the signal.'

'Good luck, everyone,' I said, then I dropped the call, put the cell phone back in my pocket, and knelt down, the rifle held between me and the wall. A flock of pigeons rose from the far side of the tracks, swinging wide around the green-gray warehouse and then away, as if they wanted nothing to do with any of us.

Ex's car pulled up on the street, its engine unnaturally loud in the comparative silence. Chogyi Jake got out of the driver's side. Midian emerged from the passenger's, moving with the same awkwardness he always did. Chogyi Jake lifted a black nylon duffel bag out of the car's diminutive trunk and unzipped it. Midian slouched to the smaller gate in the chain-link fence, then slowly, painfully knelt. I shifted my weight, the gravel crunching under me. Chogyi Jake pulled a blue silk robe from the bag, pulled it on over his clothes, then leaned down by Midian. I picked up the rifle. Through the scope, I could see the chalk in Chogyi Jake's hand, the symbols taking shape all around Midian. The vampire's eyes were closed, his hands open on his bent knees, his smile showing teeth black as fresh tar. Seeing them both in the crosshairs felt ominous, but I didn't look away.

Chogyi took his place behind Midian, one hand on the ruined scalp, the other palm raised toward the new-risen sun. When the slow, strange call of his voice reached me, I caught my breath.

The song that rose from them was one of the strangest sounds I'd ever heard. Sorrowful and accusing, it most reminded me of an Islamic call to prayer. The invisible things pressing against me shivered, paused, and then went wild. Their frenzy made me grit my teeth. I could feel them over every inch of my skin, writhing and beating against me. Chogyi Jake's call rose again, seeming to echo against itself, like someone singing a round, even though there was only one voice. Midian wasn't smiling anymore. His ruined lips were moving, his head shaking back and forth, his eyes shut. Sweat was pouring down Chogyi Jake's face and neck. I could see the rivulets glitter in the light.

The warehouse door opened with a scream of old hinges. I looked up. At this distance, the man who came out could have been anyone. I had expected him to walk unnaturally, pulled out to us like an unwilling marionette, but his steps were perfectly regular. Through the scope, I could see the dark slacks and simple white shirt below the inscribed face I had glimpsed when Ex brought me here before. Randolph Coin, or whatever had taken up residence under the dead man's skin. I placed the rifle against my shoulder the way Ex had shown me and kept my eye on Coin as he crossed the wide parking lot, reached the chain-link fence, twirled the combination lock, and opened the small gate. Something shimmered as the gate opened. For a moment, I saw inhuman faces in the air.

Coin stepped out to the street. My heart was tripping over, wild as the riders that whirled in the still air. Coin's face, caught in my crosshairs, filled me with a sense of dread and terrible, inhuman power. I heard the sound of gigantic wings again, and I didn't know if it was my imagination or something more. My breath was fast and shallow.

This was it. This was the moment Eric had envisioned. This was why he'd been killed. I took a deep breath, let it out slowly, and laid my finger on the trigger. I centered the crosshairs on Coin's chest. Chogyi Jake's song faded to silence.

Coin's lips were moving. I thought he said the words *Midian* and *Heller*. I waited for the signal, but Midian's arms remained down, Chogyi Jake still standing. Coin paused, as if listening to some reply. The tattooed mouth twisted in derision. I saw Midian's arms rise. I pulled the trigger.

Except I didn't.

Two sharp cracks came from off to my right as Ex and Aubrey fired. I saw the blue-eyed woman at the apartment, Midian firing a round into the back of her head. My finger tensed, but I couldn't pull it back. He's not human, I told myself. He killed the only person who ever tried to take care of you. He's *evil*. I heard myself grunt with effort. The rifle in my hands didn't fire.

In the crosshairs, Randolph Coin looked up. I raised my head, taking in the scene without magnification. Chogyi Jake had stepped back toward the car, the blue robe fluttering in a wind I couldn't feel. Midian was struggling to his feet.

Coin turned his head, looking down the street, then gestured with one hand like he was shooing away a fly. Two gray streaks left him, trails of smoke spiraling back along the paths of the bullets toward Ex and Aubrey. I must have shouted, because he looked toward me. When I put my eye to the scope again, his face was turned toward the little building that I was half hidden behind, his eyes shifting rapidly as he tried to find me. I centered the crosshairs on his forehead, but he lifted his palms. Eyes stared out from them—not tattoos but real, human eyes. I froze. He opened his mouth wider than I would have thought possible and shouted a single syllable.

I saw the wavefront come out from him in an expanding sphere of golden light. The concussion wasn't physical, but it pushed me back all the same. I couldn't breathe. The things pressing against me became visible for a moment, insectile and wild and nightmarish. I pulled the rifle back up, standing with it braced against my shoulder, but Coin had already stepped back through the gate. The fence was closed, and he was walking calmly back across the parking lot to the warehouse and his army. I fired now, three fast shots that did nothing but bruise my shoulder. Coin didn't even look back. I dropped the rifle and ran.

Midian lay on his back on the sidewalk, his chest heaving as he sucked in breath. Chogyi Jake was in the street, his back against the front tires of Ex's car and his eyes closed. I heard my own voice in a stream of words equal parts prayer and obscenity. I found myself kneeling in front of Chogyi Jake, his hand in mine. His skin felt cold, but his eyes opened and he smiled.

'Fine,' he said. 'I'm fine.'

'What happened? What did he *do*?'

'Won,' Chogyi said.

Midian was on his belly, crawling toward the car. His

legs were dead weight, and a slick of something too black to be blood stretched back to where he'd first fallen. I lifted and carried him the few steps to the car, sliding him into the passenger's seat as Chogyi Jake half fell into the driver's side. The sound of another engine roaring to life came from up the street, and I saw the windowless van swerving crazily toward us. It was Ex, his driving rough and erratic, coming in too late to save us. I stood up, waving him away. Get out. Get safe. *Go.*

The van slowed, stopped, turned, and then escaped. Aubrey's minivan was still in sight. It hadn't started up yet. There was no movement inside that I could see.

'Get in . . . with us,' Chogyi Jake said, but the sports car was too small. I would have had to sit on Midian's lap. Chogyi Jake motioned to me, urging me to crawl into the car.

I didn't answer. I just ran.

Aubrey sat in the second row of seats. The driver's-side window was rolled down to let him fire through it toward the gate where Coin had been. The rifle lay between the front seats where he'd dropped it. I shouted his name, but he didn't respond. I pulled open the door and climbed in. I was screaming now, but I didn't know what I was saying.

Aubrey's eyes were glassy and vacant, his hands limp as wilted leaves. He didn't even know I was there. I crawled back, half convinced he was dead. He had a pulse, though. He was breathing.

I dug through his pockets for his keys. It felt like I was fumbling with the ignition for hours. When I finally got the engine started, I pulled the minivan out into the street, my hands shaking so bad I could barely steer. I sped through the first red light without knowing what I was doing. I had to get to the highway. I had to get out of here. I had to get Aubrey to someone who could help.

Something chimed, deep as a church bell but soundless. The writhing press of riders against my skin vanished. Whatever ceremonies and rituals the Invisible College had been doing to bring the other world close were over.

They were done.

14

I sat on a low plastic chair. Aubrey's hand lay limp in mine. The sounds of the emergency room made a kind of white noise around us. Someone was coughing. A nurse was asking someone where a chart had gone. Somewhere not too far away, a child was screaming. It might as well have been silence.

Aubrey was on the bed in a cheap hospital gown, his clothes cut away. The monitor showed his heartbeat at a slow fifty beats per minute, solid and unvarying. He had enough oxygen in his blood. He wasn't dying.

He just wasn't here.

The curtain rattled and slid aside. A man in a white lab coat with a stethoscope around his neck stepped in. He was bald, wide, and he looked almost as tired as I felt.

'You're Jayné?' he asked, pronouncing it *Janey*. I didn't correct him.

'Yes,' I said.

'And you're his fiancée?'

'Yes,' I said, repeating the lie.

'Okay,' the doctor said. 'Could you tell me what happened?'

I went over the story. We'd been going out shooting.

Aubrey had said he felt a little weak, so we'd pulled over. When he stopped talking to me, I'd brought him here. It was simple, easy to remember, and as close to the truth as I was going to get. The doctor asked me a few questions about Aubrey's medical history, whether he was on any medications, if there was anything he was allergic to. I didn't know anything. I started crying while the doctor went through all the same preliminary tests that the nurse had. He explained that they were going to take Aubrey away to do some imaging. Aubrey's heart stayed at fifty beats per minute.

I'd given up hope that they'd find anything.

I let a nurse direct me to the hospital cafeteria, where I sat looking at a cup of coffee. My knee throbbed. My stitches complained where I'd pulled at the wound sometime during my flight from the warehouse. My shoulder hurt too.

'Hey. You've got a call.'

It was the fourth time my phone had rung since I'd pulled into the ambulance-only zone and screamed until a couple of paramedics helped me pull Aubrey out. As far as I knew, the minivan was still parked out there. Illegally. I tried to care.

'Hey,' Eric said. 'You've got a call.'

I pulled the cell phone out and answered, more to keep from hearing his voice again than because I wanted to talk to anyone.

'Hello?'

'Where are you?' Ex said.

'Hospital. Aubrey's in a coma or something. I don't know. He's . . . I don't know.'

'You have to get back to the house. You have to get someplace warded.'

'Okay,' I said. 'They took him off to get a CAT scan or an MRI or something, and as soon as—'

'Jayné!' he shouted. 'You have to come here right now. You're in *danger*.'

'Yeah,' I said. 'All right.'

I dropped the call and made my way back to the emergency room. It turned out someone had moved the minivan to a parking space not far away, left it unlocked, and put the keys in the visor. I didn't know who'd done it, but I figured this wasn't the first time someone had blocked up the entrance. I was vaguely grateful that they hadn't just towed it away.

I pulled out, found my way onto Speer heading northeast, and tuned the radio to a country station before I realized that I had forgotten my coffee at the cafeteria and also that I didn't know how to get home from here. I just tried to keep my mind on driving until I reached Colfax, turned left, and passed the University of Colorado on my right. Then I knew more or less where I was. I did a U-turn at Eighth Street and headed home.

It was a little past noon now, the temperature rising up into the nineties. The air smelled like gasoline and tar. The traffic was thick but not slow, and it seemed to take all my attention just to keep up with it. My body seemed to know better than I did what needed to be done. I let reflex take over, and I was a little surprised under half an hour later to find myself pulling up to the brick house. Eric's house. My house. The windowless van was on the street, the black sports car in the carport. The lawn looked thirsty. I wondered when I was supposed to have watered it.

I walked in the front door and dropped my keys on the side table. Ex came out from the kitchen, a shotgun held at half ready, like he didn't know whether to expect a friend or an assault team. Which was probably reasonable. We stared at each other for a long moment. He seemed tired. His white-blond hair was pulled back into a ponytail tied with a strip of leather. His black shirt was torn at the cuffs. He looked angry, but not with me.

He looked haunted.

It happened on his watch, I thought to myself. He did his best, and this is what came of it. Poor little tomato.

I took his hand without realizing I was going to. He looked surprised for a second, then squeezed my hand gently. He started to say something, stopped, and looked down.

It's all right, I wanted to say. Except that it wasn't.

'How is he?' Ex asked.

'Stable,' I said. 'Just not in there.'

'It's the fucking Voice of the Abyss,' Midian rasped from behind Ex. 'If he hadn't done that bullshit with the dog, he'd have held it together. You know. Maybe.'

Midian sat at the table. His shirt was off, and a bandage wrapped his wasted belly. Blood dark as India ink was soaking through.

'I thought Coin was supposed to be vulnerable,' I said.

'He was,' Midian said with a grimace. 'Fucker was barely able to ignore everything we threw at him and cripple us before he went back inside.'

'Is that supposed to be funny?' I asked.

'What do you want to hear, kid?' Midian said. The gravel and whiskey voice seemed almost compassionate. 'We took our shot. It didn't work out.'

'Where's Chogyi Jake?' I asked, a sudden stab of panic hitting me.

'Meditating,' Ex said. 'He's okay. I think he's okay.'

'So what the fuck happened?'

'We made some assumptions,' Ex said.

'And?'

'And it turned out Coin was a little more paranoid than we thought. He was protected. Personally protected, not just by the wards they had on-site,' Ex said. 'From what we can tell, he was ready for exactly the forms we were using. He suckered us.'

'Meaning someone ratted us out,' Midian said. 'My guess? Eric may have spilled a couple of beans on his way down.'

'And now their initiation rite's done, so they aren't tied up with that anymore. Coin has a couple hundred of his people free to act against us. And he's not locked to any particular location, so we don't know where he is,' Ex said. He sounded tired. 'We knew it was a risk.'

My shock was starting to wear thin, numbness giving way to something less gentle.

'Actually,' I said, 'I'm pretty sure "Oh, and we might all die" wasn't part of the discussion when I was in the room. I thought you guys knew what you were doing.'

'Well,' Midian said, his voice sharp and grating, 'maybe you should have spent a little more time planning and a little less playing at the mall and getting your ashes hauled.'

'Stop it,' Ex snapped, but it was too late by then. Midian was rising to his feet, one bone-thin hand pointing toward me. His lips drew back from the blackened teeth, and his voice buzzed with anger and physical pain.

'Look, kid, I don't care if you want to candy-ass your way through life. You've got the cash. Do what you want. You want to take over Eric's plans and then let everyone else do the work because they're older than you are and they've got cocks? Fine with me. No trouble. But I've got a half a liter of crap leaking out of me right now that should have stayed inside, and I'm not in the mood to hear you bitch that the plan you couldn't be bothered to make for yourself didn't work out.'

'I said *stop it*,' Ex said, stepping between me and Midian's accusing fingers.

'I don't need that shit,' I yelled. 'I just got back from the hospital. Aubrey could have died because of this. He might be dying right now. You don't know.'

'I knew Eric Heller, kid. I worked with him. He was hard-fucking-core,' Midian went on. 'You lost a man. That's normal. Wouldn't even have slowed Eric down, but you're about as hard as fucking marshmallow, aren't you? You want my advice? Get your sad ass out of here. Go hang out at Cabo or whatever you people do. Coin'll track you down. He'll kill you. But at least you won't be in *my fucking way.*'

The sound of Ex chambering a shotgun round silenced us both. He had the barrel leveled at Midian's face. The vampire seemed to notice the gun for the first time, yellow eyes going wide, then narrow.

'I'm going to ask you to sit down,' Ex said. 'I'm not going to ask twice.'

Midian sank back into his chair, sneering but silent. Ex followed his descent with the gun. I leaned against the counter, arms crossed like I was hugging myself. I hated the tears tracking down my cheeks. They felt like traitors. Ex didn't look back. It was only the shift in his shoulders and the gentle tone of voice that showed he was talking to me.

'There wasn't anything you could have done differently.'

'She could have pulled the trigger,' Midian said. 'Or didn't you notice that you and the smiling professor were the only ones who actually fired a round?'

In the silence that followed, I watched Ex's back go stiff, the angle of his head move half a degree as he considered this. I wondered if Midian was right. If I'd fired, maybe it would have overwhelmed Coin's defenses. I closed my eyes, and I could feel the metal curve of the trigger against my protesting finger.

'Resisting the urge toward violence isn't a bad thing,' Chogyi Jake said. I opened my eyes. He'd changed from the blue robe into a simple white T-shirt and blue jeans. His skin had an ashen tone that worried me, but his smile was the same as ever. 'The question remains, what are we going to do now?'

'I think we're still safe if we stay inside the house,' Ex said, not lowering the gun. 'Eric's wards kept them away from here when they were searching before the ceremony.'

'The Invisible College is stronger now. How long do you think the wards will hold?' Chogyi Jake asked, leaning on the counter beside me. I could feel the warmth coming from his skin, and the smell of fresh soap.

'We can prop them up. But no, not long,' Ex admitted. 'We have to go to ground. Stay where the Invisible College can't find us until things blow over. I've been thinking about it. It makes the most sense to split up. Jayné's got the resources to get out of the country, and Eric's sure to have some other places as protected as this one. It's just a question of finding which one.'

'And you?' Chogyi asked.

'I've got some ideas,' Ex said.

'And Aubrey?' I asked. My voice was shaking a little, but I wouldn't let that stop me. 'Aubrey isn't going anywhere the way he is now. Even if we got the hospital to discharge him.'

'I'm working on that,' Ex said. 'I think there are some ways I might be able to break the curse Coin put on him. Midian's right. If he hadn't already been weak, he probably wouldn't have suffered any worse than I did. And since I got hit at the same time, there may be a connection that I can work with—'

'Or maybe the bluebird of happiness will come down and shit on your head,' Midian growled. 'I've been trying to break one of Coin's pulls since your great-grandfather was a dirty thought.'

'I didn't say it'd be easy,' Ex said, 'but I've got some ideas—'

'I know how,' I said. 'I mean, we all know how to do it, don't we?'

Ex looked back at me now. The shotgun tracked down to the floor. Chogyi turned to me, his expression questioning. I shrugged.

'We kill Coin,' I said. 'That'll break all his enchantments, right? Midian's and Aubrey's both. Plus whatever got Eric after him in the first place.'

Midian coughed out a derisive laugh.

'Hey, kid. We went after him today when he was at his weakest, and maybe you didn't notice, but we got our asses handed to us. He's about a hundred times stronger now than he was at six this morning, and he doesn't have anything else to distract him.'

'Okay,' I said. 'So it'll be hard. But we still have decades of research that Eric did. We still have Midian and that Cainite resonance whatever it is. We've got the three of us, and—'

'No,' Ex said. 'We tried, and we failed. We're going to hide out now. Maybe later, when it's not so dangerous, we can think about going back on the offensive, but right now, we can't. It would be suicide.'

'Then you don't have to do it,' I said.

Three pairs of eyes were on me. Ex, shocked. Chogyi Jake, considering. Midian, amused. I felt my chin lift.

'Jayné,' Ex said. 'You don't have to prove anything here. What happened wasn't your fault. It was mine.'

'It's not about fault,' I said, willing myself to believe the words as I spoke them. 'It's just about what we do next, right?'

'Let's sleep on it,' Ex said. 'I'm pretty comfortable that the wards will hold for tonight at least. Let's not make any decisions until we can calmly, rationally look at what happened.'

Chogyi Jake nodded in my peripheral vision. I felt my mouth harden. I was being a brat. Midian's words had hit me deeper than I wanted to admit, as did the guilt at Aubrey's half-death and my own failure at the warehouse. I was trying to show them all that I was just as hard-core as Uncle Eric even though they knew I wasn't. And I knew too.

And underneath that, I knew I had to try.

'Okay, we'll wait until tomorrow,' I said. 'But after that, I'm killing him.'

I called the hospital from my bedroom. The intake nurse had put my name and cell number in Aubrey's chart along with the lie that I was family and his contact person. The person on the other end couldn't tell me much except that Aubrey had been admitted and they were keeping him under observation. When they offered to have the doctor call me back when he had a minute, I said yes and let the call drop.

All around me, Eric's things loomed like ghosts. His shirts, his furniture, his magazines. I turned on my laptop, checked my e-mail, Googled unsuccessfully for anything that talked about gunshots being fired in the Commerce City suburb of Denver, and tried to think of something else I should look for, some piece of data that would turn the whole world right again. I wound up staring at the screen with a feeling that there wasn't enough air in the room.

I wanted to cry, but I was also tired of crying. I wanted to scream and throw things and make the world be fair, but I didn't know what I meant by the world anymore. The fact was I'd let myself look forward to this day, to after-Coin. I'd let myself imagine a future where maybe I'd have friends, even a lover, and money and safety and options. Instead of that, I was locked down, hiding under Eric's undetectable protections while the people who'd killed him walked free.

The disappointment and despair were as familiar as coming home.

I wasn't sure until the second time that I'd actually heard the knock at the door. I said to come in. Ex walked in slowly, his hands in his pockets, his eyes shifting onto anything besides me sitting cross-legged on the bed. He leaned against the wall beside the dresser. From where I was, his face was both toward me and echoed in profile in the mirror. He looked like a magazine cover.

'How serious are you about going after Coin?' he asked.

I didn't know what to say, so I didn't say anything. After a few seconds, he seemed to find an answer in the silence. He drew a long breath and let it out slowly.

'I think that you shouldn't,' he said.

'I kind of have to,' I said.

'Aubrey.'

'That's part of it, yeah. I got him into this. If it wasn't for me, he wouldn't have been so vulnerable. He wouldn't be where he is now.'

'And you're in love with him.'

I looked down at my laptop screen.

'Things with him really aren't as straightforward as all that,' I said, trying to lighten the tone. 'Aubrey and me . . . I don't know. I have a problem dating someone with a wife. Maybe it'll work out. Maybe it won't. But I won't know as long as he's in a coma, right?'

'You do what you have to do to protect the people you care about,' Ex said.

I smiled and nodded because I thought he was talking about me and Aubrey. I thought the gray, sorrowful tone in his voice was him giving up on talking me out of trying again. I didn't understand that he was actually apologizing until morning came and I found out Ex had gone and taken the guns and all of Eric's books with him.

15

The rage felt good. I broke every plate in the kitchen, china shattering against the tile floor. I screamed every obscene word and phrase I knew and then started inventing. I tipped the chairs over and threw a full coffee cup against the living room wall, leaving a dark stain on the paint and a gouge in the plaster. My muscles felt warm and loose and I was about three inches taller than normal, the righteous anger puffing my body larger and stronger and making me sure of myself. I nursed it because I knew that when it was gone, there wouldn't be anything left.

Midian and Chogyi Jake didn't try to stop me or restrain me or talk sense. Midian just sat on the couch, his wrists still bound, his belly still bandaged. Chogyi Jake followed me in silence, standing witness to my violence with the same impartiality he'd had during my meltdown at the shopping mall. I shouted at him a few times too, but he didn't react at all, and it started to take the momentum out of my tantrum.

When I lost that too, I sat on the stone hearth in front of the empty fireplace—my elbows on my knees, my head in my hands—and cried. The house was trashed. It was going to take hours just to clean it up. Part of me wanted to go get the broom and dustpan and start putting it all back together, if only to prove that I had a little control over something. Most of me just wanted to sit there and give up.

'He meant well,' Chogyi Jake said. His voice was soft.

'He's a fucking asshole,' I managed between sobs.

'He's a fucking asshole who meant well.'

I glanced up. Coming from anyone else, the amusement would have been an insult. Coming from Chogyi Jake, it seemed like compassion. Midian coughed, then winced. His bound hands went to his side. Shirtless, he looked like something from Jim Henson's worst nightmare, his flesh ropy and dark and implausible. The bleeding had slowed, but whatever Coin had done to him was a long way from being healed. The same could be said of all of us.

'I thought we couldn't leave the house,' I said. 'I thought it wasn't safe.'

'It isn't,' Chogyi Jake said. 'Ex is risking himself to keep you from harm.'

'Or to keep me under his fucking control.'

'Yeah, well,' Midian croaked. He always sounded like something in his throat was about to come loose. 'Who'd have guessed a Jesuit priest would be paternalistic.'

'Ex-priest,' I said.

'Whatever.'

'Rest,' Chogyi Jake said. 'This will all be much better if we can regain some sense of our center.' His eyes were bloodshot. I should have been taking care of him, not the other way around.

'Are you okay?' I asked.

'I'm tired,' he said. From him, it was like an admission that he was near collapse. I realized that I didn't know how deeply our failure with Coin had hurt him. I felt bad that I hadn't thought to ask.

The house had become a submarine, dead on the ocean floor. Everything looked the same, apart from the damage I'd done. But the air was different. The light that pressed in at the windows trapped us. Whatever magic Eric had put on the building to keep us safe, I could feel it weakening, and I didn't know how much of that was true and how much was just my own growing fear and hopelessness.

I sat in the kitchen, my stomach too knotted for food or coffee. Chogyi Jake went to each of the windows and doors, chanting and pouring out lines of rice and salt. Propping up the wards. Buying us time.

I pictured Aubrey sitting across from me. His honey-colored hair. His bright eyes. His fingers closed around mine. In my imagination, all the anger and weirdness from our failed date was gone. I wanted badly for it to be true. Tears ran down my cheeks. I let them.

'I blew it,' I said to my imaginary Aubrey. 'I don't know how I managed to fuck everything up again, just like always.'

My hands were rubbing my thighs, the palms pressing into the denim hard enough for the friction to warm them. To hurt a little.

'I think I have to run away now,' I said. 'I've lost you and Ex. And Midian, kind of. I mean since he turns out to be one of the bad guys, that kind of takes him off my assets column. So . . .'

My hand was tapping on my thigh, just a light movement, like a kid tugging at her mother's dress. I watched my own fingers, my mind mostly empty, but aware of something happening in the background. Some thought that was struggling to bubble up from my subconscious.

'I'm down to nothing,' I said. 'Taking on Coin now is a hundred times dumber than when we did it before. I don't have the books. I don't have the rifles. I don't have the magic bullets. I've lost . . .'

I put my hand into the pocket of my jeans, looking for something without knowing quite what it was. It came back out with six hundred-dollar bills. Some of the change from my shopping spree. I looked down at the money. Benjamin Franklin looked back up at me.

'I've lost everything,' I said, but the conviction was gone from my voice. I shuffled the bills one after another. The thought wasn't quite formed yet, but I was starting to sense a vague shape. Midian coughed.

I stood up with the weird feeling that I was floating. My backpack was sitting by the front door. I unfastened the straps. Aubrey's keys rested on top of the undifferentiated mess of my life.

'Chogyi!' I shouted.

I held the keys as he came down the hall. Midian was silent. I could feel him listening to us.

'I need to go out,' I said. 'How dangerous is that going to be?'

'Very,' he said.

'What about that thing where I didn't set off the alarms in Midian's apartment? Do you think that'll make it harder for Coin to find me too?'

Chogyi paused, considering. 'If it's difficult for one magic to see you, it may be a general effect. And you didn't fire the rifle, so Coin's wards haven't interacted with you directly.'

'You're not sure, though.'

'No.'

I took a deep breath.

'I'm going to risk it,' I said. 'If I'm not back by nightfall, plan without me.'

I almost expected him to stop me. I don't know why. I trotted out to the minivan and headed north quickly, before I lost my nerve. Half an hour and a certain amount of dithering later, I parked on Brighton Boulevard where it bellied up next to the railroad tracks. I sat in the minivan, looking to the east, past the boxcars and toward the warehouses. I got out with a sense of unreality, locked the door behind me, and set out across the tracks. A homeless guy leaned against a huge black trash bag half a block down. I paused, remembering what Ex and Chogyi Jake had taught me. I drew up my qi, placing it just behind my eyes. The homeless guy was still just a homeless guy.

Ten minutes later, I was crouching where I'd been before, the flaking wall against my back, my heart tripping over itself. My throat was dry. I leaned over to peer at the warehouse. The buses were gone. Only half a dozen cars remained. I looked for people, but didn't see anyone. I made myself stay still as I scanned the ground. It had only been one day, and in a part of the city that stayed pretty much dead as a cod all weekend. The chances were that it would still be where I'd dropped it.

I saw it. The rifle lay flat, its barrel still pointing roughly toward the warehouse. I inched forward, one eye on the warehouse, one on the rifle. The sun had left it almost too hot to touch, but I got my hand around it and trotted back to the cover. I tried to remember how many times I'd fired while Coin walked back from the carnage. Three, I thought.

One round still waited in the chamber, one in the magazine. Carefully, I lifted the cartridges out, feeling the carved designs squirm against my fingertips. I dropped the nasty little things into my backpack, tucked the rifle under my arm, and jogged back to the minivan.

Despite Ex's best efforts, I had two bullets made for killing riders. It was a thin victory, but I took pride in it. I drove back to the house with a growing sense of possibility.

When I got there, I swept up the ruined dishes. I cleaned the coffee stain off with a rag and warm water while Midian sat on the couch, watching me with silent, dead eyes. I stood back, considering the wall. After a little scrubbing, the biggest problem was that the cleaned bit now looked brighter than the rest of the wall. I looked around, suddenly aware of all the little ways that the house had fallen into disrepair during the time I'd been in it.

'Well,' I said. 'Okay.'

'Okay?' Midian asked.

I looked at him, then went to the kitchen and came back with a carving knife in hand. The yellow eyes tracked me uncertainly.

'If I let you go, are we going to be cool?' I asked.

'You're serious?' he asked. 'I'm a fucking vampire, you know.'

'Eric was willing to work with you,' I said. 'And besides, I kind of like you. So are we going to be cool or not?'

'As long as we want the same thing. After that, we'll have to see how it plays out,' he said. And then, 'Hey, kid. At least I'm not bullshitting you, right?'

I answered by cutting the rope around his wrists. He rubbed the desiccated, time-dark flesh and looked up at me.

'For someone who's totally fucked, you're looking pretty chipper,' he said.

'Yeah, well,' I said. 'I'm going to clean the place. You want to whip us up some dinner?'

The vampire shrugged, then stood up.

'I'm on it,' he said.

I dug a vacuum cleaner out of a closet and set to getting all the coffee cup fragments out of the carpet. I threw out the tray Midian had been using for his dead cigarettes, gathered up all the dirty glasses and dishes that had found their way to the flat surfaces of the house, and brought them home to the dishwasher. The bright spot on the wall kept bothering me. There was only one thing, I decided, to be done about it. I got my laptop out from the bedroom, hooked it up to Eric's modest stereo speakers, and cranked up some music. China Forbes sang an old Carmen Miranda tune, and I started washing down all the walls in the living room while I danced to it. About twenty minutes and two walls later, Chogyi Jake came out from the back, surprised to see something happening that wasn't about ruining the flatware.

'I'm not cleaning the main bathroom. I've been using my own,' I said over the section of 'Dosvedanya Mio Bambino' that they lifted from 'The Happy Wanderer.' 'All that mess in there is you guys.'

Chogyi Jake tilted his head in obeisance, just on the friction point between mocking and sincere. I went back to the walls and saw him a few minutes later, heading from the kitchen to the back bathroom with a bucket and a sponge. If Midian's return to freedom was an issue, he didn't bring it up.

The music went from the Cuban-dance-band-meets-chamber-orchestra of Pink Martini to a mix CD I burned from my first-semester dorm mate's music. The old familiar Goth-punk songs didn't depress me the way they usually did. A scent equal parts butter, beef, and wine wafted out of the kitchen. When I finished with the walls, I went back and stripped the sheets off all the beds and gathered up my own old laundry. On my way through the kitchen toward the laundry room, I stopped to admire Midian's upcoming feast.

'It's all tapas,' Midian said. 'For one thing, we're down to not enough groceries for anything big. And for another, you need new plates.'

'Check. New plates,' I said with a nod. 'I'm on it.'

He shook his head in apparent disgust.

'I think mood swings run in your family, kid,' Midian said, but he smiled when he said it.

We ate dinner early, the sun still high in the late summer sky. I'd found a bottle of red wine that went pretty well with Midian's spread. Cheese and tomatoes, strips of fried beef, toasted French bread with a spread of garlic and olives. The three of us sat around the kitchen table. Outside, the day was blisteringly hot.

'So,' Midian said, looking at me through the red swirl of wine in his glass, 'you want to tell me what happened to change totally fucked girl into Little Mary Sunshine? Because right now, I'm thinking bipolar.'

'Working meditation is always useful,' Chogyi Jake said around a mouthful of garlic and olive.

'I think we call that petty control over your immediate physical environment,' I said.

'That's as good a name as any,' Chogyi Jake said. 'The thought is the same. It's a way to bring yourself together. Cope with anxiety and fear.'

'It's not just about making the place smell less like a cheap bar? Which reminds me. No more smoking in the house.'

'Hey!' Midian said, putting down his glass.

'You want to go outside and see if the magic anticultist wards cover the backyard, that's up to you,' I said. 'But not in the house.'

Midian frowned, considered for a moment, then nodded.

'I'm not hog-tied and sleeping with a shotgun pointing at my skull,' he said. 'I can deal with the trade-off. But back to the issue at hand.'

'Well, I was feeling pretty screwed over,' I said. 'And now I'm not.'

'Yeah,' Midian said. 'That's the part that's confusing me. Because from here it's still looking pretty bleak.'

I wiped my mouth with a paper napkin and leaned back in my chair. My backpack was on the counter by the phone book, and I reached for it while I spoke.

'When that fucking asshole Ex took off,' I said in my best calm, reasonable voice, 'I felt like he'd taken my only shot at dealing with Coin. I didn't have anything anymore. You know? But today I realized that's not true. I've got the two of you.'

'Yeah,' Midian said. 'And a powerful-as-fuck wizard trying to kill you. Is this a very special *Blossom*? Did I miss the part where we all learned and hugged and grew?'

'I can still tie you back up,' I said. Midian raised his hands in mock surrender.

'You were saying,' Chogyi Jake said.

'Right. Well, the two of you,' I said. 'And I have these.'

I placed the rifle cartridges on the table with a soft tap. Midian moved back an inch or two, but Chogyi Jake scooped one up, rolling it in his fingers as he examined the graven symbols. When he looked over at me, his brows were raised, inviting me to go on.

'And,' I said, 'I have a *lot* of money . . .'

16

I left the house in the best outfit to survive the shopping fiasco: a deep blue blouse with black slacks and a jacket. With my hair up and a little tasteful eyeliner and lipstick, I thought I looked the consummate professional. Right up until I reached my destination.

I drove carefully, one eye on the road, one on the rearview. Every time I stepped out of the house I felt like a field mouse watching for hawks. Every driver on the road might be one of Coin's people. Every kid on the street could be watching for me. I hated it, but I didn't let it stop me. I didn't feel even vaguely safe until I got to my lawyer's office.

It was as intimidating as anyplace I'd ever been. Stained walnut walls had the sense of solid wood. The receptionist dressed like she was running for president. The waiting area was discreetly away from the front door so that I wouldn't have to suffer the indignity of breathing the same air as the UPS guy. The couch was upholstered in raw silk and the coffee was served in a French press with almond cookies. The time-killing magazines on the table were no older than two weeks, and I counted six different languages and three alphabets. None of them had a 'Best and Worst

Dressed' feature on the front. I wondered whether the *Economist* ever had a fashion issue.

I felt like an impostor.

I'd been waiting twenty minutes, each one more nerve-racking than the one before, when my lawyer came in. She wore a gray suit with a shell-pink blouse and a smile that could have been genuine.

'Jayné!' she said, pronouncing it *Jane*. 'I'm sorry to keep you waiting. I was in a meeting.'

'It's my fault,' I said, standing up. 'I should have gotten an appointment. It was just—'

'Nonsense. You're always welcome. Come back to my office and tell me what I can do for you.'

Her office straddled the line between reassuring softness and a level of intimidation that bordered on class warfare. Her desk was carved wood, her carpeting was soft and lush in a way that made me think of tapestries, the north wall was an apparently seamless sheet of glass that looked out over Denver only because there wasn't anyplace grander nearby. There was no computer on her desk. She was apparently too important for things like that. The receptionist, or someone so like her I couldn't tell the difference, put my coffee and cookies on the corner of the desk for me and vanished.

'I've been meaning to call you,' the lawyer said, sitting at her desk. 'There are a few things I'll need your signature for. Nothing pressing, you understand. We just want to have everything in place before the quarterly statements are due.'

'Anything I can do to help,' I said.

If my fairy godmother had been a shark, she'd have smiled like the lawyer did then.

'Is everything going well, then?'

'Actually,' I said, 'there's something I wanted to talk to you about.'

She leaned forward, her expression calm and interested. I had the impression that if I'd read off the phone book, she could have quoted it back to me. My mouth felt dry.

'What we talk about,' I said. 'What I say to you? It's protected, right? Confidentiality and all that?'

'Yes,' she said. 'So long as you weren't actually planning to commit a crime. In the good old days, that was absolutely confidential as well, but rights erode, dear. It's their nature.'

'Okay.' I took a deep breath. 'I think I know who killed my uncle. It was a guy named Randolph Coin. And I need to find out everything I can about him. The thing is . . . the thing is he runs some kind of cult called the Invisible College. I don't want to take anything to the police, and I don't want anyone to know that I'm looking into his stuff. Does that make sense?'

'Coin is spelled like nickels and dimes?' the lawyer asked.

'Yes. Just like it sounds.'

'Do we know anything else about him?'

'He was at a warehouse in Commerce City this weekend,' I said. 'He has a lot of tattoos on his face, but . . .'

But he can hide them using magical spells, and he has a

bunch of wizard-ninjas who do his bidding, and he's not really human at all, because this evil spirit has actually taken over his body. I wondered if the lawyer could have me declared insane and take away all the money.

'. . . but he's really good at covering them up,' I finished lamely.

The lawyer made a noncommittal sound in the back of her throat before she spoke.

'All right. I'll see what we can do. In the meantime, how's everything else working out?'

'I was thinking that we could find out who rented the warehouse,' I said. 'Even if it's not him, it's got to be someone connected to him. And I don't know if it's legal to track down what kind of plane tickets he's bought, or if he's even . . .'

She was looking at me with the kind of amused indulgence I was used to seeing on grandmothers watching puppies gambol on the lawn. I took a sip of my coffee. It was really good.

She tapped the top of her desk gently with her fingertips and mispronounced my name. I corrected her, and she didn't miss a beat.

'Jayné,' she said correctly. 'I don't know how much you remember about Ronald Reagan's tenure in the presidency?'

'I was four,' I said. 'When he left office, I was four.'

Her brows rose about a millimeter.

'You make me feel old, dear. The phrase you need to know is *plausible deniability*. You've told me what you need. I'll find it for you. The less you concern yourself with precisely how the information was gathered, the simpler it will be.'

'Um,' I said.

'I know some very talented people,' she said. 'And really, I'm sure you're much too busy to micromanage every step of something as menial as this?'

I suppressed a grin.

'Of course,' I said. 'I'm sorry. I just got enthusiastic.'

'Enthusiasm is a wonderful thing,' she said as if she was agreeing. 'As soon as I have anything that might be useful, I'll have a report drawn up. I assume sooner is better than later.'

'Yes, please.'

'Excellent. And, since I have you here, could I put upon you to sign a few little things for us? Once we have these out of the way, I can move ahead on the property transfers with much less bother for you.'

If she'd pulled out a scroll of human skin covered with Latin and asked me to sign in blood, I probably would have done it. Everything was paper and ink, though, and there was only a little Latin.

I got back to the house feeling a bit high. With the front door closed behind me, I took a silent bow and Chogyi Jake and Midian applauded. Afterward, I sat on the couch and gave them the blow-by-blow of the meeting. Chogyi Jake looked pleased, but the circles under his eyes were getting darker. He didn't make a point of it, but I knew he was pouring himself into keeping the wards around the house strong. I wondered how many times he had saved us already without my even knowing about it.

While the pair of them cooked, I went to the back bedroom and turned on the laptop. I had a list of things I wanted to look up—what exactly a *vârkolak* was being near the top of the list. I waited while a metric assload of spam downloaded to my inbox. Nothing for me. Nothing personal. I checked my brother's blog, but he hadn't posted anything in months. I thought about checking back with my former friends again, but the more I turned the idea over, the more pathetic it seemed. The world had moved on. Several times. There wasn't any point.

A *vârkolak* turned out to be something about halfway between a vampire and a werewolf, or a vampire without any sign of its bestial nature, or a werewolf that doesn't change shapes. There was a whole lot of information, and no way to know whether any of it was more reliable than going out to Midian and asking him. And that was the same problem I had with the bigger issue of Coin too.

I needed an angle. Coin had all the power right now. That had to change. I had gone through five or six promising-looking boards without finding anything solid about the Invisible College in general or Randolph Coin in particular when my old chat program popped a window open. That hadn't happened in weeks, and the screen name wasn't one that I recognized. Once I parsed it, though, it made sense.

Extojayne: Ping

I felt the blood go out of my face, and my heart ramped up. The first thing I felt was shock at Ex's sudden virtual arrival. The second thing I felt was pissed off. I leaned forward, fingers hovering over the keys. I tried to decide what I wanted to say. *If* I wanted to.

Extojayne: Are you there?
Jayneheller: I'm here. How did you find this account?
Extojayne: It's your name. It wasn't hard. Are you OK?

I could hear Ex's voice, could see the concern in his face as he asked. It only made me angrier. No, I wanted to say, I'm getting a little sick of being betrayed by the people who I thought were my friends. No, you fucking thief. I cracked my knuckles and summoned up my best sarcasm before answering.

Jayneheller: I'm great. Thanks.
Extojayne: Good. Is Midian with you?
Jayneheller: He's not in the room, if that's what you mean. He's off cooking. As always. Mind telling me where you are?
Extojayne: I'm all right. I'm worried about you.
Jayneheller: You really show it. But it wasn't the question I asked.
Extojayne: I can't stay on long. I'm worried. The assassination attempt. I think the College's blowback may have gone past Midian into the other one.
Jayneheller: The other one? You mean Chogyi Jake?

Extojayne: Chogyi Jake. Has he been acting normal? Is he there too?

Jayneheller: Yeah, we're all here. What do you mean blowback? Where are you?

Extojayne: Don't worry about me. Nothing's changed. Give me a status report. I need to know where things stand.

I'd gotten as far as typing Who are you to demand anything of me when my fingers stopped. I felt the jaw-clenching anger shift in me like a car starting to fishtail on ice. I stared at the screen.

Extojayne: Jayne? Are you there?

My hand reached out and tapped the backspace key, cutting back my message word by word.

Who are you

I erased the whole thing and started over, my chest tight with fear.

Jayneheller: Well, we've gotten the go-ahead from the guy with the rabbits. And your buddy from Texas should be here tomorrow about noon.

I hit send and waited. The icon showed that whoever was on the other end of the chat was typing. If it was Ex, he'd ask me what I was talking about.

Come on, I thought, *ask me what I'm talking about.*

Extojayne: Good. What else?

I stared at the screen for what seemed like hours but was only a few seconds. My hands shook so hard I could barely type.

Jayneheller: Someone's calling. Gotta go.

I turned off the computer and sat on the bed for a while with my hands trembling. It was them. I'd been talking to one of them. They knew that Ex had been working with me and that he wasn't here, or else they wouldn't have tried to pass themselves off under his name. I didn't know how they'd figured that out.

They didn't know he'd taken everything in an attempt to stop me from moving against Coin again; otherwise they wouldn't have asked how things were going. I didn't know why they *hadn't* figured that out.

And they knew Chogyi Jake's name and that he and Midian and I were all together because I'd just told them.

I wondered if it was possible to track an instant message back to where it had physically originated. Maybe it was all relayed through a server over at AOL, but I had the sense it was peer-to-peer, in which case they'd have the IP address of the network here. They wouldn't be able to translate that into a street address without hacking the living snot out of Eric's service provider. They were evil wizards. Getting into a router configuration might not be beyond them, but then again, Eric had done a pretty thorough job of keeping the house off their radar. Chances were good that the service record would keep the address obscured. I wished that

Eric had left me some record of what exactly my defenses were.

I'd known that they were out there. I'd known they were looking for us. Actually catching sight of one of the hunters shook me more than I'd expected it to. I started to wonder how big a risk I'd been taking when I went to see the lawyer. How were Coin and his people going to come after us now? Would he go after my family? I tried to imagine my mother at the mercy of tattooed wizards possessed by evil parasites. It would pretty much confirm everything my parents thought about me, and that was the lowest reason on the list for keeping it from happening.

In the kitchen, Midian and Chogyi Jake were talking about different mythological loci and the relationship between choice and will. A couple hours ago, I'd have cared. Instead, I sat down at the table with my head in my hands until they both went silent.

'You okay, kid?' the vampire asked.

'I don't think so,' I said.

17

I slept badly, every passing car or creaking wall startling me awake. At three in the morning, I came within two digits of calling home and telling my parents to take my brothers and get out of the house. The only thing that stopped me was knowing that they wouldn't do it. I lay on the bed, drifting in and out of unpleasant dreams, and watched the curtains turn light again with the approaching dawn. At no point in the night did I even move toward turning on my laptop.

Midian and Chogyi Jake had been pretty quiet after I told them about the fake Ex, but neither had given me any grief for being taken in, even briefly. We agreed that the three of us would use the word *elephant* someplace in the first sentence or two if we were ever communicating across the net, and Midian made a joke about policy being the surest evidence that something had already been fucked up.

The doorbell rang at eleven in the morning, and the sound knotted my guts. Midian, watching television with the captioning on and the sound off, rose from the couch. Chogyi Jake came in from the kitchen. The doorbell rang again.

'You want me to get my Luger?' Midian asked.

'You two get back out of sight,' I said. Chogyi handed Midian a knife, nodded to me, and faded back into the kitchen. Midian stepped into the hallway where he couldn't be seen from the door. I put my hand on the knob, took a breath, let it out, and pulled the door open.

The courier had already given up, the little red station wagon pulling away from the curb. A gray cardboard box squatted on the red bricks. I picked it up, still half expecting it to be a trap. The report inside was eighty pages long, professionally bound, with nothing on it to indicate that it was meant for me or produced by my lawyer. Everything about it was plausibly deniable. I went to the dining room table and sat down. After a couple minutes, I told Midian I'd read him the good parts if he'd stop hovering over my shoulder.

Randolph Eustace Coin was born in Vienna in 1954, son of a grocer. His family moved to America in 1962, taking up residence in an ethnically homogeneous enclave in New York City. He attended public school without any particular sign of excellence, though he was supposed to have been a pretty good clarinet player.

I looked up.

'How does Coin put a curse on you in seventeen eighty whatever it was if he's not born until the nineteen fifties?' I asked.

'He was in a different body at the time,' Midian replied with a shrug. 'It's not like your lawyer can track which flesh has who inside it.'

'Ah,' I said. 'Right.'

In late summer of 1972, Coin disappeared.

The Randolph Coin who emerged six years later was a different man. While seen socially with members of something called the Zen Theosophy, he'd never espoused any particular beliefs in public apart from a general support for public education and a concern about overpopulation. A footnote pointed out that while they come from similar teachings, the Zen Theosophists weren't directly associated with the Theosophical Society and accepted the teachings of Alice Bailey, which seemed to mean something to Midian, because he nodded when I said it.

Over the next two decades, Coin had appeared in the company of religious leaders, poets, cranks, and captains of industry and finance. A list of names was included, and I recognized about half. It was never clear how he made his money, though he was on the board of two political consultancies, an international aid foundation, and a scientific equipment supply company. As far as the world was concerned, Coin was one of those entrepreneurs whose lofty status made it hard to say what they really did. While he might have had some kooky friends, he himself was a man of no particular beliefs.

The report skipped a page.

The Invisible College was a fraternal society with its roots in the sixteenth century, when it was most closely associated with John Dee and the Rosicrucians. There had been some kind of violent schism within the College associated with World War II, but details were few and far between.

The membership roll wasn't ever made public, but rumor put the group's size at between one hundred and six hundred people at any given time. It wasn't clear from the references to it whether it was a religious order, a scientific lobbying group, or an internationalist think tank. Other members had apparently included Aleister Crowley, Harry S. Truman, and Alan Turing.

'Turing?' Midian asked. 'Go back. When was Coin born?'

'Nineteen fifty-four,' I said.

'Yeah, but what day?'

I flipped back through the pages.

'June seventh,' I said.

Midian chuckled. It was a low, wet sound.

'What?' I asked.

'Turing offed himself the same day,' Midian said. 'Probably just a coincidence. Keep going.'

'There isn't much more in this section,' I said.

'What's next?' Chogyi Jake asked.

I turned the page. The remainder of the report might as well have been printed on gold plate. It was perfect. Copies of Coin's movements for the last week, including his visits to the warehouse where we'd tried to kill him, his home address (which to judge from the footnotes was a very big secret), descriptions of his cars, photographs of his body-guard. He was the big guy I'd seen with Coin at the warehouse that first time with Ex. The report ended with an estimated itinerary of his movements for the next week and a half and a footnote explaining that all predictions in the report needed to be considered approximate. The apologetic tone of the note made me wonder if they were used to an expectation of clairvoyance.

An appendix had copies of original documents, including notes from a doctor's visit last year. Coin had gastric reflux. Somehow that detail, with its sense of intimacy and vulnerability, reassured me the most. I felt like I was getting somewhere.

'Okay,' I said. 'So we know where he is. We have an idea where he's going to be. That's a start, right?'

'Would have been nice to have someone who knew a little more about riders digging into these assholes, but on the whole . . .' Midian said. 'So, kid. What's your next move?'

Here were the problems.

First, Coin knew we were out here, and that we wanted to kill him. The enemy was already on high alert. That was a bummer.

Second, the wards around the house were starting to fail. Chogyi Jake was doing his best, but even without his saying so, I could feel the air pressing in against the walls. Twice I'd half heard the sound of Coin's monstrous wings. And Chogyi was only wearing thinner. The longer we waited, the less hope we had.

Third, Coin had a lot of people—many of them with freaky supernatural powers—around to protect him. We'd managed to get around that last time by making our attack when everyone was tied up with the big nasty ritual. That part had worked, but the rest of the plan failed spectacularly.

Which brought me to the last issue: Coin had a bunch of freaky supernatural powers himself, and could probably only be killed with the two magic bullets that he'd already shrugged off once.

That last one looked like the worst, so I put off thinking about it and started at the beginning, looking for ways to misdirect the Invisible College. My first thoughts didn't go over all that well.

'Run away?' Midian said. 'You're serious?'

'We can't do anything if he's got the whole city locked down,' I said.

'You're remembering that the last time, it took maybe twenty minutes between when you broke the wards and the assassination squad showed up,' Midian said.

'I've been out twice,' I said. 'The gun and the lawyer, remember? So far, nothing.'

'Your protections don't apply to us,' Chogyi Jake said.

'Ex went out.'

'Ex has resources that may help him,' Chogyi Jake said. 'And . . . even then, we can't assume he's survived.'

'Okay,' I said. 'So we don't run.'

'*We* don't run,' Chogyi Jake said. 'You still can.'

'So let's look at the second thing,' I said. 'Coin's minions.'

'It would be a good idea to get rid of them,' Midian agreed. 'Either get Coin away from them or else spread 'em out thin enough that getting to the guy isn't like wading across the beach at Normandy.'

'So how do we do that?' I asked.

Chogyi Jake's sudden laughter was rueful and warm.

'We run,' he said. 'When you're ready with whatever else there is to do, Midian and I draw off the Invisible College by stepping out of the house and heading directly away from wherever the real drama is taking place.'

'Yeah, that's a good plan,' Midian said, making it clear with his expression that he both agreed and thought we were doomed if that was our best strategy.

'But,' I started, then let it trail away.

But I need you. But you'll get hurt. But I can't face him alone. There wasn't a way to finish that sentence that didn't seem weak. Yes, taking out Coin was up to me. No, it wasn't anyone else's job to make it easy. I'd tried the strategy where I relied on other people, and it had brought me here.

This was my job. I'd do it.

'Okay,' I said. 'So that's the start of a plan, right? You guys will draw off the Invisible College so I can get to Coin.'

'Great,' Midian said. 'And then you can punch yourself in the face a few times to confuse him. Maybe break an arm. I mean, don't get me wrong, kid. I'll do what I have to do, but now you're down to a shitload of money, whatever cantrips we can teach you, and a couple of bullets. I'm not sure what that's going to get you. Odds-on bet is you still get your ass kicked.'

'Let me think about it,' I said.

I thought for two days and by Thursday came up with

nothing. Every hour, the house pressed on me. We were hiding under our rock, and if I was in a little less trouble than Midian and Chogyi Jake, it was only a little. I didn't turn my laptop back on, not even to check e-mail or play solitaire.

I made one furtive trip to the grocery store, scuttling through the soup aisle with my qi pulled up to my eyes, looking for tattoos and danger so intently I had a hard time shopping. When I was home, I meditated with Chogyi Jake. I practiced some simple cantrips with Midian. Here was how to project your qi to intimidate people who didn't have any protection and why not to try it on people who did. Here was how to wrap yourself in qi as a protection. It felt more like a motivational speaker's affirmations than magic, but Chogyi and Midian assured me that there would be more advanced work that grew out of it. And even that wasn't enough to keep the close, hot summer air from bearing down on me.

At night, I lay in the darkness wondering where Ex was, whether he'd found someplace safe or gotten killed. I thought about Aubrey and my family and my former friends back at ASU.

I had to take Coin out. Ex couldn't help me. Eric couldn't help me. Midian and Chogyi Jake could only draw off as many of the Invisible College's wizards as would fall for their distraction. I could sneak into his mansion, except that I was pretty sure I couldn't. I could stand on the street and call him out, except he'd beat me. I could lure him into an ambush, except that as long as he had a few minions left to send in his place, he wouldn't come for the free cheese in any trap I could think of. The sheets knotted themselves around me as I shifted. The pillows grew hot and uncomfortable, each new configuration bringing only a few minutes' relief.

I crawled out of bed Friday morning to a blasting dawn. Light pressed in at the blinds like water spilling into a submarine. I sat on the edge of the mattress feeling sticky with old sweat, bored, frightened, and bored with being frightened. My stitches itched, but the wound in my side was mostly closed up, deep pink flesh fusing back into some semblance of normalcy. My knee was a mottled green and yellow, my body struggling to clean out the old blood, but it didn't hurt to move it anymore. I pulled on a bathrobe, put my hair back in a bun held in place by a couple pencils, and went out to the main room. Midian stood before the back window, looking out at the slowly browning grass of the yard.

'I can't do it,' I said.

'Yeah, I know,' he said, not looking back. 'If the two of us weren't fucked six ways to Sunday, there'd be a chance. Taking someone out like this is at least a three-man job. Probably more.'

'Maybe we could find some way to hide you guys? A ritual cleansing or something?'

'Then you've got no way to draw off the minions, and we're still screwed.'

'Yeah,' I said. 'Where's Chow Yun Fat when you need him?'

'Who?'

'Chow Yun Fat. You know. Hong Kong action film star. He was in *The Replacement Killers* and *The Corruptor.* And *Hard-Boiled.* That's the one where he had the gunfight while holding a baby. It was thoroughly over the top, but it was great.'

'I thought you led a sheltered life. How'd you get into gun opera?'

'College,' I said. 'I had a boyfriend. Cary. He was into it, so I was too.'

'Huh. Fair enough. So how does the baby figure in?'

'There's this cop and he's . . .'

Something in the back of my head fell in place with a click I could almost feel.

'And?' Midian said.

'Hang on a minute.'

I went back to my room for the cell phone, my head suddenly feeling like champagne. I felt too nervous to go at it straight so I started by calling the hospital to check up on Aubrey. There was no change, and I was both relieved that he was all right and worried that he was still incapacitated. Then I called my lawyer and left a message with her receptionist, asking for any updated information about Coin's schedule in the next week or two. It was only after that that I went back through the list of incoming calls and found the number that Midian had reminded me of.

The voice-mail message was short, and Candace Dorn's voice was pleasant. I waited for the beep.

'Candace. Hey, this is Jayné Heller? Look, I'm in a little

trouble. I may be in pretty big trouble. I need to ask Aaron for a favor. Could you have him give me a call? Thanks.'

I dropped the connection with a sense of excitement that bordered on dread. I had money, and a few cantrips, and two magical bullets.

And a cop. I had at least one cop. Maybe more, if he had friends he trusted.

And I wasn't finished yet.

I knew what I needed to do. The idea of calling Candace had opened up a whole new set of options, and no matter how much I hated them, I couldn't afford to leave any unexplored. It was to keep my friends alive. When I put it that way, my feelings didn't matter all that much.

It took me twenty minutes to find the number. I probably could have done it with two Google searches, but I still didn't want to boot up the computer. Eventually I got through directory assistance the old way, a computer with a vague East Coast accent patching me through. I listened to the ringing, my heart beating fast. I was hoping for more voice mail. It didn't work out.

'Hello?' a woman's voice said.

I opened my mouth, but nothing came out. I swallowed down the knot in my throat.

'Hello? Is anyone there?' she said, preparing to hang up.

'Hi,' I said. 'You don't know me. My name's Jayné. Jayné Heller. Eric Heller was my uncle. He died. Someone killed him, and . . . um . . . anyway. I need help. I need your help.'

She didn't say anything.

'Aubrey's in trouble,' I said. 'He could die.'

There was a moment's silence. I could hear her breathing. When she spoke again, her voice was grim.

'Where is he?'

'Denver,' I said. 'He's in the hospital.'

'I'll be there tonight,' his wife said.

18

I met her at the airport just at sunset. In person, Kim looked a little less like Nicole Kidman. She wore gray slacks and a simple cream blouse that would have looked perfectly in place at a baseball game or a boardroom. Her eyes were a sharp blue, her mouth tight and a little angry. She came through baggage claim without pausing at the carousel, a generic black carry-on wheeling behind her and a tasteful black purse on her arm. She only looked around for a moment before homing in on me. When she stood before me, her head cocked to the left, her eyes clicking over me like a specimen she was trying to identify, I was surprised to see she was half a head shorter than me.

'You look like him,' she said. She spoke sharply, like she was trying to bite off the last letter of every word. 'I mean, not *like him* like him. But the family resemblance is there.'

'Thanks,' I said.

'I didn't like Eric. I always knew that something like this was going to happen.'

'Well, he's dead now, so I guess it won't happen twice,' I said, more harshly than I'd intended. 'And he wasn't the one who got Aubrey in trouble. I was.'

'Aubrey is always the one who gets Aubrey in trouble.

It's his superpower. Are we waiting on something? I don't have any other luggage.'

I nodded and led the way back out to the minivan. Kim was silent, but her shoes tapping on the concrete behind me seemed to carry accusation and disapproval. I was probably overreacting. She didn't say anything about my driving Aubrey's car, so either she didn't care or she didn't know it was his. We'd known each other for ten minutes, and I was already certain she wasn't the sort of person to hold back an opinion.

'We're staying in Eric's old house,' I said as we pulled out of the parking space. 'It's got protections on it, and the Invisible College is looking for us pretty hard, so I'm trying not to go out if I don't have to.'

'I want to go to the hospital,' Kim said. 'I need to see him.'

'Aubrey's all right,' I said, fumbling with a parking stub and a few loose dollars to pay the charge. 'I called the doctors again just before I came out here, and they said—'

'I need to see him,' she said again.

'I don't think it's safe.'

'I didn't ask if it was.'

I clenched my teeth. I didn't want to go back to the hospital. But she was here because I asked her. Because I needed her.

'Fine,' I said. 'But we can't stay long.'

The hospital was out of our way, and we didn't talk. The few times I glanced over at her, her eyes were on the city sliding by. I wondered whether I should have told her about my night with Aubrey, whether her story about their marriage would match the one he'd given me. I parked on the street, and Kim was out of the car almost before the engine died. I had to trot to catch up with her.

Aubrey's room hadn't changed much since I'd left it. His heart rate was steady and slow. His mumbling roommate still mumbled. Kim stood beside him, looking down with her eyes half closed. Her expression betrayed nothing.

'How long has he been like this?' she asked.

'Since last Saturday,' I said, 'so a week tomorrow.'

A nurse came into the room, a strong-looking black woman in her midfifties. I remembered her vaguely from the earlier times I'd been here. She smiled at me, kindness and sympathy in her expression, and started changing out the roommate's saline drip.

'Excuse me,' Kim said. 'Where's his chart?'

'I'm sorry,' the nurse said, 'but we can't give out his medical information to—'

'I'm his wife. You can give it to me,' Kim said. The nurse looked surprised and glanced at me. I shrugged and nodded. The nurse's eyebrows rose a millimeter, but she gave no other sign of surprise. Fiancée and wife visiting together was apparently not the strangest thing she'd seen that day.

'I'll see if I can get the doctor for you,' she said, and went back to her task. I went to look out the window, feeling awkward and out of place. I didn't see it when the nurse left. Kim didn't speak to me. I let the silence press on me for as long as I could stand it.

'He'd been in a fight a few days before,' I said. 'A rider

217

took over this guy's body, and we wound up in a fight. Aubrey did something that knocked the bad guy out, but it weakened the connection between him and his body. When Coin fought back, it hit Aubrey really hard. That's why . . .'

That's why he's hurt and I'm not. That's why you're here. That's why this is all my fault. Kim made a small sound of agreement so perfunctory that I didn't know whether she was aware of it. She touched Aubrey's cheek with the detachment of someone preparing for a dissection, then ground the knuckle of her right index finger into Aubrey's sternum, hard enough to make the bed under him creak.

'Hey!' I said. 'What are you doing?'

'Sternal rub.' She nodded to the heart monitor. Fifty-five. 'He still responds to pain. That's very good. It would have been better if he'd flinched, but this is something.'

'Oh,' I said.

'I don't hurt him for the joy of it,' she said.

I didn't know how to respond, and a second nurse came in the room to save me. He was a huge man, wide as a horse across the shoulders, with a shaven head and broad lips. He looked at me, his eyes barely widening. I had the sudden, overwhelming memory of the tattooed attackers breaking into Midian's apartment and the moment of surprise that followed breaking in the door.

I've seen him before, I thought, my body already in motion. I scooped up the little plastic visitor's chair and swung hard. The huge man blocked the attack but fell a step back as I remembered where. He was the one who'd been with

Coin that first day when Ex took me to see the warehouse. He was part of the Invisible College.

It was a trap.

'Kim!' I shouted. 'Run!'

She was already moving. She slipped over the murmuring man's bed, putting one of us on either side of the false nurse. I tried to remember how to use the training Midian and Chogyi Jake had given me while I kicked at the man's kneecap. He moved fast as a cat, taking the impact on his shin instead. He drew in a deep breath, and I felt a prickling that had nothing to do with the physical as he drew in his willpower.

Kim punched at his back. He staggered, surprise on his face. I shouted as I turned, kicked like something out of a martial arts film, and drove my foot into the bridge of his nose. Something gave, and the huge head snapped back, the man dropping to the floor like we'd Tasered him. Kim unclenched her fists. There was blood where her fingernails had cut into her palm.

'There are probably others,' I said, but she was already heading out the door and I was already following her. The black nurse was heading toward the room, with a look of concern and annoyance. We blew past her. At the intersection of two halls, I paused, drawing my qi up behind my eyes, feeling the shift in my consciousness, and then swept the halls before and behind us. The world had taken on an almost surreal level of detail. I could see the dust hanging in the air, hear the high-pitched whine of the computer monitors harmonizing poorly with the hum of fluorescent lights, smell the corruption and shit under the antiseptic hospital scent, feel my clothes grating against my body. Kim paused, looking back at me. She wore contact lenses. I hadn't noticed that before. She looked at my eyes, and I could see she understood what I was doing.

'Well?' she asked.

'None here. None that I see.'

'Stairs or elevator?' she asked, gesturing down one of the hallways. A bank of brushed-steel elevators stood at the end of the hall like temple guards, a marked stairwell beside it. The leftmost doors began to open, and I caught a glimpse of tattooed skin.

'Stairs,' I said, 'but not the ones down there.'

We ran. I felt things tugging at me, the wizards of the Invisible College pulling at me with their minds, the separation between reality and Next Door thinning. As we dodged angry doctors and confused patients, I tried to keep myself between our pursuers and Kim. I thought that if Eric had put some protections on me, they might shield her too.

We found another stairwell and Kim started down it, but I caught her hand.

'Up,' I said. 'Let them pass us by.'

She nodded. We ascended. We'd gotten a floor and a half up when the door we'd come through burst open. I froze and then slowly turned back, ready to launch myself at any attacker. But the wizards' footsteps retreated, heading down toward the first floor. Some grunting marked when they ran into some poor bystander on the stairs, and then we heard a metal door slamming open. The sound was so assaultingly loud, the echoes in the concrete shaft so disorienting, that my focus failed, my qi dissipated, and my senses began to return to normal.

I was shaking. Behind and above me, Kim's breath was ragged.

'Let's go find another stairwell.'

'Okay,' she said.

I led the way up another flight of stairs, but the door there required a pass code, so we kept going up. On the sixth floor, we got lucky. A nurse was going out the door, and we caught it before it could close. We stepped into the new ward, walking quickly but not running. We got a couple stares, but no one tried to stop us. I put my hands in my pockets, lifted my chin, and tried to look like I knew where I was going. We passed rooms with men and women lying in bed, the low-level murmur of televisions punctuated by groans and weeping.

As we turned a corner, Kim took a quick double-step to come next to me. At the end of the corridor, an exit sign glowed green.

'I shouldn't have insisted that we come here,' she said. It wasn't phrased as an apology. It was like she was telling me some trivial fact I might not have known.

'I shouldn't have let you,' I said, and we reached the new stairwell. I opened the door with a clank, cutting off whatever she'd begun to say next. I went down the stairs quickly, leaning over at each landing to look for hands on the ascending rails below us. If there was anyone there, they were being quiet.

'They'll be watching for us,' she said. 'They'll be watching the exits.'

'I know,' I said.

'You have a plan?'

'I'm thinking of one,' I said. It wasn't true. Between immediate animal panic, concentration required by my still-unfamiliar magic, and anger at Kim, I hadn't come up with anything more sophisticated than get down and get out. I wasn't about to tell her that.

We got to the ground floor and stepped out into the wide lobby from a passage I had never noticed on my previous visits. The place was built like a labyrinth, which was probably why we'd gotten this far without being discovered. Weird architecture and blind luck weren't going to help much now. Three men stood at the information desk, talking into cell phones, but their eyes didn't have the veiled awareness that comes from being in a conversation. They were looking for something. For us. Two were young men, broad across the shoulders and thick in the neck. The third man was smaller, older, with his back to us. When he turned, I wanted to scream.

Power radiated from Coin like heat from a fire. His face was set in an expression of cold concentration. Bubbling panic rose up in my throat. He was here. He was waiting for me. I smelled something like burning.

'What?' Kim murmured. 'What is it?'

I hoped Midian had been right when he'd said I was hard to notice. I took her elbow and angled her down a side hallway. I didn't dare look back, but no one seemed to be coming after us. We passed a gift shop full of stuffed animals and snacks, the cashier looking at us incuriously as we passed.

'Do you think they've spotted your car?' Kim asked.

'Probably,' I said.

'My things are in it.'

'Yes, they are.'

We turned left. Signs offered us paths to the emergency room, the bathrooms, security. I walked toward the emergency room and slid through a set of doors marked HOSPITAL PERSONNEL ONLY. Curtained cubicles lined the wide room, the sounds of crying and pain making a hellish background. No one challenged us. We weren't an obvious problem, and we were in the land of great big obvious problems. I peeked past the intake nurse and toward the lobby.

The big man from Aubrey's room was sitting by the emergency entrance, his expression deathly grim, black eyes still starting to form where I'd kicked him. Two men and a thin-faced woman were sitting with him. I backed up. The trap was sprung, and we weren't getting anywhere. A soft chiming sound announced the arrival of an oversize elevator. I was trembling.

The wide steel doors slid open, and four paramedics pushed out a gurney. The woman being wheeled past was drenched in blood, her neck encased in a stabilizing collar like something from an Egyptian tomb. The shreds of her jeans trailed after her like rags. Her eyes were blank. The paramedics moved quickly, professionally, into the emergency room. The doors clapped closed behind them even before the elevator began to close. The feeling hit my gut, a fist of fear and hope that tried to take my breath away.

'Come on,' I said, pulling Kim into the elevator.

'What are . . .'

'That one,' I said, nodding to the injured woman. 'She came from upstairs.'

The doors hissed closed and I slid my fingers over the worn plastic buttons until the numbers stopped getting higher. There was one unnumbered button at the top. It was marked *H*. I pushed it.

'Medevac,' Kim said.

'Yeah,' I said. 'There's a helicopter up there.'

The elevator lurched, dropped a few inches, and then started to rise. I willed it to go faster, but the numbers continued their stately progress.

'He's your lover, isn't he?' Kim asked.

'What?'

'Aubrey? He's your lover.'

'We went out once,' I said.

'I still care for him,' Kim said. Her chin jutted out, but her eyes were all apology. I stared at her, and a floor later she looked down. 'I haven't told him that since . . . since we split. He doesn't know.'

'Okay,' I said.

'I thought I should tell someone. In case we're about to die.'

I didn't mean to take her hand. It just seemed the right thing in the moment.

'I can see that,' I said, and then, 'I was really hoping to

have a little more time before we got into the heavy emotional intimacy thing.'

'Me too,' Kim said, and shrugged. 'Sorry.'

'It's a fallen world. You do what you can.'

The elevator lurched again, stopped. We turned toward the doors together, our hands still clasped. When they opened, the helipad was before us, the beacons burning red in the darkness. The transport helicopter was still there, two men in uniform standing before it in obvious conversation. No wizards descended upon us. No sense of riders pressing in from Next Door assailed us.

I didn't know what I was going to say, but as we walked forward, Kim dropped my hand, squared her shoulders, and stepped forward.

'You,' she barked as we came near. 'You're the pilot?'

The nearer man's head snapped straight. His companion edged away as if hoping to avoid the conversation.

'Yes, ma'am,' he said.

Kim dug in her purse for a moment, then handed the man an identification card. I saw her picture on it and the words *Grace Memorial Hospital*. The place she worked in Chicago, I thought.

'I'm here consulting on a very delicate transplantation,' she said. 'I need you to take us to the airport.'

The pilot glanced down at the identification card, back over Kim's shoulder at me, and then down at the card again. He was shaking his head even before he spoke.

'I can't do that, ma'am. We're a medevac unit, not a transport. I'm not allowed.'

'It's important. A child could die,' Kim said, and I felt something when she did. A prickling on my skin like someone had brushed me with a feather. Even with the August heat still radiating from the tarmac, I had goose bumps. The pilot shuddered, nodded, and turned to his helicopter, then paused.

'There isn't room for you in the cockpit, ma'am,' he said. 'We're gonna have to strap you two down.'

Kim paled, but nodded. I saw her swallow. The pilot waved to his companion, and the two trotted to the helicopter's sides to prepare little fiberglass pods, just big enough for a dreadfully injured person.

'Magic?' I asked. 'That was a cantrip?'

'It isn't hard,' Kim said. 'People want to do what they're told. Men especially want to help women, and God knows you're pretty enough that he wanted to show off. I just . . . nudged him a bit. It's not like telling him we aren't the droids he's looking for.'

I laughed, relief giving the sound a warmth I was surprised to feel. Her smile was less wintry.

'I don't think I've said thank you,' I said. 'For coming. For helping me with this. For helping Aubrey.'

Her expression went thin and brittle. It would have been as if the moment's vulnerability in the elevator had never happened, except that I saw something softer in her eyes.

'If we survive all this, I'm going to kill Aubrey myself,' she said. 'Or at least wound him seriously.'

'Fair enough,' I said. 'Of course, we're not out of here yet. The helicopter could still get shot down by the Invisible College.'

'Cheerful thought,' Kim said, and the pilot waved us over.

They strapped me in first, wide canvas bands with industrial steel buckles cinching me in against the aluminum frame. A fiberglass pod closed over me like a coffin; a small clear space let me look out and up at the swimming stars overhead. The pilot climbed into the cockpit and started up the engines. I could feel it through the frame of the helicopter when his companion closed the pod on Kim's side. The engine whined, and the rotors began to turn. The noise was so overwhelming it was like silence.

Like a balloon with its string cut, we rose into the sky.

19

'Where's the minivan?' Midian said.

'We lost it,' I said.

'You *lost* it?'

The taxi was pulling away from the curb. I closed the door and put my backpack on the coat hanger. The house smelled like old laundry and popcorn. Kim stared at Midian and then, shaking her head, excused herself and headed down the hall toward the bathroom.

'How do you lose a minivan?' Midian said as I walked into the living room.

'There we were running down the highway, and I said, "Holy shit, Kim, I think I know why we're getting so tired." Look, if it's important, I'll buy us another one.'

Chogyi Jake emerged from the back. It might only have been that I'd been out in the world or that I was still coming off the adrenaline overload of my time in the hospital, but I thought he looked worse than when I'd left. The strain of holding up Eric's protections was showing in his face. I remembered a news program I'd seen when I was a kid with men in yellow rain slickers piling sandbags against a flood. They'd had the same exhausted eyes.

'I was starting to get worried,' he said.

'Yeah,' I said. 'So was I. It's okay, though. We're here.'

'What happened?'

It was easier for me to retell the story to Chogyi Jake than to Midian. He listened intently and without comment. I left out how Kim had insisted on going and that I'd caved, making it sound instead like it had been a mutual lousy decision. I also skipped the part where she told me she was still in love with Aubrey. Kim came back into the room about the time I got to the part where the helicopter landed at the airport and the two of us went to look for a taxi. I saw her glance at Midian, her face perfect for the poker table.

'You don't get to go out without a chaperone anymore,' Midian said.

'Bite me,' I said, and he grinned as if it was a joke. I only figured out what was funny about it after the fact.

'Kim,' Chogyi Jake said. 'I'm glad to meet you. I think we all owe you a debt.'

'Kind of you to say so,' Kim said.

'You know about riders?' Midian asked.

'I'm not an expert, but yes,' she said. 'I worked with Eric and Aubrey when I was still living in Denver.'

For a minute or two, they compared their relative expertise on things occult. I couldn't follow much of it, but I had the impression they were each favorably impressed by the other.

'Any ideas how to beat the Invisible College?' Midian asked. Kim hesitated.

'No,' she said.

'Well, welcome to the club,' he said. 'You want anything

to eat? We're pretty much down to leftovers, but I think I can make a decent omelet with what I've got.'

Kim considered the vampire without speaking.

'He's really good,' I said. 'Seriously.'

'Then yes,' Kim said. 'That's kind of you.'

Midian shrugged and limped back to the kitchen. I retrieved the report from my lawyer and gave it to Kim. She looked over it with a calm, practiced eye while the sound of chopping and the scent of butter wafted into the room. I turned to the subject of Coin and the still-unformed plan to separate the parasite from its host.

'There are a couple of possibilities next week,' I said. 'I mean, if the projections in the report are true. There's the doctor's appointment on Monday, and he's speaking at an international aid foundation meeting on Tuesday night. I've got a request in for an updated schedule for him, though. There may be a better opportunity.'

'The problem being that any time we plan an attack based on his established schedule, we also face his established security,' Chogyi Jake said. 'It's safe to assume that he will be protected at any of these events.'

'And the last time we went up against him, he didn't even need that,' I said.

'Hey,' Midian shouted, 'how do you feel about onions?'

'Love them,' Kim shouted back, and then turned to me. 'Correct me if I'm wrong, but the failure of the previous plan was that you thought you had the element of surprise and you didn't?'

I sat on the couch's armrest and shrugged.

'Yeah,' I said. 'You could look at it that way.'

'He knew how we were going to attack,' Chogyi Jake said. 'Not that it would be rifles, but that we would draw him out from his wards and that we'd be using the Mark of Ya'la ibn Murah and the sigil of St. Francis of the Desert. And so he was warded against those specifically. The attack by Ex and Aubrey gave him a channel back to them. Jayné was only saved because she was wise enough not to pull the trigger.'

I felt a momentary stab of guilt at my failure to attack and gratitude to Chogyi Jake for putting my inaction in that light. Kim only nodded.

'Since then, they've been circling,' I said. 'Looking for us. Midian and Chogyi can't leave the house. It seems like I'm okay because of some old protections Eric put on me. At least that was Ex's theory.'

'And where is Ex?' Kim asked.

'We don't know,' I said. 'He opted out.'

Midian came into the room, two plates balanced on his arm. He presented one to Kim and the other to me. The omelet smelled of onions and garlic, and it tasted like heaven. Kim took a bite, nodded her approval, and Midian accepted it with a bow before sitting down. I'd raised my fork, preparing to speak as soon as I'd finished chewing, when Eric spoke from my backpack.

I knew I was going to have to change the ringtone. I knew that it was going to be creepy for people until I did. But Kim's reaction was still startling. Her face went white, her eyes wide. She was halfway to her feet, food forgotten, before I could stand up. She tracked me with her eyes as I crossed to the front door, dug in my pack, checked the incoming number, and answered the call.

'Candace?' I said.

'Jayné,' Candace Dorn said. 'I know it's late. Is it too late? I'm sorry I didn't call back sooner. Aaron was working a double shift, and I wanted to talk with him about your call.'

'I completely understand,' I said.

Kim lowered herself slowly back to her seat, her head bowed. Chogyi Jake was frowning at her, and Midian's ruined eyebrows had lifted. I wasn't the only one to think something interesting had just happened.

'He's here now,' Candace said. 'I'll get him.'

I had a sudden flashback to sitting at my computer talking to not-Ex.

'Candace!' I yelled. 'Hold on.'

'Yes?' she said.

'If there's someone else there . . . I mean if you're being coerced in any way, say "Yes, it's okay." '

She laughed. 'It's nothing like that. God. Were you thinking it would be?'

'I'm a little jumpy,' I said. 'You don't . . . I mean . . . I'm sorry. Could you just tell me what price we agreed on for fixing your problem? Just so I know it's you?'

'You didn't charge me anything,' she said. Her voice was lower now. I could imagine the furrows on her brow. 'Is this serious, Jayné? Should I be nervous?'

'Maybe a little,' I said.

There was a fumbling sound on the far end. Someone new came on the line.

'Jayné? This is Aaron.'

His voice was deep and masculine and made me think of recruitment ads for the Marines. I couldn't help smiling.

'Hi, Aaron,' I said. 'I'm glad to hear from you. You're doing okay?'

'I am. Had a long day today, but if there's something going down, I can get a cup of coffee and be anywhere you need me in about fifteen minutes.'

'Thanks. There's nothing going on right now, but I might need a favor pretty soon here.'

'Are you safe where you are now?'

'Yes,' I said. 'Safe as I would be anywhere. There's something going on, though. Something big. If you're around, I'd really like to talk to you about it.'

'Is it another one of those fuckers that got to me?'

'Similar idea,' I said. 'Bigger scale.'

There was a pause on the line. I heard Candace's voice in the background. Aaron grunted in a way that sounded like assent.

'Hey,' he said. 'If you really don't need me right this minute, I'm going to get some rest. I'm dead on my feet. But I'm going to give you another number. It's my emergency line, and if anything happens, you call it.'

He rattled off the number and I wrote it on the back of some junk mail. He made me repeat it back to him to ensure I got it right.

'Now you listen to me,' Aaron said. 'You saved me. You

saved Candy. You ever need anything—*ever*—you call me. You're family now.'

'Um,' I said, oddly touched by the ferocity in his voice. I'd only ever known the guy as a German shepherd. 'Thanks. You bet. Why don't you call me when you wake up. Maybe you guys can come over?'

'I'm already there,' he said, and we ended the call. I programmed Aaron's emergency number into the phone and put it back in my backpack. When I returned to the couch and my cooled and thus somewhat rubbery omelet, Kim had regained her composure.

'That the other resource?' Midian asked.

'Yeah,' I said. 'We did a favor for a cop. It might be useful.'

Kim nodded. Small white dots had appeared at the corners of her mouth where her lips pressed tight. I glanced at Chogyi Jake, and he gave me the smallest possible shake of the head. *Don't push her. Not now.*

'Okay,' I said. 'So anyway, we've got a couple things going for us. Aaron's one. We have Kim now. We know where Coin's going to be more or less, and we can get more digging done on him if we want it.'

'It's not enough,' Midian said with a sigh. 'We had Aubrey and Ex before, and me, and tofu boy here. And you. And all the juju Eric put on you. And we got dicked over.'

'Yes, but that was the point I was making before,' Kim said. 'The one thing you thought you had and didn't was surprise. They were working under the assumption that you would all be coming at him under something similar to the original plan. You did. They won. This time will be different.'

'You think so?'

'This time you actually *can* surprise them,' Kim said.

I crawled into bed just before two in the morning, my body humming between the two poles of fatigue and residual adrenaline. The pillows were cool. The soft babble of a news channel in the front room meant Midian was taking the first watch. The ceiling above me seemed to glow a little, like an old television turned on but without a signal.

I willed myself to sleep, but with no effect. I was bone-tired and twitchy. I was scared and bored and uncertain. I was ready to pop. I had Kim now, and after our time at the hospital, I was even pretty sure I could count on her. Not bad, considering I'd slept with her husband. Her husband who she still loved.

I wondered where Ex was, if he was safe. If he was alive. I wanted him back with us, his angry blue eyes and his assured, in-control way of holding himself. Even when he was wrong, he was never uncertain. Having Aaron, Candace, and Kim helped. Understanding better how my inheritance from Eric gave me options helped. But I was getting tired of the people I needed going away. Ex. Aubrey. Cary. My father. My family.

Eric.

Somewhere in the city, the thing that looked out Randolph Coin's eyes was waiting for me. Watching. I wondered if the rider ever got bored, got distracted, looked away. I tried to put myself in Coin's place. Eric Heller had been gunning for me and died for the offense. Eric's team had taken up his cause and failed. The enemy wasn't gone— one of the fallen was in the hospital as cheese in the mousetrap, and another had already run. Would Coin know how many had been in the conspiracy by the warehouse? Would he know what resources I had?

I shifted, pulling the pillow over my head. The murmur of the television grew quieter so that I wasn't sure anymore whether I was hearing or imagining it.

If I were in his position, what would I expect of my enemy? Well, I'd expect us to run like hell. Just the way Ex had. Maybe we'd try to save our fallen, but the trap around Aubrey had failed once. In Coin's place, I'd think that gambit had failed. Would I still keep watch on Aubrey?

A scene from an old movie came to me. One of the Vietnam films my older brother had liked to watch when our parents left him in control of the house. Someone in the band of brothers had been shot by the enemy and left in the open, his screams the bait to lure the others out where they could be killed. Yes, I'd leave a guard on Aubrey. And I'd cover the roof next time.

The problem was . . . well, there were a lot of problems. I wanted to know exactly what Coin and his people were capable of, but my brief lessons in riders and qi and magic pretty much confirmed that was going to take a lot more time than I had. I could rely on Kim and Chogyi Jake to give me their best guess. I didn't know how good that would be, but I didn't have anything better. I wanted to know what Coin's plans and intentions were so that I could navigate my way around them, but it wasn't like I could ask him.

I wanted to misdirect him, to point over the Invisible College's collective shoulder and sucker-punch them when they turned to look. But I couldn't even do that.

My eyes flew open as the thought came to me.

Or maybe I could.

I got up, dug my laptop out from under a pile of old clothes, and stared at it without opening the case. My fingers twitched toward it. They hadn't tracked me the last time I'd talked to the fake Ex. I hadn't admitted that I knew he was a fake. Maybe there was a way. Maybe I did have a way to lie to Coin and the Invisible College. I opened the screen, my finger hovering over the power button. Was this stupid? Was this something I needed to talk to the others about?

I put on my robe, tied it in a square knot at my waist, and stalked out to the main room. Midian was on the couch with a cigarette in one hand and a beer in the other.

'I thought I said not to smoke in the house,' I said.

'You did,' the vampire said. 'I've only been doing it when I was pretty sure you wouldn't see me.'

'I let you guys make the calls last time, and we failed.'

'Old news, kid.'

'I'm not doing that anymore. Eric left everything to me. Not you, not Aubrey or Chogyi Jake or Ex. Me. This is my show now.'

Midian took a long, slow drink from the can, then held

the cigarette to his mouth. The ember went bright as he inhaled, then back to its dull orange glow. The yellowed ivory eyes narrowed.

'What's bugging you?'

'I'm making a decision,' I said. 'I think it's the right thing to do.'

'But?'

'But if I'm wrong, I might tip our location to Coin and get us all killed.'

'You want to talk about it? Roust tofu boy and what's-her-name out of bed, chew it over.'

'No,' I said. 'I'd only convince myself not to do it.'

'So was there something you wanted from me?'

'No, nothing,' I said. 'I just thought I should tell someone that I'm making the decisions now.'

'Even the risky ones,' he said.

'Especially the risky ones.'

Midian looked up at me from the couch. Almost imperceptibly, he nodded.

'You sound like the old man when you say that,' he said. 'Welcome to command, General.'

I nodded curtly, drew myself up an inch or so.

'Put out the cigarette,' I said, and went back to my room.

There were two hundred spam messages, but Thunderbird killed ninety percent of them, and I deleted the rest by hand. There was a note from my little brother, Curt, asking how and where I was, but the tone of it seemed more like his usual whine than something urgent. I pulled up my chat program.

There were half a dozen people online just then that I knew, mostly from ASU. Including my old boyfriend. His screen name showed he wasn't idle, so he was talking to someone. Just not me. Extojayne, on the other hand, had been listed as idle for days.

Jayneheller: Ex! Where the fuck have you been? Why the fuck haven't you been calling? We've been out of our minds here!

I sat back on the bed. This was stupid. This was a mistake. I should never have done it.

Someone on the other side started typing.

Extojayne: Complications. Nothing serious. I'm fine. Sorry I've been out of touch. What's the status there?

I flexed my fingers like claws. I shifted the mouse over and turned on the logging feature. Better to have a transcript of this so I could keep my lies straight. And I might as well start with something they already knew.

Jayneheller: The rabbit thing fell through. You were totally right about that one. Sorry I gave you grief. The big news is we tried to get Aubrey, but it was a no-go. The Invisible College folks are on that place like white on rice. We barely got away.

Extojayne: We?

Jayneheller: Me and Kim. The others weren't there. I don't think we're going to be able to get Aubrey out of that. I hate to leave him behind, but I just don't see what else we can do.

239

Extojayne: I understand. I'm not happy about it either, but you're
    probably right. What else? What's the news on Texas?

I grinned. He was buying it. All vestiges of exhaustion
were gone. I felt like I'd just had eight cups of coffee and a
jelly roll. I could keep going with this bullshit all night.

Jayneheller: Texas looks good. If we can get to Mexico, I think we'll
    be all right. You keep them distracted for a few more days, and
    we'll be just about ready to make a run for it. Cool?
Extojayne: I can do that. But let me know the details. I don't want to
    do something that would get in your way.
Jayneheller: You betcha.

Hey, Coin. What's that over your shoulder?
Go ahead.
Look.

20

The second report came from the lawyer in the morning, about half an hour before Aaron and Candace arrived.

I had cut the conversation with the fake Ex off after about fifteen minutes with the promise that I'd be in touch again soon. Afterward, it had been hard to sleep, so I didn't drag myself out of bed until almost noon. My eyes felt gritty and my mind was stuffed with cotton, and the scent of Midian's coffee was like the promise of spring in February. I struggled with last night's square knot on my robe, gave up, and pulled on a pair of blue jeans and one of Eric's white shirts. It was a little too sheer for polite company and the only bra I could find was way past laundry day, so I put one of his suit jackets on too.

Kim and Chogyi Jake were sitting across the kitchen table from each other, engrossed in a conversation about the relationship between parasitism and immaterial beings. It seemed to center on whether riders were really using people as a means to reproduce or if they had some other agenda. Midian took a look at me, chuckled like a chain saw, and poured me a cup of coffee.

'You still need new dishes, kid,' he said. 'We're eating off bakeware here.'

'I'll get right on it,' I said.

Kim glanced at me, her expression closed and unreadable. Her hair was in place, her makeup perfect. I was willing to bet her bra was clean, and we'd lost her bag the day before. It was hard not to see the emptiness of her expression as criticism, and it stung a little. I'd thought we were working on being friends. But then I remembered her moment of candor at the hospital and her reaction to Eric's voice. There was more going on than I knew about. I tried to keep my paranoia in check at least until the caffeine could work its way into my blood.

'Look,' I said. 'There's something I did that you guys should know about.'

I recapped Extojayne for Kim, then explained my plan to use the plant to mislead Coin. Chogyi Jake smiled all the way through it. I found myself wishing he would frown sometimes or express disapproval, just for variety's sake. I topped off my cup.

'It's a risk, but I think you're wise to take it,' Chogyi Jake said.

'Thanks,' I said.

The doorbell rang, and Kim started at the sound. So did I, a little. Midian sighed.

'I'll get the gun,' he said, but by the time we got to the door, the courier was gone.

The new report was as anonymous as its predecessor, but shorter. It was little more than an itinerary for Coin over the next seven days, starting with going to church tomorrow and ending with a concert next Friday night, with a footnote disclaiming the reliability of the list, and pointing out that things change. Like I needed to be reminded of that.

'What about Tuesday?' Kim said. 'He's speaking at the convention center downtown. If we make our fake escape during that, we might be able to catch him coming out.'

'If he thought we were worth bothering with,' Midian said. 'He might just send his bully boys.'

'Let me work on that with Extojayne,' I said. 'If we make the cheese pretty enough, he might come out. It'll take away some of his backup anyway. Are we sure about Tuesday night, or is there anything on the list that looks better? Where exactly is he supposed to be speaking?'

My cell phone went off. Kim only tensed at Eric's voice this time. When I answered, it was Candace saying that she and Aaron were coming up to the front door, and not to freak out.

Candace Dorn had changed from the first time I'd seen her. Her face looked stronger, more confident. She held herself with less reserve. It's amazing how not having your boyfriend beating the crap out of you improves your appearance. Aaron, at her side, was a little under six feet tall with dark hair cut close, shoulders broad enough to build small townships on, and a demeanor that leaned in toward the world. Everything about him had me reaching for my license and registration.

I had my hand out to shake his, but he stepped inside my arm and lifted me up in a bear hug that had my ribs creaking. When he put me down, Candace echoed the gesture in a less painful way.

'I hope you don't mind that I came too,' she said. 'I've gotten to where I can stand to let him go to work, but this . . . after last time . . .'

'I totally understand,' I said. 'Come in. Both of you. I have some people I'd like you to meet.'

Kim and Chogyi Jake greeted Candace and Aaron. Midian had the good taste to look uncomfortable, the only inhuman beast in the room. We sat in the living room, all six of us, and I launched into what felt like the hundredth retelling of the situation—the Invisible College, Eric, Coin, Aubrey, Ex, Extojayne, Chogyi Jake and Midian's house arrest, the bullets designed to kill riders, the reports on Coin's schedule, everything. I talked for twenty minutes, Chogyi Jake, Kim, and Midian interrupting occasionally to clarify one point or another, Candace and Aaron asking infrequent questions. Along the way, I started to notice something that unnerved me.

Without discussion or conscious intent, the room had divided. Candace and Aaron sat at the end of the couch, Kim leaning against the wall beside them, while Chogyi Jake sat at the far side of the hearth and Midian haunted the doorway that led to the kitchen. I remembered an image I'd seen in science classes—a cell pulling itself apart, dividing in two. Along one wall was the team I had assembled—Kim to work the magic, Aaron to provide the muscle and knowledge of violence, Candace to help however she could. Along the other, Midian and Chogyi Jake were the survivors of the team I'd begun with when I first dropped down this rabbit hole. Apart from giving advice and history and perspective, there was nothing for them to do. I was leaving them behind.

I didn't want to.

'Seems like the first thing we ought to do,' Aaron said, 'is drive his route. We know where he's going to be Tuesday night. We know where he lives. It'd be a good idea to know what's in between point A and point B, right?'

'I'd thought of that too,' I said, pulling myself back from the strange sorrow that had distracted me. 'I printed out some MapQuest directions.' I pointed to them on the coffee table. 'According to those, it's about a twenty-minute drive from Coin's place to the convention center. I don't know that he'll be taking the computer's route, though.'

'That's why you've got locals,' Aaron said with a grin. 'We'll figure it out. The bad guys have seen you and Kim?'

'Yes,' I said. 'Not very well, though. The only one who really got a look at us was the one I kicked.'

'You two should sit in the backseat all the same,' Candace said. I must have looked surprised at her tone of voice, because she shrugged and went on. 'It makes you harder to see. Basic tactics.'

I began to wonder if I'd underestimated the woman.

'All right,' I said. 'I don't know that it's a plan, but it's at least moving toward one. Give me a couple minutes to get presentable.'

Aaron nodded, but he was looking at the MapQuest printouts. Candace leaned over his shoulder, her brow furrowing.

'You don't think he'd take Speer?' Candace said.

'I'd take Colfax and I-25,' Aaron said. 'I don't know why you'd want to keep to surface streets.'

'What about heading out Federal and going south?'

'Better than Speer,' Aaron agreed.

I snuck back to my room. I didn't figure there was time for a shower, but I did my hair up in a bun and put on clothes that looked less like I was dressing myself out of Eric's secondhand shop. Jeans, T-shirt, tennis shoes. I even dug up a mostly cleanish bra that wasn't so dark it would show through the white of the tee. I hung my leather back-pack on one shoulder and considered myself in the bathroom mirror. Halfway to respectable, me.

I couldn't restrain myself and checked e-mail before I went back out. There was nothing. I turned the laptop back off.

The debate of routes from Coin's place to the speaking engagement had turned into a full-on council of war while I was gone. Aaron was squatting on the floor in front of an unfolded map of the city, marking out a route in yellow highlighter. There were already other paths in green and blue. Kim was on the couch alone now, leaning forward and listening intently to Candace and Aaron debate. Chogyi Jake was still on the hearth. I touched his shoulder and nodded to the kitchen. We went past Midian without disturbing the planning session in progress.

Chogyi Jake's expression was concerned, but there was still the hint of laughter at the corners of his bloodshot, exhausted eyes. I had the impulse to take his hand, but didn't do it.

'I wanted to apologize,' I said. 'I know there's not a real reason to, but I wanted to do it anyway.'

'I accept,' he said without hesitation. 'What was it you were apologizing for?'

'Going without you,' I said. 'For putting this whole thing together and not having you be part of it.'

'I have my role,' he said. 'With the Invisible College tracking me, I wouldn't have been much use for this part.'

'I know that,' I said. 'It's just . . . I don't want you to feel like I cut you out. I don't want you to feel like I'm leaving you behind or something. I'm . . .'

I gestured ineffectively. Chogyi Jake gently pushed my hands back down toward my sides.

'You've had to put a lot of people behind you, haven't you?'

'Yes,' I said.

'Your mother and father. The friends you had in college.'

I was more than a little embarrassed at the tears that sprang to my eyes.

'Okay,' I said. 'Putting too fine a point on it now.'

'What you've done here? It's exactly the sort of thing Eric would have chosen. This was the way he lived. When a situation arose, he gathered the people he needed to address it. When the work was complete, he moved on. If you're taking up his work apart from this one last project of his, it's going to be the kind of life you lead too.'

'But he had friends. He had people he could count on. People he could trust,' I said. And then, 'Didn't he?'

'I don't know,' Chogyi Jake said. 'He was a difficult man

to know well. Perhaps he'd seen too much. I know you much better than I ever did him. And I care for you more.'

I grabbed a sheet of paper towel and wiped my eyes. Chogyi Jake stood silently, bearing witness without offering to hold me or turning away. I loved him a little bit for that.

'Okay,' I said. 'So here's the thing. I care about you too, and I've got to go do this thing. And I know you can't do it with me. But it's not because you aren't really, really important to me. Okay?'

'Okay.'

'And you're going to be here. In the house. When I get back?'

'I am.'

'You aren't going to take off on me.'

'I'm not.'

'Fucking *promise*.'

He grinned.

'I fucking promise,' he said.

I took a deep breath, then another, then another, letting each one out slowly until I was back under control. Chogyi Jake was smiling gently. He looked tired. If I'd let myself think about it, I wouldn't have done it. I leaned in and kissed his cheek the way my mother used to when I was a kid. He laughed.

'Okay,' I said, loud enough for it to carry into the living room. 'Let's get this show on the road.'

The heat was worse than it had been before. Candace drove a two-year-old Saturn sedan, and even with the air-conditioning turned up high enough that Kim and I had to lean forward to hear and be heard, the backseat still felt like a sauna. On the streets, the trees seemed to wilt under the press of sunlight. Pedestrians reclined at the bus stops like prizefighters between rounds.

'There's supposed to be a cold front moving in,' Aaron said over his shoulder. 'It always gets like this right before the heat breaks.'

I squinted into the sun.

What does the secret lair of an evil wizard look like? It was two stories high with a red tile roof and stucco I could only think of as Realtor beige. Across the street, there was a wide park where improbably green grass looked like a very short jungle. We circled the block once, Aaron watching the house as if it might move. Kim murmured under her breath, and I had the feeling she was doing something not entirely natural with her will.

'Okay,' Aaron said. 'Here's the thing. There are a lot of different ways he can go from here to there. I'm thinking that our best option is to take him out close to one of the ends. Either here when he's heading to the speaking thing or downtown when he's leaving afterward.'

'There are going to be more wards and protections here,' Kim said.

'On the other hand, there are going to be more innocent bystanders downtown,' I said. 'If there's going to be a fight, I'd rather have it someplace where no one's likely to get hurt. By mistake, I mean.'

'If we find the right site, it won't be an issue,' Candace said.

'You sound like you've done this before,' I said.

'Nah,' she said, with a nod toward Aaron. 'I've just been hanging out with him too long.'

We spent two hours driving different routes back and forth between Coin's neighborhood and the convention center. The convention center itself was a huge glass-fronted building like an aquarium built for people. The streets downtown were busy and almost all one-way, usually not the one we wanted. There were two places—one near the convention center, the other down near Coin's house—that particularly excited Aaron's interest.

Kim, sitting beside me, seemed to grow more and more withdrawn through the day. At about half past three, I called a break, and Candace drove us a couple of blocks to the Rock Bottom Brewery at the Sixteenth Street mall. We sat on the patio so that we could actually hear one another. In the shade, it wasn't too bad. With a cold beer, it was better.

'Okay,' I said after we'd ordered some food. 'What have we got so far?'

'I think we can take him out by the convention center without there being too much risk of it spilling over,' Aaron said. 'It'll mean taking him by surprise, but—'

'But he's a rider,' I said. 'He can do things that a human being can't. We have to figure that in.'

'I've been thinking about that,' Kim said. 'He's going to outclass us when it comes to magic. There's no way around it.'

'What options can you give me?' I asked.

Kim sipped her beer, then wiped her mouth with the back of her hand. It was the least cultured and controlled gesture I'd seen her make.

'My toolbox is smaller than you're used to,' she said. 'I quit working with Eric before Aubrey did, so I just don't know as much. In a way, that makes it easier because there isn't much to choose from. I can attack Coin. Try to break the bond between the rider and the body it's in. It's unlikely to work by itself, but if he's also being assaulted physically at the time, there might be a chance. Or I can protect the group by making us difficult to focus on, which has the advantage of giving our side more time. But it doesn't do anything about his protections, which I expect are going to be difficult to penetrate no matter how much time we buy ourselves. Or . . . or I can damp down *all* the unnatural activity in the immediate area.'

'Tell me about that last one,' I said.

'It's a simple ceremony,' Kim said. 'The name for it is Calling Malkuth. It doesn't take a lot of finesse or preparation, which is an advantage because I'm not very good at this. It's fairly easy, since it's essentially calling forth normalcy, and bringing things back to their natural state is simpler than pulling them out of it. I don't think it would be wise to count on me for anything fancy.'

'What's it do?' Aaron asked.

'It invokes the material world,' Kim said. 'It makes riders less powerful. Which means it will affect the body-guard too. We can't forget about him. It also restricts the kinds of things other people can do. Normal humans who've been trained would find it harder to cast spells or express their will in nonphysical ways.'

'What's the downside?' I asked.

'It's indiscriminate,' she said. 'I can't just affect their side. So you wouldn't be able to do anything either.'

'Okay.'

'And I don't know what it would do to the protections Eric put on you.' That she looked down when she said it was enough to show that this was her real objection.

'Tell me about *that*,' I said.

'Well. Chogyi and Midian both said that there have been things about you . . . that you've been surprisingly good with some kinds of fighting, that you're harder than usual to locate using nonmaterial means. If Eric had protections on you, Calling Malkuth would diminish them. And then I don't know that afterward they would come back.'

'What if she wasn't there?' Candace asked. 'If Jayné didn't come, then she wouldn't need to be there when you did the—' She waved her hands like a stage magician.

'I'll be there,' I said. 'If it's a risk, that's fine. I'll take it.'

'No. Don't just make a snap decision like that. Think about this,' Kim said. 'We don't know all of what Eric's done. We don't know what other work we might be interfering with. I don't want . . . I don't want to be responsible for breaking something I can't fix.'

She shrugged, and I understood what she wasn't saying. I was her husband's lover. There was a whole side of her that wanted nothing more than to see me hurt. She didn't trust herself.

'Okay,' I said. 'I'll think about it. But right now, it's the option that sounds the best to me.'

The food came. I hadn't realized how hungry I was until my first mouthful. Then I couldn't stop. The sun pressed down on the world. A constant trickle of sweat ran down between my shoulder blades. It was Sunday. The last day in the worst week of a life that had a couple other real contenders.

Maybe Tuesday wasn't the right time. Two days didn't seem long enough to really plan out what I was going to do, all the possibilities and contingencies. All the things that could go wrong. I paid the bill with cash when it came. There was still a part of me that shuddered a little bit at a single meal that cost over fifty dollars. A month ago, it wouldn't have been something I could afford. Now it was subliminal. Next month, it could be up to whoever was catering my funeral.

The street mall was permanently blocked to cars. We'd parked in the structure underneath the restaurant, so when we left, the direction was down. The garage was pretty full, but also offered the kind of cool that comes with being underground in the unkind heat of August. We angled for Candace's sedan, and I fell into step beside Kim. She looked over at me, then away. A motorcycle whined.

I didn't know what was happening until Aaron had already pushed me down between two cars. Candace and Kim were crouched low and following. A pistol had appeared in his hand as if from nowhere. The motorcycle's engine dropped to a lower hum.

'What?' I whispered.

'The bike,' Aaron said. 'It's been following us. I wasn't sure before. The thing is the guy on the bike keeps changing.'

'More than one person?'

'He changed in the middle of traffic,' Aaron said. 'He was a big black guy, and then about half a block later, he was an Asian chick. I thought maybe it was just similar bikes, but . . .'

I moved forward. The motorcycle was at the end of the row, pointing vaguely toward the exit. The man sitting on it was craning his neck, looking for something. Looking for us. He pulled something small and plastic out of his pocket, looked at it, frowned, and put it back. He was maybe in his early fifties, with salt-and-pepper stubble and a long, greasy ponytail. I gathered my qi, drawing it slowly up to my eyes. The image shifted. The glamour washed away, pony-tail and stubble and decades flowing away from the man. I said something vulgar.

'Stay here,' I told Aaron, then stepped out into the aisle, walking down the oil-stained concrete like I owned it. On the motorcycle, our shadow saw me. His expression went from surprise to chagrin to anger in less than a breath. By the time I reached him, he had braced the cycle with his legs and his arms were crossed.

'What do you think you're doing?' I shouted over the low roar of the engine.

'I was going to ask the same of you,' Ex said.

21

He looked near exhaustion. His hair, tied back in a ponytail and held with a thick rubber band, was limp and greasy. His face was grayish around the eyes, like someone who's been working around smoke and soot so long it's been ground into the pores. Without the glamour, he was wearing a white shirt that looked as worn as he did, with old jeans and black boots.

I crossed my arms.

'I'm doing what we should have done from the start,' I shouted. 'You want to kill the engine on that thing, or should we talk about this really loud and in public?'

His expression soured further and he nodded to the back of the cycle, ordering me on. I raised an eyebrow and didn't move.

'I'm not having this conversation here,' he said.

I turned and spat on the ground, then walked back to Aaron, Candace, and Kim. They were still hunkered down behind parked cars, but the fact that I had talked to the mysterious stranger without the pair of us devolving into a street fight seemed to reassure them all.

'It's Ex,' I said. 'You three get back to the house. I need to talk to him. I'll meet you there in an hour.'

'You're sure?' Aaron said. The gun was still in his hand, though pointed professionally away from anyone. His glance over my shoulder offered to beat the living shit out of Ex. Part of me appreciated the thought.

'I'll be fine,' I said. 'I want you guys to talk to Midian and Chogyi Jake. Tell them about the Calling Malkuth plan, and see what you can brainstorm as far as strategies.'

'We're doing it?' Candace asked. 'Tuesday night is the time?'

'I don't know yet,' I said. 'See what you can work out. I'll see what I can do about getting Ex over whatever his problem is.'

The others looked at one another for a moment, then Aaron slid the gun back into an ankle holster I hadn't noticed before. I walked back to Ex. He reached into a small side bag and pulled out a black helmet, holding it out to me as I came near.

'Where's yours?' I asked.

'I'll be fine,' he said. 'Put it on and we'll go.'

I got on the back of the bike, the helmet weighing down on my neck, and tucked my leather backpack into the side bag. Ex leaned forward, gunning the engine. Resenting the physical contact, I leaned forward, put my hands on his sides, and got ready for launch.

I hadn't been on the back of a motorcycle since I was sixteen, and even then it hadn't been more than a few slow blocks with a guy from church. Ex's launch felt like an amusement park ride without the amusement. Before we'd gotten out of the parking structure, I'd forgotten all about

Coin and the Invisible College, Kim and Aubrey, and riders in general. All my attention was on shifting my weight the right way so that the pavement wouldn't rise up and rip my skin off. My arms slid forward, and within a couple blocks, I was holding Ex closer than I'd ever held anyone I wasn't looking to sleep with.

The streets slid by, the wind of our passage drying the sweat off my arms almost before it was there. Despite the heat of the day and the punishing weight of sunlight, I felt cool. I only wished that I had refused the helmet. The air would have felt good against my face.

Ex turned us onto Colfax, and then, to my unease, onto I-25 heading north. The Sunday traffic was light, and speed turned the asphalt to a gray blur beside me. I found I could tell from the subtle movement of Ex's body when we were going to change lanes or shift direction. Before long, I was matching him without thinking.

Back on the surface streets, the houses were low and comfortable looking, the shops mostly strip malls. I felt sure enough of myself at the slower-than-highway speeds to lean back and allow a little air space between me and Ex's back. The front of my T-shirt where I'd pressed close to him was sweat-soaked and I suspected less opaque than I would have liked. I didn't want to have the coming showdown looking like I was trying to win a contest at a sports bar.

I didn't need to worry about it. By the time Ex slowed the cycle down to a putter and angled us down a long dirt driveway, I was back to myself and sure of my dignity. The house on our right was a one-story ranch, white paint flaking at the eaves. It was the sort of place where I expected to see a family living. I wouldn't have been surprised to see a swing set out back and children in the yard. Ex coasted past it.

The garage in back was huge. Three cars would have fit in it easily. But instead, it was fitted out as a little apartment. Ex's shining black sports car sat close to the eastern wall. A canvas cot that looked like it came from World War II rested against the back wall beside the open door of a bathroom almost too small to turn around in. Ex killed the engine, dropped the kickstand, and got off the bike. I got off too, pulling the helmet off as I did. My legs were trembling.

The smaller details of the space began to register with me. The books in Latin and French stacked under the cot. The crucifix reverently hung by a small, dirty window. The mixed smells of dust, motor oil, and old laundry. Ex leaned against his car, his arms folded, his expression stern. In context, it was all I could do not to laugh.

'Okay, I need to know two things,' I said. 'First, tell me that's not your parents' house up front. Second, tell me you didn't spend all your money on the cool car just to impress girls.'

Ex looked puzzled for a second, then glanced around at the ad hoc apartment as if seeing it for the first time. He seemed chagrined, but he covered it quickly.

'The house belongs to a friend. He lets me rent this when I need a place to stay.'

'When you need a place to stay?'

'It's not like I'm carrying a mortgage,' Ex said.

I couldn't help it. I laughed. Big, strong, authoritarian Ex, with his black clothes and shining sports car, lived in a garage. Ex's expression darkened.

'Let it go, Jayné,' he said. 'You are risking your own life and the lives of everyone who was at that restaurant with you today. The first thing you need to do is tell me what you're planning, and the next thing you need to do is call it off.'

'How is it,' I said, ignoring him, 'that Eric has enough money to buy a small island, and the rest of you are living like college students?'

'That's what I'm telling you! Will you listen to me? Eric was the real deal. He'd been doing this for years. He was connected. Chogyi Jake, Aubrey, me. We were his gophers. We were the day labor he took on when he needed an extra pair of hands.'

There was real pain in his voice. It sobered me. I looked at the cot, the books, the crucifix. I tried to see beauty in it.

'Why are you following me?' I asked.

'Because someone has to keep you safe.'

'They know you've left me,' I said. 'The Invisible College? They know you left.'

'They caught sight of me a couple times,' he said. 'And now that I'm out of the house, I'm not under Eric's wards and protections. Even if they don't know exactly where I am, they can tell that much.'

'And yet you're still alive,' I said.

'I am.'

'Luck?'

'Partly,' he said. 'I've got a talent for not being found.'

'You're going to stop following me,' I said. 'You're in or you're out, but not this halfway crap. It's creepy. You scared me today. I thought you were them.'

'I could have been. Coin has his people all over the city looking for you. He knows you're up to something.'

'He doesn't know what,' I said.

I walked to the window. A simple weeping Christ on a rough wooden cross. The floor before it was cleaner than the rest of the place. Like someone had knelt there often.

'We were idiots to think we could win where Eric failed,' Ex said. 'We were blind and proud, and we've paid the price for it. You have to stop this before it gets worse.'

'Pride?' I said. 'You think that's what went wrong? We were too full of ourselves, and so God saw to it that we didn't win?'

'I didn't say that.'

'But it's what you meant.'

I gave him a few seconds to object. He didn't. Instead, he walked toward me, his hands out to his side, unconsciously echoing the figure on the cross. I'd spent a fair part of my childhood watching my father work himself into rages, and the feel of this was different. This was desperation.

'Eric overestimated, and he got killed for it,' Ex said. 'We overestimated, and Aubrey paid the price. I'm not going to see you be the third.'

'I might win,' I said.

'You won't. You'll plan the best that you can, and be as

260

clever as you can be, and call on all the help you can find, and Coin will still beat you. You know it, and you're ignoring it because you're in love with the man in that hospital bed, and you think that maybe, *maybe*, you can pull off a miracle and get him back.'

He paused. I waited.

'You don't have to prove anything,' he said. 'Not to anyone.'

Ex was close to me now. The smell of his body wasn't unpleasant. He seemed to shake with the force of his emotion, a controlled violence that was pounding through him like a deep internal storm. I didn't feel threatened by him at all. I was oddly touched.

'I'm not taking Coin out because of some kind of sick, desperate love for Aubrey. I'm doing it because I think he'd have done it for me. And because Eric was the only one in my whole life who ever really looked out for me. And I'm doing it for myself. Because I can.'

'Don't,' Ex said. 'Don't try. Be safe.'

I stepped into his open arms and hugged him. His body went stiff with shock, and then softened. He wrapped his arms around me. I felt him sigh deeply, his ribs expanding and falling back. I rested my head on his broad shoulder. Through the dirty window, I saw a sparrow take wing, a brown-gray blur rising into the sky.

'Thank you,' I said.

He nodded, his cheek against my forehead. I squeezed him tight, then stepped back and let him go.

'You should take me home,' I said.

'You're dropping this,' he said. 'You're walking away.'

'Nope,' I said. 'If I go down, I'm going down with my teeth around that fucker Coin's throat.'

His eyes widened, his face went a shade paler. He looked past me to the crucifix like an actor who needs someone to feed him his next line.

'I know you're trying to take care of me,' I said. 'In your stupid, patriarchal, Neanderthal way, you think this is how you treat your friends. But I've already got a daddy, and I walked away from his bullshit too. Now take me home.'

'You don't understand,' he said as I stepped past him toward the bike.

'I do,' I said. 'I just disagree.'

Back at the house, I stood on the porch, sweat cooling on the back of my neck, and watched Ex drive away. I thought maybe he turned and looked over his shoulder at the last moment, but I might have been making that up. I went inside.

Voices came from the living room, Midian and Kim talking over each other. For a second, it sounded like a fight. Then it only sounded like excitement.

When I stepped in the room, all eyes turned to me. Kim and Chogyi Jake were sitting on the floor off to one side, a notebook open between them with designs and symbols that seemed to shift and move when I wasn't looking straight at them. Midian was sitting on the coffee table, Candace and Aaron on the couch.

'Hey, kid,' Midian croaked. 'We were wondering if you were coming back.'

'I live here,' I said.

'How's the padre?' Midian asked.

I shook my head.

'Yeah, well,' Midian said. 'Probably for the best. He got on my nerves.'

'What have we got?' I asked.

Aaron cleared his throat, leaned forward, and started talking. The initial plan to take Coin out close to the convention center had hit some snags. We'd been working under the assumption that Coin would be heading back to his place, but Midian had pointed out that that wasn't necessarily true. So they'd been working out other strategies.

All the plans made some assumptions. First, that we could draw off the vast majority of Coin's minions, both by Midian and Chogyi Jake picking the right moment to break cover and get themselves chased and by feeding a little clever misdirection to the fake Ex. All of that was just to get Coin and his bodyguard out where we could take a crack at them.

The best-looking option thus far involved getting two cars, one with Candace at the wheel and Kim in the back, the other with Aaron and me. We could follow Coin when he left the convention center. Once we were sure where he was going, it wouldn't be hard to get the two cars close to him. Kim would damp out Coin's powers, Aaron would run him off the road (he'd been trained in that sort of thing and had no lack of confidence in his ability), and then he and I would finish things off with the bullets I'd recovered from our first attempt. Candace and Kim would pick us up, and we'd vanish into the night.

'It's cleaner than it looks,' Aaron said. 'There were three guys that got killed in the last five or so years with the same MO. They were all traffickers. Coin's a higher tax bracket than those guys were, but the chances are when the Denver cops see this, they'll assume he was involved and not look at it too hard.'

'Hey,' Midian said, tapping Aaron on the knee with one skeletal hand. 'Tell her what they call that. This is great, kid. You know what the cops call it when some mad fuck who needs to die gets aced by a civilian?'

'What do they call it?' I asked.

'Misdemeanor murder,' Aaron said. 'It happens. We get someone who everyone knows has been selling crack in the school yard, but we could never prove it. Someone does the obvious thing. There's just not much point in spending the resources on the investigation.'

'Don't you just *love* that there's a name for that?' Midian cackled. 'Renews my faith in mankind.'

Actually, it creeped me out, but I put my reaction aside.

'Are you sure we can make this look like a drug hit?' I asked.

'I'm sure,' Aaron said. 'I'm going to borrow some things from the evidence store back at home. We can drop it in Coin's car when we leave. Or in the one we're driving. If it's on the scene, the guys down here will put it together. They're not dumb.'

I nodded. It occurred to me for the first time that I had

put all my time and concentration into killing Randolph Coin, and none at all into getting away with it. This was going to look like murder, and I couldn't really tell the judge about riders from the Pleroma unless I was pushing for an insanity plea. Sobering thought.

'But the car that we use to run him off the road,' I said. 'That's an issue, right?'

'Actually,' Candace said, 'we can kind of kill two birds with one stone.'

'There's a place just north of Boulder,' Aaron said. 'There's no business going on there, but we're all pretty sure it's a way station. A safe house the bad guys use to move drugs and girls from the West Coast out east. We've never had enough to get a warrant, dig into things.'

'Okay,' I said, pulling the word out to three syllables.

'So the second car,' Aaron said. 'I'm going to borrow it from the guy who owns the house. If it's involved in a homicide in Denver, I'm pretty sure we can shut down everything else the fuckhead's up to too.'

I laughed and sat down on the hearth.

'We may be a force for good in the world after all,' I said. 'What about the Calling Malkuth thing?'

'I think it will work,' Chogyi Jake said. 'It isn't a configuration I'd seen before, but everything that Kim's showed me fits together well.'

'There is a problem,' Kim said, her head turned to Chogyi and away from me. 'Jayné's protections. I don't know what this will do.'

'Don't worry about it,' I said.

'It is a consideration,' Chogyi Jake said.

'It really isn't,' I said. 'Are we thinking we'll have two rifles?'

'One for each of us,' Aaron said, nodding.

'One per bullet,' Midian said. Then, 'You know, kid, you aren't the world's best shot. And the last time you were looking down a barrel at Coin . . .'

'That was last time,' I said. 'This is point-blank. I can't miss.' And this time, I was going to pull the trigger.

'So we're on?' Midian asked.

I hesitated, wondering what Ex would have thought if he'd come in. If he would have been swayed by it. If he would have thought I stood a chance, or been just as certain that I was fooling myself. I couldn't answer those questions, and they didn't matter anymore. Ex's opinion wasn't as important as mine.

'We're on,' I said. And then a moment later, 'Hey, can you guys ride motorcycles?'

22

My covert Monday morning coffee run failed. I went out alone in Chogyi Jake's van, picked up a few bags of food, and headed toward the nearest Starbucks, my mind on a cup of coffee and a slice of pound cake, and I almost didn't see the trap. Two middle-aged women sitting at the entrance, smiling and talking to each other. When I pulled my will into my eyes, their glamour faded, the tattoos on their faces and hands appeared, and I turned the van back out of the parking lot, shaking almost too hard to drive.

They were closing in.

I didn't tell anyone about it when I got back to the house. Aaron and Candace were back up in Boulder, taking care of things on that end. Midian was cooking. Chogyi was meditating and chanting, adding more spiritual sandbags to the levee. Kim was strewing ash and salt around the house until we ran out. Then she started pacing, her mouth set in a permanent frown. I sat on the couch, staring at the map of Denver and the calamity of streets that met downtown and trying not to think about how stupid it would have been to die at the coffee shop.

I hadn't slept well, waking up at four in the morning with the unshakable certainty that I'd found a flaw in our plan. As I came more awake, the objections turned into fluff and dream logic—something about how safety cones were orange and all we had was yellow paint. By the time I'd shaken off the sense of panic, I'd also stopped being anything near sleepy. It had been Chogyi Jake's turn to sit watch, and I'd sent him off to bed, made a cup of green tea, and watched television with the sound off until dawn came creeping through the window.

I knew Coin was there, as close as my laptop or waiting in the street. I couldn't tell anymore whether I was feeling the pressure of his magic eating away the safety of the wards, or if it was just my own paranoia. With my spare nervous energy, I started writing a list of the crimes I was about to be party to. *Murder. Theft. Discharging a weapon inside the city limits. Reckless driving.* When I got to *possession*, I started laughing so hard I had to put the pen down.

I wanted to call the hospital, to find out if Aubrey was still okay. If he was still the cheese in their mousetrap. I wanted to go back to Ex's garage apartment and kick his ass or talk sense to him. I wanted to be with Aaron and Candace when they stole the car from the safe-house jerk. I wanted to know how to clean a rifle so I could take mine apart and put it back together a couple thousand times in the course of the day. I wanted my uncle back. I wanted to talk to my mother.

More than anything else, I wanted Kim to stop pacing.

'Hey,' I said. 'You got a minute?'

Kim looked at me like I'd asked if she was a biped. I gestured to the couch. She sat. Her eyes were bright blue and hard as marbles. I had a brief vision of the woman who'd attacked me that first day, wide blue eyes, the Slavic accent asking *Who are you?* I tapped Kim's knee with the flat of my hand.

'Are you going to be okay with this?' I asked.

'I'll be fine,' Kim said. 'It's you I'm worried about.'

'It's okay,' I said. 'If I lose whatever protections Eric put on me in order to break the Invisible College, then—'

'No,' Kim said. 'I mean, how did he find you?'

I blinked. It took a couple of breaths before I understood the question.

'Ex, you mean?'

'If that's his name. You're supposed to be hard to locate with magic, right? So how did your priest friend evade the Invisible College, move to his own little bolt hole to keep a low profile, and still know where we were?'

'Maybe he's good at it?' I said. 'He does know where the house is.'

'Then he's been out there, sticking himself out like a flag?' Kim said, her voice fast and hard. 'Because if they can see him, and he's close by, then it's just as good as them knowing where you and Jake and that whatever-it-is that does all the cooking are.'

'*Vârkolak,*' I said. 'Midian's a *vârkolak.*'

Kim shooed the word away. I started to marshal my thoughts. If the Invisible College could use Ex to find me, they would have done it already. The fact that there weren't ninja wizards breaking down the door was plenty of evidence that we were okay. Plus which, one more day wasn't going to matter. Either we'd have succeeded in breaking the College, or we'd be so deep in trouble nothing was going to help.

Except that Kim knew Ex wasn't a bad guy. Self-important, overbearing, and burdened by an unrealistic idea of his own responsibility, yes. Dangerous to us, no. This, I thought, was her version of waking up at four in the morning worrying about orange safety cones.

'Freaked about tomorrow?' I asked.

She shook her head, then a moment later she nodded.

'This is why I left in the first place,' she said. 'Eric and his covert world. The things he would do. That he would have us do. And now here I am, back in the middle of it. And he's not even here.'

There was a deepness in the way she said the last phrase. *He's not even here.* Longing. Sorrow. Emptiness. She wasn't talking about Eric anymore. She meant Aubrey.

'What are you going to do if we win?' I asked. 'What are you going to do afterward?'

'Go back to work,' she said. 'They think I'm still in Chicago. I've been calling the front office on my cell phone every morning, holding my nose and telling them I still don't feel well. They think I've got the cold from hell. But there's a budget meeting on Thursday, and I have to . . . I have to be there for it.'

Kim seemed to deflate. She stared at the television. It was an advertisement for something, but I couldn't guess what the product was. Abstract happiness, maybe. I cleared my throat.

'I'm not in love with Aubrey,' I said. 'I have a crush on him. He's really cute, and really nice. And he can dance.' I took a deep breath and let it out slowly. 'The thing is, I'm not really in the best place to be making that kind of decision right now. A couple weeks ago, I was a college dropout hoping I could land a job waiting tables at Applebee's. And now I'm—'

I gestured at the house, the walls. Kim looked at the place as if it was a real indication of who I had become. She nodded.

'That isn't the only question, though,' she said. 'You can't be sure what he feels for you.'

I wanted to object, to tell Kim that Aubrey clearly didn't love me or want me or whatever it was she was afraid of, but we both knew I'd be making it up. This wasn't the time to close my eyes and pretend the world was what I wanted it to be.

'I don't know what he feels,' I said. 'We were on kind of iffy footing when it happened.'

A tight smile flickered over Kim's lips.

'With any luck, we'll be able to worry about all this next week,' she said.

My cell phone rang. Kim jumped a little as I dug it out of my pack. I thought of the fear in her face the first time my cell phone rang. When she heard Eric's voice. It was one of the functionaries at my lawyer's office returning my call. He'd gotten my message that morning and had a couple of questions about how I wanted him to proceed. I stuck my hand flat over the other ear and walked out back, talking it over with him.

The plan this time was a lot more complex than our last one had been. We had the cars we needed for the actual assault, or would after Aaron had completed his work stealing the one he'd be driving. I had one rifle, and the second was coming with the stolen car. I'd picked out a place near the convention center that had free wireless access. Midian and Chogyi Jake were ready to act as decoys, drawing off as many parasitized victims of the Invisible College as they could.

The trick was to not let my decoys get killed over it. And that meant making sure they were moving quickly and unpredictably. The good news was that that required only money, and I had that.

'Okay,' I said as the lawyer's functionary finished talking. 'Can you e-mail me the address of the airstrip?'

'It's on its way,' he said. 'And the motorcycles will be there between noon and two o'clock tomorrow.'

'Great,' I said.

'Is there anything else I can do for you, Ms. Heller?'

A cadre of priests chanting exorcism rites. The number of a really good pizza joint. Some groceries.

'No,' I said. 'I think we're good.'

I dropped the connection and went back into the kitchen. Midian was leaning over a wide metal bowl with a whisk in one hand and a bottle of brandy in the other.

'Everything's taken care of,' I said. 'You'll be out of here on a bike fast enough to outrun the cops, and there's a flight chartered to get you out of the city. All you need to do is get there alive. Or. You know. As alive as you get.'

272

'You're a class act, kid,' Midian said. 'You want to taste this sauce? I'm not sure it's working.'

He held out a wooden spoon dripping with something brown and sweet smelling. I tried it.

'It's working,' I said. 'That's really good.'

The vampire grinned crookedly and took a drink of the brandy. I went back to Chogyi Jake's room and knocked gently on the door before I opened it. He was sitting perfectly still in the middle of the floor. The drapes were lowered, casting the room in a soft twilight. It occurred to me that I'd almost never seen Chogyi Jake when he wasn't smiling or on the verge of it. His face was soft as sleep, expressionless and peaceful. As I watched, he drew in a deep breath and let it sigh out between his teeth. His dark eyes opened.

'Hey,' I said.

'How are you?' he asked.

'Nervous,' I said. 'I mean, not ten-thousand-dollar-shopping-binge nervous. Just, you know, ready. I've got a way out for Midian, and I'm getting a second cycle for you.'

'Just like Ex,' he said. 'The three bikers of the apocalypse.'

'I'm not above stealing a good idea,' I said. I stepped into the gloom and sat on the edge of the bed. 'I had a close call this morning. I don't think I'm going out again. Until . . . you know. Until. How about you? You all right?'

'I'll be fine,' Chogyi Jake said, looking up at me.

'But not fine yet,' I said.

'Frightened,' he said.

'You? I didn't think you got scared,' I said, trying to make it sound like a joke.

'Everyone gets frightened,' he said. 'And tired. It's been a hard week. I can't . . .'

He shook his head.

'It's good that this will be over soon. The wards are going to fail. Soon.'

I nodded. Maybe I'd known that.

'Can I ask you something?'

'Yes,' he said.

'Do you think I'm doing the right thing? Or am I just going to get us all killed?'

Chogyi Jake leaned forward, stretched, and rose to his feet. The stubble on his scalp was getting longer. In the dim light, it looked like a black halo close against his temples.

'Interesting phrasing,' he said. 'Do you really think that what makes an action right or wrong is how it turns out?'

'I think that's got a lot to do with what makes it stupid or not, yes,' I said.

'Ah. That's a different question. I thought you meant whether we were doing a good thing instead of an evil one. You mean good tactics rather than poor?'

I sighed.

'I'm not sure what I mean. Except I'm afraid of what happens if we fail out there.'

'It would be more pleasant to win. But even if we don't, that doesn't mean that the effort was wrong.'

'Has anyone ever told you that you are really freaking

274

terrible at pep talks? You could just pat me on the head and say it'll all be fine and not to worry.'

'It'll all be fine,' he said, patting me on the head. 'Don't worry.'

'Okay. That so didn't work,' I said. 'But thank you. For staying with me. For trying to do this.'

'It's who I am,' he said.

'Thanks for being you,' I said.

'You're welcome. And thank you for becoming who you needed to be,' he said.

He leaned over and took my hand in his. I was amazed by how warm he was. We stayed there in silence for a few seconds, then, as if by common decision, went back out to the main room.

Aaron arrived in the middle of the afternoon behind the wheel of a black Hummer S2. The car was like a Jeep on too many steroids—muscular, masculine, and vaguely un-healthy. I watched as he backed it in under the carport. A few seconds later, Candace pulled up to the curb, her car snuggling in behind Chogyi Jake's van. Aaron hopped out of the stolen Hummer with a grin.

'I've got a sun cover in the back,' he said. 'Help me get it over this thing, would you?'

'It went okay?' I asked, following him toward the back hatch.

'Perfect. Jerk's probably still wandering around the parking lot wondering what just happened,' Aaron said, then paused and turned to me. His face was serious. 'I know this isn't protocol. There's about a thousand reasons I shouldn't be doing it, and that it's illegal and I'm one of the good guys is pretty much at the top of that list. But I have to tell you there is nothing in the world better than taking one of these can't-catch-me motherfuckers and screwing him into the ground.'

'Yeah,' I said. 'I can see how that might satisfy.'

Aaron nodded to himself and opened the back of the car. Together, we unfolded the thick blue plasticized canvas and spread it over the car. It felt like we were making a bed together. I wondered if my life of crime was going to be full of those kinds of little insights. Kim and Candace helped out at their end. When the evidence was covered up, Candace went back to her car for the extra rifle.

Inside, the house felt small and tight, but also strangely festive. Midian laid out a table full of quiche and teriyaki chicken, rice pilaf and green beans with almonds, cream puffs with caramel sauce. Aaron and Candace, still clearly riding a wave of excitement that followed their theft, brought a wild energy to the place, and the nervous tension in the house crystallized around it. We were laughing and talking even before we dug into the food. I wondered whether soldiers had the same feeling the day before a battle. Merriment driven by fear. It was a lot like love.

It was Monday night. Aubrey had been in his coma for a week. Coin and his creatures were out in the rising darkness like sharks in a tank. Ex had abandoned me. Eric was dead. The friends and family who had been my life until now didn't even know what had happened to me. And here

I had a little constructed family, a group of people who I'd somehow gathered around me to eat and laugh and drink and fight against all the evils of the world. The big evils like Coin and the little ones too.

It was Monday night, and we were killing Randolph Coin tomorrow.

I couldn't help recalling the drama and anger and pain that had preceded our last attempt to break the Invisible College. I hoped the difference now was a good omen.

I dropped out of Midian's poker game just after nine o'clock and went back to my bedroom to take care of the part of the plan that needed attention. Extojayne was online and pleased to see me. We exchanged a few lines of vague pleasantries and then got down to business. He pumped me for information, and I lied.

We were going to head south on Wednesday morning, all of us, I said. We had a big van that we'd been covering with all kinds of wards and protections so that we'd be hard for the bad guys to find. I'd looked up flights out of Albuquerque and invented an itinerary that ended with us in Mexico City on Friday morning. Whoever it was seemed to buy it all, though I did have a few minutes of irrational paranoia that Coin had seen through my disguise and the Invisible College was playing me.

I was about to call it a night—I didn't want my conversation with the fake Ex to go on long enough for me to screw it up—when a new window opened.

Caryonandon: J? You there?

I blinked at the words a few times. Cary, my old boyfriend from ASU. The one whose jacket was hanging in my closet right now. Was it a trap? Had the Invisible College tracked him down to use as a way to get at me? I bent over the keyboard, my hair hanging down like blinders, blocking out everything but me and the screen.

Caryonandon: J? I know ur not idle. C'mon. Don't be a dick.
Jayneheller: Hey.
Caryonandon: I knew you were there. I've been thinking about you a lot.
Jayneheller: Have you been drinking?
Caryonandon: A little. You want to get together? Talk?

Extojayne asked something and I told him to stand by. Then I told him I had to go, and I'd talk to him tomorrow. The last thing I did before I shut down the laptop for the night was answer Cary.

Jayneheller: Actually, no.

23

It was just past midnight when the knock came at my bedroom door. I was pretty well asleep, deep in a dream that involved a huge mountain and a sunrise that projected purification instead of light, and only half woke at the sound. I'd almost convinced myself that I'd imagined it when the bedroom door eased open. I sat partway up. I wondered where my rifle was, more with annoyance than fear.

Kim was dressed in a bathrobe that had been Eric's. Her hair was down and messy from where it had lain against her pillow. She walked toward me, hands deep in the robe's pockets. Her expression was blank. I thought she was sleep-walking until she started to speak.

'Don't say anything,' she said. 'Just . . . just let me say this. All right?'

'Okay,' I said. Sleep-soaked, my voice sounded almost as bad as Midian's.

'I didn't leave only because the riders made me uncomfortable. They did, but I wouldn't have left Aubrey in the middle of all this just because I didn't like it. If anything, my fear of them was a reason to stay.'

Her chin rose a centimeter. Her eyebrows rose too. The

expression made me think of old pictures of English queens. I half expected her to say *We are not amused*.

'I was having an affair with your uncle,' she said. 'I didn't plan it. I didn't even particularly enjoy it. It was just something that happened between us. We were on one of his covert actions, and the two of us were trapped in a cabin together for a day and a half while the *wendigo* outside dissipated. And . . .'

She sighed and sat on the edge of the bed. She shook her head.

'Eric wasn't a man I liked,' she said. 'He wasn't someone I trusted or admired. But there was something powerful about him, and I responded to it. I broke it off with him half a dozen times, but then a few weeks later, I'd be driving home and find myself turning right instead of left. Aubrey only saw that I was trying to pull away from Eric and the riders and the Pleroma. That whole secret world. We had the most ridiculous fights about the whole thing. And of course they never came to anything because I could never tell him what I really felt or the real reasons behind anything I did.'

'Did Aubrey ever find out?'

Kim shook her head.

'Eric never told him,' she said, 'and I separated from my husband and left the state in order to stop. That's what happened. I thought that someday, if Eric moved away or he and Aubrey grew apart, I could come back. And then Eric died. When you called, I didn't know whether to laugh or cry. It was finally safe for me to come back to Aubrey, and it was too late. And then I met you.'

'I didn't know about you,' I said. 'I didn't know Aubrey was married.'

'I know. But coming off that airplane . . . you're young, and you're beautiful, and you have Eric's sense of power about you. Charisma, I suppose you'd call it. I've been watching you put this all together. I think you've done all the things that he would have, but somehow you've done them gently. Kindly. You have a good heart. If you had been a shrieking bitch, it would have been simple. Well, simpler than it is, anyway.'

I sat up and drew the sheets around me like a robe. The darkened house clicked to itself, cooling. The distant hum of traffic competed with the ticking of a clock. I could still smell the last fading scents of Midian's great feast, tainted by the smoke of his cigarette.

'I'm not getting between you,' I said. 'I didn't know he was married, or I would never have gone after him. When I found out he was married, I gave him raw hell over it. And now that I know you, there's no way, Kim. There's just no way.'

'You see?' she said. 'Kindly.'

She pronounced the last word as if it tasted bad, then turned to look at me. Her pale eyes were colorless in the dim light.

'You care for Aubrey,' she said. It wasn't a question.

'He stood by me when I needed someone to stand by me,' I said. 'He's a friend. Anything more than that, I'm not swearing to.'

'I suppose that will have to do,' she said. 'I wasn't going to tell you, only I thought . . . I thought you should know.'

'Thank you,' I said as Kim stood. She raised a single hand as she went, waving my thanks away. She closed the door behind her with a click, leaving me alone and sleepless and disturbed. My fist reaction was sorrow for Kim and her loss, then a proxy anger on Aubrey's behalf, and then a deep loneliness that I couldn't quite explain, except that it had to do with Eric.

It was easy to think of him as being just Uncle Eric. I had my memory of him, my experience. Apart from seriously biffing it by assuming he was gay, I'd never considered his love life. His sex life. The other people in the world who he'd mattered to besides me. Of course he'd had lovers. Of course he'd had friends. I imagined his life being somehow neater and cleaner than my own had ever been. That was my mistake.

I looked up into the darkness and tried to remember when this bedroom had stopped feeling like his and started feeling like mine, when the house had stopped being Eric's house and started just being the house.

It was an illusion. The house was still Eric's. The fight against Coin and the Invisible College was something he'd begun and I'd inherited along with his money and property. His shirts. His cell phone.

I tried to imagine him watching me from heaven or something like it. I tried to imagine his approval, but it didn't really work. Instead, I managed to remind myself that he was gone. I wondered what it would be for Kim to be here, in the place where she and Eric had been lovers or cheaters or however they'd thought of themselves at the time.

I didn't notice falling asleep again until the sound of wind woke me. The bedroom was dim as dawn, but the clock said it was ten thirty in the morning. I pulled on a robe and drew back the curtains. The sky was gray and low enough to touch. The window was dotted with raindrops.

'Well, that's just great,' I said to nobody.

In the living room, Midian had more or less the same take. He was lounging on the couch when I came in, yellowed eyes fixed on the television.

'For a plan that really rests on motorcycles and small airplanes, there's just no better "fuck you" than a good low-pressure system,' he said.

'I was thinking that myself,' I said.

'Didn't check the weather report when you put this whole thing together, did you?'

'I'm new at this,' I said.

'It will be fine,' Chogyi Jake said as he and Kim walked in from the kitchen, drawn by the sounds of our voices. Kim was dressed in some of Chogyi's spare clothes, tan pants cinched up with a braided leather belt, a shirt the color of sand. She'd had to roll up all the cuffs, and she looked small. The only sign of our conversation the night before was a barely noticeable reluctance to meet my eyes.

'The motorcycles are going to be new,' Chogyi Jake continued. 'They'll have good tread on the tires.'

'Besides which, it's not like we've got time for a plan B,' Midian sighed.

'That too,' Chogyi Jake said. Then, to me, 'Really. It will be fine.'

'I hope so,' I said.

I had hardly finished with my shower and pulling on my clothes when the doorbell rang. The dealership was there to drop off my new toys. I signed all the paperwork and took the titles and proof of insurance forms for both bikes, along with copies of the service agreements and owner's manuals. I hadn't thought to arrange insurance for them. I made a mental note to send my lawyer flowers or a thank-you note or something, provided I was still alive tomorrow.

The cycles themselves were gorgeous. We couldn't put them in the carport since the stolen Hummer was taking up all the air, so we had them pulled up onto the front walk. Black and red and set low to the ground, these weren't machines meant for touring or taking in the countryside. They were built to be hunched over, body forward, head into the wind. They both had matching helmets and complimentary leather jackets and chaps. I wondered how much I'd paid for them that the dealership was giving me all these extras. The rain beaded on the fiberglass.

'Well, they're sexy,' Midian said, looking over my shoulder. 'I'll give 'em that.'

'Think you can handle it?' I asked.

Midian made a rough sound that might have been a cough or laughter.

'Biggest problem I'll have is keeping the girls off me,' the vampire said. 'Or, if not the girls, the teenage zit-faced boys who think motorcycles impress girls. One or the other.'

'I don't know. I'm fairly impressed,' Kim said. I raised

my hand. We ate lunch, breakfast for me, making jokes about crotch rockets and wheeled vibrators. Midian and Chogyi Jake both tried on the protective gear—black leather and helmets. It was a nervous kind of hilarity, but it helped cover the fear.

Zero hour was eight o'clock, and it was a little after noon now. My stomach was starting to get knotted. The distant throb of a headache was climbing up the back of my skull. Kim played solitaire on the kitchen table with the cards from Midian's poker game. Chogyi Jake was meditating, gathering his remaining strength for the night's pursuit. I paced, drummed my fingers on the door frames, went to the front door every few minutes to make sure the motorcycles were still there and that the Invisible College wasn't. I felt stretched tight as a drum.

Aaron and Candace arrived at 1 p.m. in Candace's car. While Kim and Candace prepared the backseat for the ceremonial Calling Malkuth, I showed Aaron the ammunition. Two bullets I'd recovered from our last failure. I hated handling them, but Aaron didn't seem more than amused by the engraved figures. He knew exactly how to clean my rifle and showed me in detail. The living room smelled of mineral oil and rain by the time we were done and he took both weapons out to the stolen Hummer. We all went over the plan again. The clock seemed to go slower just to spite me.

There were still holes. There was still chance and contingency and a hundred ways it could go wrong. What if Chogyi Jake and Midian's flight didn't draw Coin out of his meeting? What if he was in a different car from the ones my lawyer's report had identified? What if there were more people with him than Aaron, Candace, Kim, and I could manage?

What if some poor bastard who didn't know anything about all this got in the way and got hurt or killed or taken over by riders? It would be my fault. I distracted myself as best I could, but every minute that passed was a weight on my shoulders. I told myself that everything would be all right. That this time it would be different. I almost believed it.

I told myself that Aaron knew the traffic patterns of Denver, where and when something could be done with as little attention as possible. And Kim and Chogyi Jake both thought that damping out Coin's powers could give us the edge we needed. I hoped that the confidence they felt came from the strength of the plan itself, and not because they had faith in me.

At about four o'clock the rain started coming down harder, with flashes of lightning and rolls of thunder. I stood in the open doorway, watching it and willing the clouds to separate. It was such a stupid, petty thing to have overlooked. Chogyi Jake's and Midian's escapes could be thrown off by something as stupid and simple as summer rain.

'Don't sweat,' Midian said. 'It'll be gone in time.'

'Your special vampire senses tell you that?' I asked.

'Yeah,' he said. 'That and I've been watching the local news. Doppler radar, all that. Streets are going to be wet tonight. The driving'll be tricky, especially with the new tires. But it's not the biggest problem you're looking at.'

'I know,' I said.

We were silent for a few seconds, looking out into the gray. I could smell Midian's weird, cold nonscent. He shifted, crossing his ruined arms.

'You did a hell of a job, kid,' Midian said. 'I mean I wouldn't make a habit of this, but for improv, you're doing great. And . . . hell. I know I came down on you pretty hard after the whole thing went south last week. I didn't mean to kick your ass.'

'We were all stretched a little thin,' I said. 'No harm, no foul.'

'Good.'

'You think Eric would have done it this way?' I asked.

'Hell if I know. He wasn't the kind of guy you could predict. Always something going on in his head. Why? You worried about it?'

'I'm worried about pretty much everything,' I said. 'It's just that you knew him. I think everyone here knew him better than I did. He was just this force for good that swooped into my life when things got bad and then swept back out again. And then I find out about the money. And then you and riders and magic. And . . . and it just seems like every time I turn around, there's more.'

'No one knew Eric,' Midian said. 'You saw part of him. I saw part of him. The three musketeers saw part of him. No one was in on the whole show. It wasn't who he was.'

'I guess,' I said.

'You miss him?'

'I miss the part I knew,' I said. 'I just regret that I didn't meet the other parts.'

'Deep,' Midian said. 'You should write a poem.'

'Smart-ass.'

'Glad you noticed. A lot of the time my sense of humor goes unappreciated,' Midian said. 'So look, I've got the fridge pretty much filled. There's dinners in the freezer. If you need to hole up for a few days after this comes down, you'll have something decent to eat. I wrote out instructions on how to reheat it all and what goes together on the tinfoil. Just look for things written in the same color pen. That way you know it'll all fit. I leave you poor fuckers to yourselves, you'll have all the starches in one meal together.'

'Thank you,' I said. And then, softly, 'Ah, fuck.'

'Yeah,' Midian agreed. 'This is pretty much good-bye.'

'We don't know that,' I said. 'This whole thing with Coin may work. You get away, I break Coin. Maybe we'll meet up again sometime. Down the road.'

'I don't think that'd be such a good idea.'

I shifted to look at him. The desiccated flesh of his face and neck, dark as old meat. The white shirt and high-waisted pants. He hitched up his shoulders in a pained shrug.

'Don't fool yourself, kid. This has been great. We've been friends. But next time you see me, we aren't going to be on the same side. I'm one of the bad guys, remember? People like you and Ex and tofu boy? You hunt down things like me. Like Coin.'

'Yeah,' I said. I could feel tears coming into my eyes. The rain pattered hard against the pavement, thousands of tiny gray explosions like something from *Fantasia*. 'You're right.'

'Don't take it hard,' he said. 'It was good being friends. So it didn't last. So what? It's not like it ever really does, you know?'

'I know,' I said.

A thin, wasted hand rested on my shoulder for a second, squeezed gently, and moved away.

24

A little before six thirty, the rain stopped. By seven, the clouds were breaking apart, a sky of fresh-scrubbed late summer blue showing for the first time all day. Aaron handed me a ski mask and I folded it into my pack. Chogyi Jake and Midian were in their riding outfits. I nodded to them both as I slipped my backpack over my shoulder. I couldn't deal with any more emotional good-byes.

'Are we ready?' I asked.

'Guns are in the car,' Aaron said. 'We've all got masks, right?'

'I'm ready,' Kim said. She looked perfectly calm. I had the feeling I could have known her for years without learning how to read her expressions.

'Okay,' I said. 'Let's do this.'

Candace and Kim took off in her car first. Aaron and I followed about five minutes later. The traffic was thicker than I'd pictured it, but Aaron seemed pleased. We parked on the street near the Marriott on California Street, then went to the Starbucks for overpriced lattes and down to the bar. I turned on the laptop, connected to the network, and started up the chat program under a screen name I'd built just for this. True to form, Extojayne was on and waiting for Jayneheller to show. It was seven forty. He wouldn't have to wait long. We were three longish blocks from the convention center. MapQuest said it was about a third of a mile. It felt like a thousand miles away until I imagined Coin there. Then it seemed way too close.

Ten minutes later, Candace called.

'He's there,' Candace said. 'We're by his car. I saw him going in.'

'Did he notice you?'

'No,' she said.

'Okay,' I said. 'Hang tight. We'll be right there.'

I dropped the call and dialed the house. Chogyi answered before I heard it ring.

'Jayné?'

'Yeah,' I said. 'Spark it up. I'm pulling the trigger now.'

'I understand.'

'Chogyi?'

'Yes?'

'Live through this, okay?'

'I'll do my best,' he said, and hung up. I put the cell phone in my backpack and signed on as Jayneheller.

Jayneheller: Ex! Are you there?

Extojayne: Yes. I'm here. What's up?

Jayneheller: Change of plan. Coin's at the convention center right now. We're going with plan B. The U-Haul with the fertilizer bomb is on its way. We can take out his house now while it's unprotected. You should meet us at the airport ASAP. We're scrambling now.

Extojayne: Wait. I don't think this is a good idea. Can we talk about it?

Jayneheller: No time, babe. Fortune favors the bold.

I closed the laptop, took a deep breath, and nodded.

'Hornet's nest now officially kicked,' I said. 'Let's see what happens.'

Aaron actually grinned and slammed down the rest of his coffee. I put my cell phone in my backpack and left my cooling latte untouched on the table. We walked fast out to the Hummer. The stolen Hummer. With the rifles. I had to pull myself up into the passenger's seat. Aaron started the engine. I put on the seat belt like I was strapping in to drop from a plane.

If I'd guessed right, there were about a hundred things happening right now. Extojayne, whoever he was, was raising the alarm about an imaginary truck bomb cruising toward Coin's house and the enemy—meaning us—meeting at the airport. Whatever resources the Invisible College had watching for Chogyi Jake and Midian were also getting action for the first time, the two of them heading fast in opposite directions. And, with any luck, someone was calling Coin.

We pulled out into traffic. I plucked my cell phone out of my pack and called Candace. Kim answered.

'They're out,' Kim said. Her voice was a tight whisper. 'They're getting into the car now. I think it worked. It's just the two of them. Coin and the other one. The driver. The driver's huge.'

Candace's voice came over Kim's, talking loud.

'They're pulling out. We're going after them.'

'Tell Kim that's great,' I said. 'Just let me know where you guys are, and we'll fall in behind you in a couple minutes. Just don't follow too close. I'm going to put you on speaker here. Let me know if the background noise gets too bad.'

'Okay,' Kim said.

Aaron gunned the engine, cursing under his breath. The downtown traffic was thick. We passed the Sixteenth Street mall, turned right on Fifteenth and then left again on Champa. I tapped my foot anxiously. We'd been right not to try taking him out down here. Too many people. Too much traffic. Someplace else would be better. I hoped that the right place existed. Kim reported in breathlessly. Coin was on Fourteenth, going the opposite direction. I cursed.

'It's okay,' Aaron said. 'He's heading to Colfax. We'll get there ahead of him. We're going to be fine.'

We passed over the two separate streets of Speer and the creek running between them, water high from the day's rain, and curved to the left. At the intersection of Colfax, two cars kept us from turning right. Aaron murmured something under his breath and reached toward the dashboard. Looking annoyed, he pulled his hand back.

'Miss having a siren?' I said.

'Hell yes,' he said, and Coin drove through the intersection ahead of us. I didn't recognize his car so much as feel its presence in my gut. My eyes tracked it as it flowed away to my right. Candace's car flashed through the light just as it shifted yellow, speeding after Coin. Aaron leaned forward as if he could push the cars before us out of the way by force of will. We got onto Colfax, Aaron gunning the engine as we turned.

The voice that came from my cell phone was Candace's.

'We're past Eighth,' she said. 'I think he's getting on I-25.'

'He'll be going south,' Aaron said. 'We'll do this on the loop. Get in behind him and get ready to put on your hazards when we come past you.'

'Kim?' I said. 'Are you ready?'

'She's ready,' Candace said. 'I'm getting in behind him. We're about to hit the on-ramp. Where are you two?'

We were coming to the intersection at Seventh Avenue. The last one before the highway. The light was red. We weren't going to make it.

'Hang on,' Aaron said, then leaned on the horn and the gas pedal at the same time. The Hummer leapt forward like someone had goosed it as we cut across the intersection. Brakes screamed and I closed my eyes, waiting for an impact that never came. The engine roared, acceleration pressing me back into my seat. My heart was pounding like it wanted to get out. Aaron wove the great black box through traffic like he was playing a video game, cutting off a semi as we slid onto the on-ramp doing sixty.

'We're going to flip the car,' I said.

'We aren't,' he said through gritted teeth. 'This is perfect. Candy! You with me? I'm coming up right on your ass. Pull to your right.'

'Slow down,' Candace said.

'Not happening,' Aaron said. 'As soon as I get by, get in the middle of the road with your blinkers going. Don't let anyone past.'

'Okay,' Candace said.

'Put your mask on,' he told me.

We buzzed past Candace's car like it was standing still just as we passed under the great concrete bridge of a surface street. Coin's car was six car lengths ahead of us, passing under the highway itself. We barreled toward it. My hands were on my knees, gripping so hard the knuckles ached. I couldn't unclench my fingers.

There was no sound that announced Kim's cantrip. She didn't say anything or call out physically, and yet there was no question when it happened. It was like the world clicking into focus when I hadn't realized it was out before. The car in front of us, the asphalt speeding by, the Hummer with its mingled scents of new car and old marijuana. Literally in the blink of an eye, all of it went from the rich, complicated, uncertain world I knew to a gorgeously complex mechanism. All emotion was gone, all sense of morality, of uncertainty, of fear or hope or dread. I could almost see the microscopic gears that made up the universe, the laws of physics triumphant. This was what the world looked like utterly without magic or emotion or soul.

Aaron drove up on Coin's left, sliding the Hummer's nose even with Coin's back tires, as if we were going to pass him on the inside of the curve. Then, violently, he cut the wheel right. The impact jarred us, and then Coin's car was fishtailing out in front of us, the driver's side of the car at a right angle to our oncoming grill. Gray smoke came off their tires like clouds. Aaron stamped the brake as Coin's car slammed into the concrete barrier. We were stopped in the middle of the long, slow curve that would lead to the highway. Aaron undid his seat belt and pulled on his ski mask. Of course he did. It was just physics. I undid my own, snatched my rifle up from the backseat, and slid out of the car.

I walked out to kill the thing in Randolph Coin's body, and my mind was perfectly calm. I didn't remember picking up my backpack, but there it was on my shoulders. I'd need to go back for the laptop. I didn't want to leave that behind. Candace's car was coming around the curve and beginning to slow. There were other cars behind her. I lifted the rifle to my shoulder.

The driver's door burst open. The big man rushed out. There was blood on his face. Blood and ink. His pale skin was covered in markings and tattoos. He raised his hand to us, palm out, and I saw the markings on his arm writhe like living things under his skin. He shouted and something moved past me, something unreal and angry and rich with malice. I felt something like teeth touching my mind.

In my peripheral vision, I saw Aaron raise his rifle with fluid grace. The report was a single barked command. The big man staggered back. There was blood on the car behind him. The thing with teeth—invisible, abstract, magical—shuddered against me and fell away. Blood darkened the big man's shirt. His illustrated face went slack, and he slipped to his knees and then to his side, lying on the dirty street in a pose that could never be mistaken for sleep.

Aaron dropped his rifle and motioned me forward. One of the bullets was gone. Used. One of the Invisible College's riders was dead or cast out of the world. The only bullet left was in my rifle, and I walked toward the back of Coin's car. Candace and Kim stopped by the Hummer. Kim was out of the car. I ignored them.

He was there, sitting at the far side of the seat. His glamour was gone, his face inhuman with glyphs and sigils. His eyes were wide and stunned. He looked old. I lifted the rifle again and he threw open the door and fell out on the car's far side. I sidestepped to my right, moving around the car's back. Its nose was crumpled against the concrete barrier. There was no place Coin could go.

'Move it!' Aaron shouted, pointing me forward. 'Get him! We've got to get out.'

I nodded and stepped forward, around the car. The traffic on the highway above us filled the air with the buzz of tires against pavement, the thump as they crossed the expansion joints. The smell of burned rubber was thick in the air, and there was something else. Blood. Death. Something.

Coin was on his knees, one hand to his chest just over his heart, the other pressed to his forehead. His lips, red striped with the black of his markings, were moving fast. His eyes were closed. I thought at first he was praying.

His eyes opened. There was writing on the sclera, tiny words worked on the whites of his eyes. He spoke a single word, but it resonated like we were standing in a tunnel, just the two of us.

'Heller?' he said.

'Yes,' I said.

'Hurry!' Aaron shouted. I heard horns blaring and the crunch of tires on gravel. Candace's car rolling toward me. I leveled the rifle at Coin's chest. I couldn't miss at this range. Even I couldn't miss. Coin shrieked, his mouth hinging open wider than I'd imagined possible. There was writing on his tongue. His teeth were like scrimshaw. I squeezed the trigger.

I didn't have the rifle snug enough to my shoulder. The kick was like a blow. I stumbled back as Coin's body folded forward. I stepped closer, the rifle still at the ready even though there wasn't a round left in it. A curl of smoke rose from the barrel.

He looked up at me.

He smiled.

He held out his hand to show me—shining, clean, searing his flesh with the heat of the discharge—the bullet, its etched markings squirming as if they were in pain. It was my turn to shriek.

Aaron was at my side. I hadn't known he was there until he pulled me back. A black pistol in his hand fired three times, four. Coin stood up, brushing the grit and gravel from his knees, ignoring Aaron as if he wasn't there.

'The car!' Aaron yelled. 'Get in the car!'

I turned and ran. Coin shouted out words I couldn't comprehend, and something detonated. I skidded and fell on the pavement, my hands and knees skinned. I wasn't going to make it to the car.

Candace was in the driver's seat, her face pale. She'd forgotten to put on her ski mask, or else had already taken it off. I saw Kim in the backseat, her hand pressed against the window. She could have been a world away. As I rose to my feet, I wondered whether she'd gotten my laptop. It was a disconnected thought, something plucked from the middle of a car wreck.

Aaron was on the ground. Blood flowed from his nose. His eyes weren't focused. Coin stood over him, head tilted like a man considering a crossword puzzle. I knew the next thing the rider would do would be to kill him. Or worse.

It was pointless. The Hail Mary throw. I gathered my qi the way Chogyi and Ex and Midian had taught me. In the thinned universe of Kim's cantrip, it seemed weak even to me. I pushed it out my mouth as I shouted.

'Leave him alone!'

Coin looked up. His eyebrows rose. His hand moved faster than a human's. The fabric of the world pulsed. The sense of being in a clockwork of physics faded. Someone was honking. I heard tires squeal. We were causing a traffic jam. If the plan had worked, Kim and Aaron and Candace and I would already be gone, speeding south on the highway, Coin dead on the road behind us. Aaron groaned, rolled over, rose to his elbows.

'Leave him alone,' I said again. 'He isn't your problem.'

'And you are?' Coin asked. 'My problem. It's you?'

'Yeah, it's me,' I said. 'So leave him the hell alone.'

We stood there for the space of five fast heartbeats. I had time to hope that Midian and Chogyi Jake had gotten away. I heard a car door open behind me.

'You aren't Eric Heller,' he said. 'Who are you?'

I pulled off my ski mask. I'd almost sweated through it in the few minutes I'd had it on. The air felt cold against my neck. I shook my head to get the hair out of my eyes. Candace stepped into my peripheral vision, a pistol in her hand. Coin didn't even bother to look at her. His eyes were on mine. I felt something cold traveling up my spine. Aaron rose to his knees. Coin stepped forward, and Candace started firing. Four fast shots. Someone off to my left started screaming. An engine revved. Coin looked at her, his lips drawing back.

'No! Candace! Get Aaron and get back in the car!' I said, stepping between them. Then to Coin, 'Leave them out of it.'

'As you've left Alexander out?' Coin said. He meant the big one. The one we'd killed.

'Alexander was mine too,' I said. 'They were all mine. You want this stopped? I'm the one. Just me.'

Coin looked back over his shoulder, toward the body of his fallen man. I thought I saw something like sadness in his eyes. Then he turned back to me and nodded.

'Just you,' he said.

He closed his eyes, balled his fists, and shouted. The sound was deafening, a thousand times louder than anything human, and more complex. There were storms in his voice. Earthquakes. Huge beings moving underground. I felt my body tip back and thought I was falling.

When I looked down, the streets were a hundred feet below me. Aaron and Candace were gone, but I saw her car, just beginning to move, finishing the long arc to the south. I saw the tangle of cars and trucks, semis and motorcycles that had piled up behind us. The stolen Hummer, its black doors standing open. Coin's car with its crumpled hood. The huge man's body. I could even see the pool of blood.

And then it was two hundred feet below me. And then a thousand. I dropped the rifle, the small black stick flipping down through the empty air. The great asphalt cloverleaf of the highway spun in the distance. I felt a sudden regret. My plan hadn't worked any better than Eric's. I wondered what I could have done differently. If there had ever really been a way to win.

Something profoundly cold touched the back of my mind, and the gray world went black.

25

I was cold.

Slowly, I became aware of other things. My knees hurt. There was a crick in my neck. All I could hear was a soft wind. When I moved, it made a scraping sound like gravel. But mostly, I was cold. I shifted my head, and something soft and chilly moved under me. I let my eyes slit open. My backpack. My head was resting on my leather backpack like it was a pillow.

I tried to remember where I was, how I'd gotten there. I had a sense of urgency. It was all very, very important. If I could just put my mind back together . . .

I sat up. The city spread out below me, streets marked by the glowing yellow lines of their lights, the shifting red of taillights in traffic. The western sky was red and gold, the sun already set. All around me was pebbled gray gravel, wide sheet-metal ductwork on raised steel beams. Something partway between a radio antenna and the Eiffel Tower rose up to my left, a red beacon glowing at its tip.

A skyscraper. I was on top of a skyscraper. I tried to stand, but my knees were weak beneath me. I turned slowly. There was a door—green and rust with a dead bolt lock. Coin was sitting beside it. Five inches above his open hand floated a small cylinder of metal that came to a point at one end. The bullet.

The thing in Coin's body looked over at me, then back at the artifact floating above its hand.

'Nasty piece of work, this,' it said. Its voice was conversational, deep, inhuman. 'Ya'la ibn Murah and St. Francis of the Desert both. Unpleasant.'

I tried to think, to focus. I had to say something.

'Fuck you,' I slurred.

It made a soft tsk-tsk and shook its head.

'It isn't yours. I know that,' the thing said. 'Heller designed it. It's his style. Oh yes, I know my enemies. And I've known Heller quite well. You, though, I confess I didn't expect. You're Jayné, yes?'

He knew how to pronounce my name, and for the first time since I'd come to, I felt the deep, penetrating rush of fear. Far to the south, a storm cloud still hung on the horizon, lightning flashing so far away there was no thunder. Coin nodded.

'The niece,' it said. 'The heir. Eric's next incarnation. I thought we had put an end to all that, but here you are. And Alexander gone because of it. I suppose I should have guessed. Heller was the past master of putting things in motion.'

'You killed my uncle,' I said. My voice sounded steadier now.

'Yes,' Coin said.

'You're going to kill me,' I said, sure as I did that it was the truth.

The rider narrowed its stolen eyes. The bullet slid down through the air to land on its upturned palm.

'Possibly,' it said. 'If it's necessary.'

I almost had my feet back. The city below us glittered and darkened. Somewhere out there, down below us, Midian and Chogyi Jake were running for their lives. And Candace and Aaron and Kim. Every minute I kept Coin focused on me was one that its attention wasn't turned to them.

Run, I thought. *Wherever you are out there, get the hell away from here. Live.*

'How much do you know?' it asked.

'Enough,' I said. It was silent for a long moment, then nodded.

'And you have made yourself part of this,' he said. It was almost a question.

'Yeah,' I said. The thing in Coin's body sighed.

'You are a woman of great power. Great potential,' it said. 'You needn't take your uncle's path. Even with the hurt you've caused me, you don't have to die here.'

I looked at it. The ink marks on its pale flesh seemed to shift, letters forming and re-forming. Something in the pit of my stomach warmed and rose, and against my own expectations, I laughed. Coin looked nonplussed.

'You're saying I could join up with you?'

'That's an option,' it said, vaguely offended.

'Next you offer me all the nations of the world?' I asked. When it looked confused, I gestured to the wide, empty air around us. 'Temptation. High place. Devil.'

'Ah,' it said, nodding. 'No, I'm not Satan, and you've

little enough in common with Christ, for that matter. I wasn't offering to purchase your soul. Only that I would rather we not end this in violence if there isn't need. If alliance isn't interesting to you, armistice at least remains a possibility.'

'What? "Oops, my bad. Won't do it again," and you let me go?'

'Of course not. I've underestimated Heller's reach, but that doesn't make me a fool. Renounce your vengeance and there will be an agreement. A binding of intention. Then, yes, you can walk away.'

'Really can't,' I said.

Coin stood. The man's body was only a little taller than mine. The business suit looked perversely in place with the arcane designs on its skin. I raised my chin.

'You killed my uncle,' I said again, and shrugged.

'And you are determined to walk in his footsteps,' Coin said. It wasn't a question, but it was the last chance I had.

I shifted my feet, the gravel crunching under me. I was a thousand feet above the ground, facing a supernatural evil that had already said it was willing to kill me. I didn't have another bullet or a rifle with which to fire it. Eric's protections might have been stripped away by Kim's cantrip. I didn't have any friends or allies. I was alone, and if I didn't do what the thing in Coin's body wanted, I'd be killed. Or I could say no, accept whatever binding it had in mind, and live as its slave and subject until I found a way to slip my leash. If I ever did. But at least I'd be alive. All I had to say was *No, I'm not.*

'Yeah,' I said. 'Really am.'

Coin nodded, its expression resigned and unsurprised.

'This gives me no pleasure,' it said, and drew in its breath. I jumped at it, swinging low. Coin danced out of reach, lifted its hands, and shouted a single syllable. The sound was louder than anything I'd ever heard—like a jet engine about two feet from my face. There were other voices inside it. I heard a chorus of shrieking words, a high wailing, and something deep and chthonic and inhuman. Sound pushed at me like a storm wind.

I set my feet, leaning forward toward Coin's gaping mouth and outstretched arms. The gravel under me shifted as I slid backward. My mind was jumping in a hundred different directions. I tried to pull up my qi, to force my will down into the soles of my feet to stick me to the spot. There was nothing.

The edge of the building came up behind me faster than I'd expected. The raw force of Coin's will had shoved me a dozen feet or more. The parapet came up to my thighs, the void on the other side. I dropped to my knees, trying not to pitch over it. My ears rang, and my eyes felt dry and scoured, like I'd been staring into a sandstorm.

And then I was in motion. I curled to the side, pushing through my legs as I did. I landed on my shoulder, rolling gracefully through my back to end up catlike on my fingertips and the balls of my feet. There was no surprise on Coin's face. It lifted its raised fists, and I jumped to the side as the roofing where I had been burst open, pebbles flying like shrapnel. I felt something dig into my leg, but I ignored the pain. My backpack was inches from my hand, and I swept it up and threw it, the leather singing against the air. It took Coin in the belly. Nothing more than a moment's distraction, but I was running forward, teeth bared.

My blood was a song, my body a weapon. My mind let go and let my flesh take control without me. Coin blocked a claw-fingered swipe at his neck, but not the kick that I sent hammering into its knee. I wanted to see surprise in its expression, but there was only momentary pain and then grim determination. I danced back, and Coin flipped up a handful of gravel, the unnaturally powerful stones hissing past my ear like gunfire.

It didn't speak. That time was over. We circled each other, waiting for a break, a moment. A chance. I thought I saw a tremble in the knee I'd kicked. I lunged forward, but it had anticipated the move. It stepped into the attack, taking the momentum on its arm, grabbing the front of my shirt and twisting. I lost contact with the ground, flew through the air out of control. I reached down with one hand, willing myself down to the gray stones. My hand slapped the parapet as I sailed past. For a fraction of a second I was over the edge, looking down the endless drop of black glass and chrome to the distant, glowing street. Then I was hugging the wrong side of the parapet, my legs kicking against the void.

Coin stood above me, both hands raised. I could feel the air change as it gathered its will. I think I screamed, but what I remember thinking was *Oh, well. That's it.*

The world became a clockwork. My arm, slung over the edge, carried a certain mass at a particular angle. The friction of my feet against the side of the skyscraper held a particular and measurable force. Coin's hands were only hands, its will a faint echo of what it had been only seconds before. Someone had performed Kim's cantrip.

Coin stepped back, real shock in its expression now. Something metallic banged, and I got an ankle up over the parapet's edge and hauled for all I was worth. I felt weak, but it was enough. I landed hard on my side just as I heard the first shotgun blast.

Coin's back was to me now, one hand pointed as it advanced on the green door that had been closed until now. Ex stepped out onto the roof, Eric's shotgun held before him, and fired twice more. I heard Coin grunt at the impact. I saw the small figure of Kim in the stairwell behind Ex.

'Run!' I tried to shout, but it hardly came out louder than a groan. 'He'll kill you!'

The concussion wasn't physical, but it was stunning all the same. A low hum like something electrical gathering a charge, and then the blast like a head blow from a brick. The world smelled like an iron skillet left on the burner by mistake. I forced my eyes open.

Ex lay on his back, blood running from his nose, his eyes wild with fear. Kim was no more than a low shape in the doorway. Coin stood over Ex's fallen body like a punch-drunk boxer who'd put his opponent down for the count. Who'd killed him. The suit jacket had come open, and Coin's chest was raw hamburger and blood where the shotgun's load of iron, salt, and silver had struck. It shook its head, trying to orient itself. Ex tried to say something, his jaw working without sound. The sense of a clockwork universe faded as Kim lost consciousness, and I felt my own strength coming back, at least enough that I could do something more than tremble.

Something glittered at Coin's feet. There in the stone litter of gravel, something shone brass and blackness. Coin was breathing hard. I shifted, getting my weight under me again. Ex tried to raise the shotgun, the barrel making a hushing sound as it dragged across the rooftop. Coin lifted its foot with slow deliberation and slammed down on Ex's chest. I imagined that I heard ribs snapping.

I launched.

I hit Coin in the small of the back, shoulder first and all my weight and power behind it. It felt like I'd tackled a concrete post, but Coin stumbled. Ex rolled once, from his back onto his belly, the shotgun underneath him now. Coin swung at me; the back of his hand grazing my cheek was enough to knock my head to the side. I dropped, scrabbling in the gravel for the glimmer I'd seen.

My fingers found the bullet, the weird energy of the sigils dry and mobile as a snake. I clenched a fist around it and jumped back. Coin's rib cage was falling and rising like a bellows. I stayed in a crouch, the bullet in my left hand, my eyes on the enemy.

As long as it breaks skin, we're fine.

Coin stepped back, arms spread wide and eyes closed. I felt its will gathering like a high wind full of knives. The shredded flesh of its chest wept blood without drenching it. I had the time it took to draw a breath, and if I failed, we were all dead.

I stepped forward and pressed the bullet to the shot-gun wound. Something between my fingers shifted and squirmed. Coin's eyes opened in shock.

'Tag,' I said. 'You're it.'

Imagine a balloon the size of the world. Touch a pin to it. Coin's death was that loud and that sudden, and then it was over. The husk of his body fell to the rooftop, took three slow wheezing breaths, and went still. I stood there for what seemed like an hour and wasn't more than five seconds. Slowly, I crouched down. Coin's eyes were still moving, looking up at me with horror and despair and then shifting to focus on something in the distance that only it could see. The bullet rested on its ruined sternum, the metal bright and unmarked, the engravings gone. I lay back.

The gravel felt comfortable as a feather bed. When I knew I was going to vomit, I rolled to my side. When I was empty, I rolled back. Far above in the dark sky, an airplane pulsed. There was no sound of traffic. We were too high up for that. There was only the hollow sound of the breeze in my ear, and then unsteady footsteps.

Kim came into view. A streak of blood darkened her cheek. I smiled at her.

'Jayné?' she said. 'Are you okay?'

I managed a weak thumbs-up. My voice didn't seem to be working. She knelt beside me, her hand smoothing back my hair. I had the weird thought that Kim would have been a good mother. A little June Cleaver for my tastes, maybe, but perfect for someone else. There was a scrape, a cough, and a grunted obscenity as Ex started to move. It reminded me of something.

'How?' I managed.

'Your friend, Ex?' Kim said. 'He put a GPS tracking device in your backpack. It was how he knew where we were before too.'

I closed my eyes, frowned, opened them again.

'Creepy,' I said.

'Needed to happen,' Ex said. He was sitting up now, his arms around his chest. His face was pale with pain. I raised my hand and pointed a single finger at him.

'Creepy stalker bullshit,' I said. And then, 'Thanks.'

'Welcome,' he said.

'Aaron and Candace are downstairs guarding the stairwell,' Kim said. 'Can you walk?'

I nodded, sat up, shook my head, and lay back down.

'Give me a minute,' I said.

'I'm going to get the others,' Kim said. 'Don't go anywhere. Either of you. Just stay here.'

I heard her walk away. My body felt like rubber. Like chewing gum that had lost all its flavor. Ex tried to stand up, groaned, and went still.

'GPS tracker?' I said.

'Seven hundred bucks, online,' he said. 'Little smaller than a pack of cigarettes. Put it in the side pocket. Took us a while figuring elevation, though.'

'Deeply, deeply creepy.'

I tried to think of something else to say, but there was nothing left in me. Ex and the shell that had been Randolph Coin and I all communed in silence. The last rays of sun glow dimmed in the west. Ex said something about *very, very stubborn,* but I wasn't listening closely enough to know whether he meant himself or me. I turned my head to see Coin's body. With eyes closed and mouth slack, it seemed to be sleeping.

Coin seemed peaceful. I wondered if death was always like that. I wondered whether some part of Eric could see us, wherever he was. If he still was at all. Heaven or the Pleroma or Philadelphia. I wondered if he knew I'd finished the job. Would he have been proud of me? I had screwed everything up from the start, but I'd seen it through. No plan had ever worked the way we'd meant it to, but then Coin's hadn't worked out either. I imagined Eric would see that as a win.

I hoped so.

I didn't sleep, but I wasn't perfectly conscious either. It surprised me when a man's broad hands lifted me to sitting. Aaron was beside me, looking concerned. Kim was at my other side, ready to lift me if needed. Candace was helping Ex walk to the stairway.

'We need to go now, okay? Jayné? Can you stand up?'

'I killed Randolph Coin,' I said. 'I can do anything.'

Aaron grinned. He looked young when he did that. Like a little boy.

'Yeah,' he said. 'I think you can.'

I rose slowly and started toward the open stairway. At the doorway, I stopped.

'Backpack,' I said. 'I need my pack. We can't leave anything here.'

'It's okay,' Kim said. 'We've got it covered.'

'Laptop?' I said.

'Yes, we got your laptop too,' Aaron said. 'Don't worry about it. How bad are you? Do we need to go to the hospital?'

'The hospital,' I said. 'Aubrey! We need to see Aubrey!'

'It's okay,' Kim said. 'We'll take care of that once you're all right.'

'I'm fine,' I said. 'I'm perfect.'

I didn't remember walking downstairs or out to Candace's car. A bump in the road brought me back to myself, and we were driving down the highway toward the house, Aaron and Kim in the front, Candace in the back with me and Ex slumped beside her. Ex's mouth was pinched with pain, but there was a light in his eyes. I thought that was what redemption must look like. When he saw me looking at him, he smiled. When I smiled back, he took my hand.

I was asleep before we got home.

26

Later, Ex told me that Chogyi Jake had appeared on the doorstep of Eric's old house the morning after Coin had died. His motorcycle was marred by deep, white scratches on the left side, and Chogyi Jake himself had a bruise on his back that looked like he'd been whipped by a bullwhip with legs like a centipede. The forces of the Invisible College had chased him just the way we'd hoped. They'd been in pursuit before he'd gotten six blocks from the house. He'd eluded them, but only just. Midian had never arrived at the airstrip that I'd reserved for his flight out. We didn't know if he'd made it or not, a fact that haunted me for a long time. Chogyi Jake slept for fourteen hours, but I hadn't noticed at the time, since I crashed for almost twenty.

I woke in my bed, only half aware of where I was and what had happened. I'd stumbled out to the main room in a T-shirt and sweats to find Ex very slowly preparing one of Midian's frozen meals and reading a new, deeply anonymous report that had been dropped off on my doorstep.

Randolph Coin had been killed in something that looked like a drug-trade hit. His personal secretary, Alexander Hume, had also been shot and killed. The police were investigating, and it appeared that the attack was linked to a heroin and prostitution operation in Boulder. Aaron was mentioned by name as being part of that investigation.

That was the first three pages. There were nineteen others that followed. I'd wolfed down potatoes and green chili and two cups of black coffee while Ex read the report out loud. By the end, Chogyi Jake and Kim had joined us in the kitchen, all of us listening to Ex declaim the words of my lawyer.

When we'd all gone over it twice, I called Aubrey and he answered. We'd gone to see him as soon as we could, and now Chogyi Jake and I were almost done bringing him up to speed.

He looked pretty good for a guy who hadn't been in his own body for over a week. His eyes were bright, and his smile came out often and with almost no prompting. He even had his hair washed and cut. Apart from the skimpy little hospital gown, he was the picture of health. Way ahead of the rest of us. He flipped through the report, his eyebrows slowly sliding up his forehead.

'They're falling apart,' Aubrey said.

'Just the way Eric said they would,' I said. 'The Invisible College just took a long dive into an empty swimming pool. Coin was the linchpin. All of the things he'd done in the world fell apart when we killed him.'

'Including my coma. It sounds like it was quite the experience,' Aubrey said. 'I'm sorry I missed it.'

'I wouldn't be,' I said. 'It was mostly not fun.'

'All the more reason I should have been there,' Aubrey said.

'Next time,' I said, and put my hand on his knee. It was a small gesture, that touch. Not even skin against skin. Still, I could feel him tense at it, and then relax.

'I can't believe you called Kim,' he said, with something like a laugh, except it was a little forced.

'Kim's all right,' I said. 'I like her.'

The atmosphere grew tense. Chogyi Jake cleared his throat and rose.

'I'm sure there's a restroom around here somewhere,' he said, and made his discreet exit. The other bed in the suite was empty. Aubrey and I were alone. Tentatively, he took my hand. I had the powerful memory of being in his apartment, in his bed. I looked away, willing myself not to blush.

'I owe you,' Aubrey said. 'After it all went south, I would have thought you'd run. And instead you . . . you did it. You went after him. You won.'

'Well, it was that or leave you as neurologically active broccoli,' I said. 'It seemed like the right thing to do. Besides which, they killed Eric. It wasn't like I could just let it slide.'

'It was brave,' he said.

I felt a flash of annoyance, and Aubrey must have seen it. He sat back, suddenly tentative. He started to take back his hand, but I held on and tugged him toward me.

'It's not that I don't appreciate you saying that,' I said, 'but would you have said it to Kim or Ex? Or Chogyi Jake? Hell, Midian? Sure, I was a brave little bunny and rose to the occasion, but so did everyone else. Any of us could have gotten killed or worse. It wasn't just me.'

'I'm sorry.'

'And stop apologizing,' I said. 'Condescending and apologizing for it are really not the combination you're looking for. Aubrey, I'm glad as hell you're back. I missed you. But you've got to stop thinking of me as the lost little girl you met at the airport. She's gone.'

'And how should I think of you?' he asked. His voice was low. It was a charged moment. I could have said anything. Think of me as your friend. Your lover. Think of me the way you thought of Eric. Think of me as your wife's confidante.

'I'm working on that part,' I said.

The storms had broken the summer heat's back. As I left the hospital, climbed up into Chogyi Jake's van, and headed out toward the house, it felt like autumn. Still T-shirt weather, but not the assaulting sweat-down-your-back kind. It was like the city and the sunlight had reached some kind of peace. I rolled down the window as we drove, my arm lolling out into the wind of our passage the way it had when I was a kid.

Chogyi Jake and I got back to the house in the early afternoon. Ex was waiting for us, sitting on the couch with his shirt off, and a wrapping of bandages shoring up his cracked ribs. Wide bruises peeked out at the edges. His hair was loose around his shoulders, making him look vaguely angelic.

'How's the invalid?' he asked.

'Aubrey's fine,' I said. 'The doctors are a little freaked out by a guy in a coma for eight days not having a whole lot of brain damage. I wasn't going to tell them that the damage was spiritual. They don't like that kind of talk.'

'Makes them think you're a religious nut,' Chogyi Jake agreed as he closed the door.

'How are you doing?' I asked.

'I'll live,' Ex said.

'You should see a doctor,' Chogyi Jake said.

Ex shook his head carefully.

'I don't want any records of this,' he said. 'You go to the emergency room, they just ask questions. How did it happen, why didn't you come in sooner? Then there's police asking if you want to make a statement. Before long, they start putting us together with what happened to Coin. There's nothing they can do for a broken rib except wait for it to grow back together, and I can do that on my own.'

'Besides which, he's weirdly into pain,' I said to Chogyi Jake. 'Thinks it makes him a better person.'

'It's manly, at least,' Chogyi agreed, picking up on my teasing tone.

'If one of you happens to have a Percocet, I wouldn't say no,' Ex said sourly, but he also smiled. 'Aaron and Candace called to make sure everyone was all right. Things appear to be going well in their neck of the woods. I'm still having them check in four times a day until we're certain the remnants of the College haven't traced anything back to them.'

'I wish they'd stayed here,' I said. 'Eric's protections—'

'Are worn to nothing,' Chogyi Jake said. 'If they were

still pushing, they'd have broken through by now. And not being around us has a certain protective aspect too,' Chogyi Jake said.

'I know,' I said, putting down my backpack and looking into the kitchen. 'It's just I want everyone where I can see them. It makes me feel better. Where's Kim?'

Ex started to shrug, then winced and went a little pale.

'She left just after you did,' Ex said. 'Called a cab. I figure she's probably in an airplane back to Chicago by now.'

I looked from Ex to Chogyi Jake and back. There wasn't a reason to be surprised. She'd never said she was going to stay, or that she wanted to see Aubrey before she left. I had just made the assumption.

'I think she left a note or something in your room,' Ex said.

He was right. The wide manila envelope was on the bed. My name was written on it in black marker. I lifted it gently. It felt heavy, like a thick catalog or a printed schedule of classes back at school. It wasn't sealed.

Jayné:

I suppose it's a failure of nerve leaving like this. I hope you can forgive me. I've struggled with this more than you know.

I had dreamed of the day when I could come back to the life I left behind. Now that the obstacles that held me apart from Aubrey and Denver are gone, I find that there are more reasons to stay away than I had realized.

I care for Aubrey very deeply, but as I look back at the manner in which he and I fell away from each other, I can't in all honesty say I'm sure it would be different now. I know that if I stayed, if I saw him, I would be tempted to try. The rational part of my mind says that would be a mistake. And so I'm taking the coward's way out.

Tell him that I wish him well. Tell him that I blame him for nothing, and that I forgive him as I hope he will forgive me.

Take care of yourself.

She hadn't signed the note, but it was at the front of a packet of papers: close-set legal type with flat, low boxes to fill in. Divorce papers, completed with Kim's information and Aubrey's. Those, she'd signed. The only blank spot was where Aubrey would put his name and the date. Whatever relationship they'd had with each other, I was holding its end. Whatever combination of hope and lust, betrayal and blindness had led them here, it cooked down to these pages.

Except that she'd come when I called her. Not for me or for Eric, but for Aubrey. She'd risked her life for his. I flipped through the pages with my thumb, but not looking at them as much as the complexity they represented. Then I put them back in their envelope and slid it into my laptop bag.

Later. I could deal with it later.

I got online, sent an e-mail to my little brother letting him know that I was okay without going into any detail, checked some old blogs from people I used to know. Extojayne wasn't connected. I deleted him from my contact lists like I was dropping a dead mouse in the wastebasket. Then I did the same with Caryonandon.

I sat on the bed, legs crossed, laptop humming quietly to itself, and thought. My fingers ran across the plastic keyboard, Googling a phrase at random, and then doing it again in a kind of Internet-based electronic daydreaming.

I felt like the pressure was still on me, like there was something I needed to do. The idea that it was over hadn't really sunk in yet. Raw inertia kept me thinking about Coin, the Invisible College, how to keep Aubrey and Ex and Chogyi Jake safe, who I could go to for help. What I could do.

But it was over, and I could do anything.

I noticed the kinds of phrases I'd been putting into the search engines and realized I knew exactly what I wanted to have happen next. I found my cell phone, called my lawyer, and made an appointment for later that afternoon.

When I got there, still dressed in a Pink Martini T-shirt and blue jeans, and told her what I had in mind, she didn't miss a beat.

I booked us a private room at the back of what my lawyer promised me was a very good restaurant. The maître d' escorted us through the dim, well-appointed hall, real candles burning in wall sconces and live music playing in the background. The table was set for four. I'd debated inviting Aaron and Candace too, but until the investigation of Coin's death was completed, I decided it was better to keep social contact to a minimum. If Kim had stayed, I'd have brought her too.

As we ordered drinks, I considered the three of them.

Chogyi Jake, with his freshly shaved scalp and constantly laughing eyes, asked for water. It arrived in a sculpted glass bottle, freshly opened. Ex ordered a gin and tonic. He was wearing all black again, the way he had the first time I'd met him. His hair was pulled back and tied with a length of leather. Aubrey sat across from me and ordered wine. I got the same thing he did.

I raised my glass.

'If not to a job well done, at least to a job done,' I said.

'And to Jayné,' Aubrey said. 'Without whom I'd still be eating through a tube.'

'To Eric,' Ex said. Chogyi Jake didn't offer a toast, so we gave the silence a moment, then drank.

'I suppose you're all wondering why I asked you here,' I said, trying to lighten the mood a little.

'To say good-bye?' Chogyi Jake suggested. Aubrey's head lifted as if he'd heard a strange sound. Ex saw the movement and coughed slightly in scorn.

'She's got an empire, Aubrey,' he said. 'Eric had places all over the country. All over the world. You can't expect her to curl up here in Denver and never poke her nose out.'

'Besides which,' I said, 'the Invisible College is broken, but it's not dead. I was thinking it would be a good idea to get out of town for a while, even if I did decide to come back.'

Aubrey went pale. It was good to see the reaction. It made me feel better about the part that came next.

'So,' I continued, 'that's why I'd like to hire you.'

Now it was Ex's turn to look startled.

'I've got a lot of money,' I said. 'I can afford a decent yearly salary for all three of you. And Ex is right. It is an empire, and I'm still pretty much wet behind the ears. I need help cataloging things, but even more than that, I need to know what the hell it is once it's all cataloged. You guys know more than I do, and that's important—'

'We don't know *near* enough,' Ex said. 'Coin just about killed Aubrey. We were living with a vampire for days without any of us putting it together. You and Aubrey could have gotten slaughtered by the *haugtrold* before any of the rest of it even got off the ground!'

'That's important, but it's not the only issue,' I said, staring Ex down. He scowled deeply, then softened and smiled a little. I went on. 'The big thing is I know you guys. The world's still full of riders. Vampires, werewolves, demons. Whatever you want to call them. And if I'm going up against them, I want people I trust. I trust you. So there you have it. Come work for me, and we'll pick up where Eric left off, or enjoy the meal and I'll tell you how much I owe you for what you've already done and we'll call it quits. Your call.'

I took a sip of the wine and waited while it sank in.

'I have a job,' Aubrey said. 'The lab . . .'

Chogyi Jake considered his water glass as if it were a piece of fine art. Ex leaned forward. No one spoke. They were going to do it. I could already smell it. They were in, all of them.

I'd come to Denver a little under a month before, knowing nothing about riders or the Invisible College, Eric's wealth, or my role as his heir. I hadn't had anyone. Now I had all of it. Sitting in the dim elegance around our table, I could see a future worth hoping for. I watched as each of them—Aubrey, Ex, Chogyi Jake—nodded. I grinned, delighted.

My uncle hadn't had the time to train me, but he'd meant for me to have all of this, to follow in his footsteps. With a little help, I would. I'd be the one who could help the Candaces and Aarons and stand against the Randolph Coins. And even better, I'd have my friends beside me. In that moment, I was as sure of myself, as confident, and as at peace as I had ever been.

I didn't have a clue.

Acknowledgments

I would like to thank JB Bell, Sam Jones, and Andan Lauber for their help in inventing Jayné Heller and for handing me *Guilty Pleasures* back during the heyday of the Abbey. I would also like to thank Jayné Franck for lending her name. I owe debts of service and gratitude to the members of the Santa Fe Critical Mass group, including S. M. and Jan Stirling, Emily Mah, Ian Tregillis, Melinda Snodgrass, Terry England, Walter Jon Williams, Sage Walker, Vic Milan, and the auxiliary presences of Carrie Vaughn and Diana Rowland. The book would not exist without the faith and hard work of my agents, Shawna McCarthy and Danny Baror, and my editor, Jennifer Heddle. The strength of the book is very much an honor to them. Any errors are entirely my own.

extras

www.orbitbooks.net

about the author

M. L. N. Hanover is an open pseudonym for Daniel Abraham, author of the critically acclaimed Long Price quartet. He has been nominated for the Hugo, Nebula, and World Fantasy awards. He also writes science fiction (with Ty Franck) as James S. A. Corey. He lives in New Mexico.

Find out more about M. L. N. Hanover and other Orbit authors by registering for the free monthly newsletter at www.orbitbooks.net

if you enjoyed
UNCLEAN SPIRITS
look out for

DARKER ANGELS

also by

M. L. N. Hanover

1

'Hey,' my dead uncle said. 'You've got a call.'

I rolled over in bed, disoriented. A dream about meeting Leonard Cohen in a perfume factory was still about as immediate as reality. My previous day's clothes were piled in the corner of the tile floor along with the leather backpack I used as a purse. The pack's side pocket was open and glowing. My uncle Eric's voice came again.

'Hey. You've got a call.'

I untangled myself from the sheets and stumbled over, promising myself for the thousandth time that I would change the ringtone. The bedroom was still unfamiliar. The cell phone flashed a number I didn't recognize, but there was a name—Karen Black—associated with it, so she must have been in his contacts list someplace. I accepted the call.

'Unh?' I grunted into the receiver.

'Eric, it's Karen. I've found it!' a woman said. 'It's in New Orleans, and I know where it's going next. There's a little girl with Sight, and she says her sister is the next target. I don't know how long I've got. I need you.'

It was a lot to take in. I hesitated, and the woman misinterpreted my silence.

'Okay, what's it going to take?' she demanded. 'Name your price, Heller.'

'Actually,' I said. 'That's complicated. I'm Jayné. Eric's niece. He's . . . um . . . he passed on last year.'

It was Karen Black's turn to be silent. I gave her a moment to let it sink in. I skipped the parts about how he'd been murdered by an evil wizard and how several of Eric's old friends, along with a policeman who owed me a favor and a vampire with a grudge against the same wizard, had teamed up to mete out summary roadside justice. I could get back to that later if I needed to.

'Oh,' she said.

'Yeah. He left me pretty much everything. Including the cell phone. So . . . hi. Jayné here. Anything I can do to help out?'

The pause was longer this time. I could guess pretty well at the debate she was going through. I gave her a hand.

'This is about riders, isn't it?' I asked.

'Yes,' she said. 'So you know about them?'

'Abstract spiritual parasites. Come in from Next Door or the Pleroma or whatever you want to call it,' I said as I walked carefully back to the bed. 'Take over people's bodies. Have weird-ass magical powers, kind of like the magic humans can do, but way more effective. Yeah, I've got the For Dummies book, at least.'

'All right,' she said. 'Did Eric . . . did he even mention me?'

'No,' I said. 'Sorry.'

The woman on the other end of the line took a breath as

I got back under the covers and pulled the pillow behind my back. I heard Aubrey cough from one of the bedrooms down the hall.

'All right,' she said. 'My name is Karen Black. I used to be a special agent for the FBI. About ten years ago, I started tracking down what I thought was a fairly standard serial killer. It turned out to be a rider. We caught the horse, a man named Joseph Mfume, but the rider switched bodies.'

'So not so easy to track,' I said.

'No,' she agreed. 'My supervisors wanted me to stop. They didn't believe there was anything to it. And . . . well, *X-Files* was still popular back then. There were jokes. I was referred for psychiatric counseling and taken off active duty. I resigned and went on with the investigation myself. Eric and I crossed paths a few times over the years, and I was impressed with his efficiency. I've found where the rider is going to strike next, and I need help to stop it. I thought of Eric.'

'Okay,' I said.

'Can you help me?'

I rubbed my eyes with my free hand until little ghosts of false light danced in my vision.

'Hell if I know,' I said. 'Let me talk to my guys and call you back.'

'Your guys?'

'I kind of have a staff,' I said. 'Experts.'

I could hear her turning that over too. I wondered how much she'd known about Eric's financial situation. For a man with enough money to buy a small third-world nation, he hadn't flaunted it; I hadn't even known until he left me the whole thing. My guess was Karen hadn't expected Eric to have a staff.

'I don't know how much time I have,' she said.

'I'll get back to you as soon as I can. Promise. We're in Athens right now, so it may take me a few days to get to New Orleans.'

'I don't mean to be rude, but it's not that long a flight,' Karen said, impatience in her tone. 'You could drive it in eight hours or so.'

It took me a second to process that.

'Not Georgia Athens,' I said. 'Athens Athens. Cradle of civilization.'

'Oh,' she said, and then, 'Oh fuck. What time is it there?'

I snuggled down under my covers and looked at the bedside clock.

'One in the morning,' I said.

'I woke you up,' she said. 'I am *so* sorry . . .'

Amid a flurry of apologies and promises to return calls, Karen and I let each other go. I dropped the phone next to the clock and stared at the ceiling.

The last six months had offered me a wide variety of bedroom ceilings. The first at Eric's house in Denver when I was first thrown into the world of riders and possession and magic. Then the dark wood and vigas of an old ranch outside Santa Fe, then a place in New Haven with honest-to-God mirrors over the bed and red silk sheets, followed by a gray-green retro-seventies number in a rent-controlled apartment building in Manhattan that was so small I got hotel rooms for the guys. There had been a much more civilized beige with a little unprofessional plaster repair near the corner in a townhouse in London, and now the bare white with deep blue notes that said this Greek villa had been a full-on tourist trap rental before Eric bought it.

The guys had been with me the whole time, apart from a couple weeks when Aubrey had gone back to his former job at the University of Colorado to tie up some loose ends on his research. In the long, complex process of inventorying the property and resources Eric had left behind, we hadn't stayed anyplace more than two months running, and most considerably less. None of it seemed like home to me, and from experience, I knew I could stare at the dim white above me for hours and still not sleep.

With a sigh, I got up, pulled on my robe, and made my way downstairs to the kitchen. A newspaper on the cheap yellow Formica table yelled out headlines in an alphabet I didn't understand. I poured myself a bowl of cereal with little bits of dried fruit and added milk that tasted subtly different from the two percent I'd grown up with.

I heard the door of one of the other bedrooms open and soft footsteps come down the stairs. After so many months together, I could differentiate Aubrey from Ex from Chogyi Jake without looking.

'Why do you think it is,' I asked, 'that someone can on the one hand be talking you into a fight against evil spirits and semi-demonic serial killers, but then on the other get embarrassed when they figure out they woke you up to do it?'

'I don't know,' Aubrey said as he sat down across from me. 'Maybe he just didn't want to be rude.'

'*She* didn't want to be rude,' I said. 'Sexist.'

Aubrey smiled and shrugged. Aubrey was beautiful the way a familiar leather jacket is beautiful. He wasn't all muscles and vanity, he didn't spend hours on his wardrobe and hair. His smile looked lived-in, and his body was comfortable and reassuring and solid. He always reminded me of Sunday mornings and tangled sheets.

We'd been lovers once for about a day before I found out that—point one—he was married and—point two—I have a real hangup about sleeping with married men. I still had uncomfortably pleasant erotic dreams about him sometimes. I also had divorce paperwork in my backpack, filled out by his wife with her signature and everything. I hadn't told him about that. It was one of those things that was so important and central to my life that putting it off had been very easy. Every time a chance came up to talk about it, I'd been able to find a reason not to.

'What's the issue?' he asked, and I startled a little, my still-exhausted mind interpreting the question as being about the divorce papers. I pulled myself together.

'There's an ex-FBI agent in New Orleans. She's on the trail of a rider that's a serial killer,' I said, and yawned. 'Are there a lot of those?'

'Depends on who you ask,' he said. 'There are a lot of serial killers who claim to be demons or victims of demonic possession. You remember the BTK killer? His pastor said right through the end that the voice coming out of the guy wasn't the man he knew. There are some people who think that all serial killers are possessed. Serial arsonists, too. Is that the last of the milk?'

'No, there's another whole bottle in the fridge,' I said around my spoon. 'So is it true? Are they all riders?'

'Probably not,' Aubrey said. 'I mean some serial killers blame porn or bad parenting or whatever. And you can be mentally ill without there being a rider in your head. But by the same token, I'd bet that some are.'

'You'd buy it? This FBI lady has been tracking down a body-hopping serial killer, she's managed to get one step ahead of it, and needs help. Sounds plausible?'

'We've all seen weirder,' Aubrey said as he measured out enough coffee for three of us. Chogyi Jake always opted for tea. 'Do you have any reason to think it's not on the level?'

'You mean is it the bad guys setting a trap? I don't have any reason to think so,' I said. 'Also no reason not to, though. I could get a background check on her, I guess.'

'Might be wise.'

I didn't hear Ex coming. He just breezed in from the hallway. Even the T-shirt and sweats he slept in were black. His hair was loose, a pale blond flow that softened his features. Usually he wore it back.

'Since we apparently aren't sleeping tonight, what are we talking about?' he asked as he pulled out a chair and sat at the table.

'Serial killers, demonic possession,' I said. 'Same as always.'

'Jayné got us a job,' Aubrey said.

I ran down the basics again while I finished eating and Ex and Aubrey started. The coffee smelled good—rich and reassuringly heavy—so I had a mug myself. I had to give it to Greece, the coffee was great. Ex pulled back his hair into a severe ponytail, tying it with a length of leather cord while I talked. The softness left his face.

'Officially, it's one out of seven,' Ex said when I finished. 'Or that's what Brother Ignatius said back when I was in seminary. A little under fifteen percent of serial killings are the result of possession.'

'Creepy,' I said.

Aubrey and Ex looked at each other across the table. I could tell there was some kind of subterranean masculine conversation going on, and it annoyed me that I was being left out.

'What?' I said. 'It's creepy. What?'

'How are you feeling, Jayné?' Aubrey asked.

'Tired. It's . . .' I checked my watch. 'Two in the morning.'

'Three weeks ago in London, it would have been midnight,' Ex said.

'True,' I said. 'Point being?'

Aubrey held up his hand.

'We've all been busting hump for . . . well, for months now. We've got six hundred books in the wiki and at least that many artifacts and items, most of which we don't have any kind of provenance for. And we're not a fifth of the way through the list of properties that Eric owned.'

I knew all of that, but hearing it said out loud made me want to hang my head.

'I know it's a big project,' I said. 'But it's necessary. If we don't know what we have to work with . . .'

'I agree completely, Ex said. 'The thing is, someone's come to you with a problem. Sounds like it might be a little hairy. Are you . . . are *we* in any condition to take it on? Or do you want to finish the full inventory before we dive back into fieldwork?'

What I wanted was firmly none of the above. I wanted to stop for a while. I wanted to find a lovely alpine village, read trashy romances, play video games, and watch the glaciers melt. And there was nothing to stop me from doing it. I had the money, I had the power.

But this was what Eric did, and he left it to me, and walking away from it meant walking away from him too. I sighed and finished my coffee.

'If this lady's on the level, she needs us. And if we wait until we're totally ready, we'll never do anything,' I said. 'And I think we could all use a break. So here's the plan. I'll get us tickets to New Orleans, we'll go save the world from abstract evil, and afterward we'll hang out in the French Quarter for a couple of weeks and blow off steam.'

'If we've defeated abstract evil, I'm not sure how much of the French Quarter will still be there,' Ex said.

'First things first, padre,' I said, standing up and heading for the main rooms. In fairness, the padre part wasn't entirely true. Ex had, in fact, quit being a priest long before I met him. Thus the Ex. *Padre* was what a vampire we both knew had called him, and sometimes the nickname still stuck.

The main room of the villa looked like a dorm room a week before final exams. Books filled cheap metal shelves and covered the tables. Ancient texts with splitting leather bindings, paperbacks from the 1960s with bright colors and psychedelic designs, medical papers, collections of theological essays, books on game theory, chaos theory. Grimoires of all arcane subjects waiting to be examined, categorized, and entered in the wiki that the four of us were building to support our work as magical problem solvers. Our laptop computers were all closed, but plugged in and glowing.

I sat at mine and opened it. It took me about three minutes to dig up an old e-mail from my lawyer listing all the addresses of Eric's properties, and about thirty seconds from there to confirm that I did indeed own a house in New Orleans listed as being in the Lakeview neighborhood, and valued at eight hundred thousand dollars, so it probably had enough bedrooms for all of us. I wondered what it would look like.

I smiled to myself as I got on the travel site and started shopping for the most convenient and comfortable flights back to the States. The truth was, even as tired as I was, the prospect of going somewhere new, opening a new house or storage unit without having the first clue what we'd find gave me a covert thrill. Yes, it all flowed from the death of my beloved uncle, so there was an aspect of the macabre, but it was also a little like a permanent occult Christmas.

Well, except when evil spirits tried to kill me. I had some scars from those that kept me in one-piece bathing suits. But nothing like that had happened for months, and by the time I had four flights booked from Athens International to the Louis Armstrong International Airport, I was feeling more awake and alive than I had in days. Probably the coffee was kicking in too.

It was four in the morning and still a long way from dawn when I called Karen Black.

'Black here,' she said instead of hello.

'Hey. It's Jayné Heller here. We talked a few hours ago?'

'Yes,' Karen said.

'I've talked to most of the guys, and it looks like we can get there in about two days. So Thursday, middle of the morning, but I'll call you as soon as we're in and settled. That sound okay?'

'That's great,' she said. I could hear the smile in her tone, and I smiled back. Always good to save the day. Her next words were more sober. 'We should talk about the price.'

'We can do that once we get there,' I said.

'I can do that,' she said, and paused. 'I don't mean to. . . . When I called before, I was a little scattered. I didn't say how sorry I am to hear about Eric. It was rude of me.'

'Don't sweat it,' I said. 'And thanks. I was . . . I was sorry to lose him. I'm a little thin on family generally speaking, and he was pretty much the good one.'

'He was a good man,' she said, her voice as soft as flannel. To my surprise, I found myself tearing up a little. We said our good-byes and I killed the connection.

I spent the next hour with the fine folks at Google, reading up on serial killers who had claimed to be demons. I got a little sidetracked on a guy called the Axeman of New Orleans who'd slaughtered a bunch of people almost a century ago. In addition to claiming to be from hell, he said he'd pass by any house where jazz music was playing, which seemed a lot more New Orleans than lamb's blood on the lintel.

Chogyi Jake woke at six, a habit that he maintained in any time zone. His head hadn't been shaved in a few days, and the black halo of stubble was just starting to form around his scalp. He smiled and bowed to me, the movement half joking and half sincere.

'Getting an early start?' he asked, nodding at the dun-colored landscape drawing itself out of darkness outside our windows. The Aegean glowed turquoise and gold in the light of the rising sun.

'More like an early finish,' I said. 'There's been a change of plans.'